MURDER
IN BERMUDA

WILLOUGHBY SHARP
(Portrait from the book jacket of *Murder of the Honest Broker*)

MURDER
IN BERMUDA

WILLOUGHBY SHARP

COACHWHIP PUBLICATIONS

Greenville, Ohio

Murder in Bermuda, by Willoughby Sharp
© 2013 Coachwhip Publications
Introduction © 2013 Curtis Evans
No claims made on public domain material.
First published 1933.
Front cover: Lily © Svetlana | SV Photo

ISBN 1-61646-198-5
ISBN-13 978-1-61646-198-0

CoachwhipBooks.com

CONTENTS

DEATH'S DILETTANTE

THE DETECTIVE NOVELS OF WILLOUGHBY SHARP

Curtis Evans

DETECTIVE FICTION of the Golden Age (c. 1920 to 1940) is known for the glimpses it affords readers of the rarefied world of leisured wealth. Yet the clever scribblers who produced those charming tales of classical detection during the years between the two world wars typically drew inspiration more from their vivid imaginations than from real life. For most writers of the period (not to mention most readers), the old moneyed and sophisticated Peter Wimseys and Philo Vances, who with such sublime self-confidence exquisitely swanked their well-bred ways though the gilded pages of Golden Age mysteries, were winsome figments of romantic fantasy.

William Willoughby Sharp (1900-1956), however, was an author of Golden Age detective fiction who actually lived the sort of life that Dorothy L. Sayers and S. S. Van Dine wrote about in their books.[1] Although Sharp was born in New York City, at the time of his birth his paternal ancestors had been prominent in Norfolk, Virginia, for a century. His grandfather was a United States Naval

---

[1] To be sure, after his 1920s detective novels became bestsellers in the United States, S. S. Van Dine (Willard Huntingdon Wright) lived lavishly—so lavishly, indeed, that after the popularity of his novels declined in the 1930s he could not keep up the lifestyle to which he had grown accustomed. See John Loughery, *Alias S. S. Van Dine: The Man Who Created Philo Vance* (New York: Scribner, 1992).

Academy graduate who commanded the Confederate gunboats *Beaufort* and *Neuse* during the Civil War and headed the Confederate Naval Ordnance Department, while his great-grandfather was a Norfolk attorney and the president of the city's Exchange Bank.

In the 1890s William Willoughby Sharp's father moved to New York City, where he worked as a clerk in the office of J. P. Morgan. Starting his own firm on the strength of a loan from J. P. Morgan himself, the senior Sharp became an extremely successful and wealthy stockbroker. He married Dora Adams Hopkins, a "beautiful young widow" of distinguished antecedents originally from Atlanta, and the couple had two children, a son and a daughter. The elder William Willoughby Sharp held his seat on the Stock Exchange for three decades. When in 1926 he was hit and killed by a taxicab as he crossed West Eleventh Street, Greenwich Village, he was returning home to one of those elegant brownstone row houses that so often serve as sites of the complex killings in Philo Vance's refined murder cases.[2]

Giving some idea of the social standing of the elder Willoughby Sharp in New York, his stepdaughter married Gilbert Eliott, a stockbroker and heir presumptive to a baronetcy, while his daughter married Russell Grace D'Oench, the son of Albert Frederic D'Oench and Alice Grace, a daughter of William Russell Grace, the fabulously wealthy former New York mayor and founder of the great chemical conglomerate W. R. Grace and Company. (At his

[2] *Utica Herald Dispatch*, 6 August 1903, 6; *New York Times*, 28 October 1926. William Willoughby Sharp's father, grandfather and great-grandfather all were named William Willoughby Sharp. Sharp gave his own son the traditional family name as well. The male lineage of the Norfolk Sharps is as follows: William Willoughby Sharp I (1801-1871), William W[illougby] Sharp II (1826-1910), William Willoughby Sharp III (1863-1926), William Willoughby Sharp IV (1900-1956), William Willoughby Sharp V (1936-2008). On the Sharp family genealogy see http://familytreemaker.genealogy.com/users/b/r/y/William-Bryson-VA/WEBSITE-0001/UHP-0022.html. Dora Adams Hopkins was the daughter of Flournoy Woodbridge Adams, a member of the Georgia legislature. Her first husband, named for the former vice president of the Confederacy, was Alexander Stephens Livingston. Joseph Gaston Baillie Bulloch, *History and Genealogy of the Habersham Family* (Columbia, S. C.: R. L. Bryan, 1901), 65.

WILLOUGHBY SHARP
Photograph courtesy of the St. Paul's School Archives, Concord, NH

death in 1904 Grace left an estate of $25 million, or over $650 million today.) Their son Russell "Derry" D'Oench married Ellen "Puffin" Gates, who at Vassar was a classmate and friend of Jacqueline Bouvier (the future Jacqueline Kennedy). Their impending nuptials inspired Bouvier to pen a poem about them, the first lines of which run: "Puffin and Derry in wedded bliss soon will be/Vassar will miss her and so will we."[3]

Derry's uncle, the younger Willoughby Sharp, attended St. Paul's School, an elite New Hampshire prep school, where he played football (second string in the Delphian Club) and served as assistant editor on the *Horae Scholasticae*, the oldest literary school or college magazine in continuous publication in the United States. Already displaying a literary bent, Sharp during 1917-18 contributed to the *Horae Scholasticae* poetry of a rather higher order than that which Jacqueline Bouvier later penned in praise of Puffin and Derry. Lines from Sharp's "Changing Colors" suggest his early interest in the maritime world and foreshadow the setting of his first detective novel, *Murder in Bermuda* ("Rosy coral and black rock shells/Lay where the gleaming sun-fish glide/'Mid crimson sea-flowers and violet stones/Where carmine conchs and blue crabs hide/In the depths of the tossing sea"). With the entry of the United States into the Great War, however, martial subjects predictably came to fore in the young man's poetry. Sharp's longest and most impressive poem, "The Soldiers' Mass," evinces awareness on his part of the horrors of war, yet also expresses his faith in the "saving grace" of God. The last of Willoughby Sharp's war poems, "A Nation's Awakening," written in support of direct American intervention into Europe's armed struggle, is a fervent expression of Wilsonian idealism. Sharp denounces Germany, a "vandal" country that holds to "that vile, ruthless maxim—might makes right," for inflicting "Belgium's agony" and "Kultur on the seas"; and he rejoices that at last the "New World has responded

---

[3] *New York Times*, 28 October 1926, 25 January 2012; Edward Klein, *All Too Human: The Love Story of Jack and Jackie Kennedy* (New York: Pocket Books, 1996), 27.

to the plea/Of justice, freedom and democracy." This final war poem was published in the *Horae Scholasticae* on May 30, 1918, not long before Sharp graduated from St. Paul's School. Upon his graduation, Sharp put his words into action, enlisting in the United States Marine Corps.[4]

In 1919, Sharp, now a nineteen-year-old war veteran, matriculated at Harvard, where for a couple years he studied English literature. During this time he also wrote some crime stories for the pulps. One of Sharp's stories, "Dead Men Tell No Tales: A Story of Circumstantial Evidence," which originally appeared in *Munsey's Magazine* in June 1921, is included as an appendix to this volume. A dramatic tale of the trial of a pathetic clerk for the murder of his employer, "Dead Men Tell No Tales" dared to suggest to *Munsey's* readers that lady justice can be capricious. Had personal experience of war and its aftermath blunted the youthful idealism that Sharp voiced in his prep school poetry?[5]

After leaving Harvard and returning to New York, Willoughby Sharp for much of the 1920s appears to have lived the more jaded sort of life of the wealthy young man-about-town. An altercation in which Sharp was involved in 1922 at the fashionable Club du Montmartre, an all-night club located at Broadway and Fiftieth Street, gives us an interesting glimpse of his life at this time. With his friends John ("Jack") Boissevain and Louis Bertschmann, Sharp at around three in the morning left a dance at the Hotel Vanderbilt

[4] St. Paul's School *Alumni Horae* 36 (Spring 1956), 69; "Changing Colors," St. Paul's School *Horae Scholasticae* 50 (May 1917), 152; "The Soldiers's Mass," St. Paul's School *Horae Scholasticae* 51 (December 1917), 63; "A Nation's Awakening," St. Paul's School *Horae Scholasticae* 51 (May 1918), 181. Both the *Alumni Horae* and the *Scholasticae Horae* are located in the St. Paul's School Archives, Concord, New Hampshire. My thanks for her assistance to Lisa Laughy, Assistant Librarian, Ohrstrom Library, St. Paul's School.

[5] St. Paul's School *Alumni Horae* 36 (Spring 1956), 69, St. Paul's School Archives, Concord, New Hampshire. *Munsey's Magazine* had a circulation of around 60,000 in the 1920s. On *Munsey's Magazine* see Peter Haining, *The Classic Era of American Pulp Magazines* (London: Prion Books, 2000). My thanks to Bill Pronzini for alerting me to the existence of this early Willoughby Sharp story, written by Sharp when he was only about twenty years old.

to join a supper party being given by Henry Rau at the Montmartre. "A lot of nice people were there, including Prince Engalitcheff," Sharp confided to the *New York Times* reporter who came to interview him at his parents' brownstone to get his side of the story. Unfortunately, when the three chums reached the Montmartre, the doorman denied them admittance, claiming that the club was closed (in fact this was not true, as Rau's party was still ongoing). When the doorman tried to shut the door in their faces, Jack Boissevain inserted his cane between the door and its frame, allowing the determined trio to push through the portal into the entrance hall. The doorman, according to Sharp, responded by punching Boissevain and then punching Sharp, "very hard." "Naturally," declared Sharp to the sympathetic *New York Times* reporter, "we were not looking for any such treatment in a place that caters to ladies and gentlemen, so that we were taken by surprise." Sharp went down on the floor and was held there by the two Montmartre elevator operators while the doorman continued to punch him, giving him a black eye and a bloody nose. Extricating themselves from the affray, the three young men contacted the police, but by the time a sergeant and four policemen had arrived at the scene of the late battle, the doorman had fled the premises. "Propped up in bed . . . with a piece of gauze covering his injured nose but failing to conceal his black eye," Sharp explained that he had been moved to speak out about the incident "not on my own account, but because of the example, and because this is not the first time the same kind of thing has happened there [at the Montmartre]."[6]

Willoughby Sharp seems to have garnered sympathy over the affair at the Club du Montmartre, but he is said to have scandalized his family when he married a divorced former Ziegfeld chorus

---

[6] "Society Men Beaten in Montmartre Row," *New York Times*, 22 February 1922. Later that year the Club du Montmartre became a favored target of federal prohibition agents. See "Uncle Sam Starts War on Hip Flasks," *New York Times*, 18 August 1922; "Dry Squads Raid Broadway Clubs," *New York Times*, 30 September 1922; "Dry Up Broadway is New Police Order," *New York Times*, 8 December 1922. Montmartre habitué Prince Vladimir Nicholae-witch Engalitcheff (1901-1923) was the son of a Russian vice consul and his Chicago department store heiress wife. He graduated from Brown University

girl, Muriel Manners. Be that as it may, the Sharp-Manners union was a decidedly happy one and the couple eventually had four children, a son and three daughters. Sharp ceased dabbling in pulp fiction and in 1925 became a member of the New York Stock Exchange, courtesy of his father, who gifted him with a seat on the Exchange on the occasion of his twenty-fifth birthday. In 1928, two years after the death of his father, Sharp with Dudley Harde and Dudley Brown Harde established the rather forbiddingly named brokerage firm Harde & Sharp. The Sharps resided in a Park Avenue apartment with a bar that, most conveniently in the era of prohibition, could be folded back into and out of a wall. Painted with lions and tigers (though no bears), it was known as the Circus Bar. Here Willoughby and Muriel kept what their son described as "a kind of open house," entertaining "their friends and friends of friends and friends of friends of friends."[7]

Of course the great party was destined to come to a halt with the stock market crash. Sharp's son recalled that his father mordantly told him concerning this period in history that upon leaving his office at One Wall Street he always would look "up over his shoulder . . . in fear of being hit by people who jumped to their

in 1922 and joined a brokerage firm in New York. The next year he died very suddenly and unexpectedly in New York at his luxurious twelve-room Fifth Avenue apartment, supposedly of heart failure. F. Scott and Zelda Fitzgerald met the Prince in 1921. "We came to New York and rented a house when we were tight," reminisced Zelda to Scott in a rambling 1930 letter. "There was Val Engelicheff [sic] and Ted Paramour and dinner with Bunny [Edmund Wilson] in Washington Square and pills and Doctor Lackin and we had a violent quarrel on the train going back, I don't remember why." Jackson R. Bryer and Cathy W. Barks, *Dear Scott, Dearest Zelda: The Love Letters of F. Scott and Zelda Fitzgerald* (New York: St. Martin's, 2002), 67. F. Scott Fitzgerald partly based the character Prince Val Rostoff in his 1925 short story "Love in the Night" on Vladimir Engalitcheff. Robert L. Gale, *An F. Scott Fitzgerald Encyclopedia* (Westport, CT and London: Greenwood Press, 1998), 363. My thanks to Helen Szamuelly for helping me disentangle the various incorrect spellings of Engalitcheff.

[7] Linda Montano, "Interview with Willoughby Sharp," *Performance Artists Talking in the Eighties* (Los Angeles and London: University of California Press, 2000), 307; *New York Times*, 29 September 1922, 2 December 1934, 25 January 1936. The daughter of a wealthy Broadway play producer, Muriel

death from the building." In 1931, "not liking the outlook on Wall Street," Sharp sold his seat on the Stock Exchange and moved with his family to the island of Bermuda, marking a new direction in his life. There the family lived off judicious sales of costly pieces of jewelry that Willoughby Sharp had bought his wife back in the 1920s. After a couple years in Bermuda, Sharp felt inspired to compose his first detective novel, in which he imagined murder taking place on the peaceful island. Predictably enough, he titled the novel *Murder in Bermuda* (1933). Sharp wrote his second mystery, *Murder of the Honest Broker* (1934), in Bermuda as well, but during the summer of 1934 he went over the proofs while staying at New York's Calumet Club. Later that year, after the publication of *Murder of the Honest Broker* in August, the entire Sharp family returned to New York to stay and Sharp entered into a publishing partnership with a fellow New Yorker, Claude Kendall, the man who had published his two detective novels.[8]

Although forgotten today, the publishing firm *Claude Kendall* was a quite interesting business venture that sprang up and managed to thrive for a time amidst the onset and prolonged duration of the Great Depression. Older than Sharp by a decade, Claude Kendall, the man behind the company, was born in 1890 in the small city of Watertown, located in northwestern New York, near Lake Ontario. His father, Martin Kendall, was employed by the

---

Manners claimed to be a descendant, though her mother, of the mid-nineteenth-century actress, poet and essayist Adah Isaacs Menken (1835-1868), but this is a problematic claim, Menken's sons having died in infancy. Of mixed race parentage, Menken, who was probably originally named Adah Bertha Theodore, as a celebrated actress came to know many of the literary luminaries of her age, including Charles Dickens, Charles Swinburne, Alexandre Dumas and Walt Whitman. *Infelicia*, her sole book of poetry, published shortly after her death, was dedicated by her to Dickens. Possibly Muriel Manners, whose mother was Janet (Menken) MacMahon Manners, was descended from the family of Alexander Isaac Menken, a Jewish musician who was the first husband of Adah Bertha Theodore. See Michael Foster and Barbara Foster, *A Dangerous Woman: The Lives, Loves and Scandals of Adah Isaacs Menken, 1835-1868, America's Original Superstar* (Guilford, CT: Lyons Press, 2011).

[8] Montano, "Interview," 308; *New York Times Book Review*, 2 December 1934.

H. H. Babcock Company, one of the largest carriage manufactur-
ers in the United States. The young Claude was considered a live
spark, working as a "carrier boy" (i.e., paperboy) from the age of
ten and serving on the student council at Watertown High School.
At his high school graduation ceremony he was the student chosen
to recite Abraham Lincoln's Gettysburg Address.[9]

Claude Kendall began life in modest circumstances in a rather
out-of-the-way corner of the world, but he soon moved on to much
bigger things in life. His ticket out of Watertown came when, after
briefly working as a stenographer in a hardware company, he
landed an administrative position at the Mount Washington Hotel, one of great turn-of-the-century grand resort hotels, located
in the White Mountains at Bretton Woods, New Hampshire (in
1944 the hotel famously was the site of the Bretton Woods Confer-
ence, which established the International Monetary Fund). There
Kendall met investment banker M. H. Rice, who hired Kendall as
his personal secretary and took him to Europe for four months.
After the pair returned to the United States, Kendall settled in New
York City, where he was employed by Charles R. White & Co., an
investment banking firm, and for two years attended New York
University. When the United States entered World War One,
Kendall enlisted in the navy and was commissioned an ensign.
After the war he joined the United States Shipping Board as a
supercargo officer, in which capacity he traveled to both Europe
and East Asia. He then was hired by Standard Oil Company and
spent five months representing the company's interests in
Tampico, Mexico. After this latest foray into foreign fields he was
hired as a staff correspondent by the United Press and assigned to
South America. Finally returning to New York in the late 1920s,
Kendall charted an entirely new career course by founding his own
publishing house in 1929.[10]

[9] *Watertown Daily Times*, 24 May 1907, 26 November 1937. The articles
from the *Watertown Daily Times* cited in this essay come from the Claude
Kendall clippings file made available to me by Lisa M. Carr, librarian of the
Watertown Daily Times.
[10] *Watertown Daily Times*, 26 November 1937.

The first publication of Claude Kendall was *Uncle Sham*, a controversial critique of American culture by an Indian national, K. L. Gauba, who had been greatly incensed over the publication a couple years earlier of *Mother India*, a book by an American author, Katherine Mayo, which was scathingly critical of India's culture, particularly on account of the treatment of Indian women. The nettled Gauba responded in kind about the United States, often in frank and indelicate language, provoking the United States Customs Service to confiscate review copies of the book that had been sent from India to the United States, on the grounds that the writing was obscene. Having a keen nose for controversy, Kendall successfully published the book in the United States, putting his nascent company on the publishing map with a fine flush of notoriety. *Uncle Sham*'s dust jacket blurb boasted that Gauba's book revealed the "pools of nastiness, obscenity and vice" underlying "the smug morality of the United States." Curious readers—many of whom likely had never even stuck their toes in the water, so to speak—wanted at least to glimpse these pools. *Uncle Sham* sold well, quickly going through several printings.[11] Not for nothing was Kendall using this advertising motto on the *Uncle Sham* dust jacket:

Claude Kendall
Books That Sell

[11] *Foreign Affairs* 8 (October 1929) (review of *Uncle Sham* by William L. Langer), at http://www.foreignaffairs.com/articles/80378/kanhaya-lal-gauba/uncle-sham; *The Pittsburgh Press*, 3 August 1929, 6 (reprint of Lowell Mellett editorial against the proscription of *Uncle Sham*); K. L. Gauba, *Friends and Foes: An Autobiography* (New Delhi: Indian Book Company, 1974), 87. In her introduction to the 2000 University of Michigan Press edition of *Mother India*, Professor Mrinalini Sinha calls *Uncle Sham* "the most famous . . . of nationalist responses to *Mother India*" (p. 54). Claude Kendall quickly followed *Uncle Sham* with a second opportunistic publication of a work making a riposte to a notorious book of moment: Henry von Rhau's *The Hell of Loneliness*, an "impudent and delightfully scampish" parody of Radclyffe Hall's landmark 1928 lesbian novel (then banned in England), *The Well of Loneliness*.

Over the next few years, Kendall published a succession of what often were termed "spicy" or risqué books, attractively bound, printed and, frequently, illustrated. The most notorious and the most successful of these works were four novels by Tiffany Ellsworth Thayer ("Tiffany Thayer"). With several hundred thousand copies sold during the early 1930s, the Tiffany Thayer novels, particularly *Thirteen Men* (1930) and *Thirteen Women* (1932), earned Claude Kendall a great deal of publicity. Other controversial books from the early 1930s that bore the Kendall name include: the first American edition of Octave Mirbeau's *The Torture Garden*, a primary text of the Decadent Movement originally published in France in 1899; *Mademoiselle de Maupin*, an American edition of Théophile Gautier's gender-bending 1835 novel about a real-life infamous French female cross-dresser; G. Sheila Donisthorpe's *Loveliest of Friends*, a novel dealing with lesbianism; Cecil De Lenoir's *The Hundredth Man: Confessions of a Drug Addict*; Beth Brown's *Man and Wife,* about prostitution and the divorce racket; Lionel Houser's *Lake of Fire*, fairly described as a "bizarre tale of identity theft, mutilation, lust and murder, provocatively illustrated with strikingly explicit woodcuts"; and, last but certainly not least, Frank Walford's *Twisted Clay*, a lurid tale about a psychopathic, patricidal lesbian serial killer that was banned by government authorities in both Canada and Australia. Kendall also unsuccessfully attempted to secure the American publication rights for James Joyce's *Ulysses*, which had been banned in the United States on obscenity grounds since 1920.[12]

---

12 "She loved . . . and killed . . . both men and women," promised *Twisted Clay's* salacious dust jacket blurb. With *Twisted Clay* comprising a trifecta of casualties of moral outrage were Thayer's *Thirteen Men* and Donisthorpe's *Loveliest of Friends*, both of which also were banned in Canada. *Vancouver Sun*, 23 January 1932, 3. On Houser's *Lake of Fire*, see the summary found at *Golden Gate Mysteries: A Bibliography of Crime Fiction Set in the San Francisco Bay Area*, at http://bancroft.berkeley.edu/sfmystery/summaries/houslake.html. Sylvia Beach, the publisher in France of *Ulysses*, demanded from Kendall $25,000 for the novel's American publication rights, a figure that Kendall termed "absurd." Kendall doubted he could recoup the cost of both a $25,000 payment to Beach and litigation over the novel in American

Like its star author Tiffany Thayer, whose books F. Scott Fitzgerald—no Puritan he—disparaged as "slime . . . in the drugstore libraries," the firm of Claude Kendall developed *something of a reputation*. Newspaper notices that Claude Kendall books received in the 1930s often emphasized what was viewed as decidedly racy subject matter. Middle American reviewers seem to have been especially scandalized. One such individual in Greensburg, Indiana, (population under 6000 in 1930) deemed Thayer's *Thirteen Men* "morbid" and complained that "not even the Russians could pack more unhappiness in a single volume." In Salt Lake City, a reviewer for the *Deseret News* observed sardonically that Roswell Williams' *The Loves of Lo Foh* "will never be discussed at a ladies literary tea" and was "hardly suitable for the entertainment or education of budding youth." An especially incensed Midwestern reviewer for the Lawrence, Kansas *Journal-World* huffed that Tiffany Thayer's *An American Girl* was "an obscene novel without any merit whatever" and that Beth Brown's *Man and Wife* was "a worthless novel without any point or reason." For his part, Walter Stanley Campbell—a University of Oklahoma English professor who was Oklahoma's first Rhodes scholar and, under the pseudonym Stanley Vestal, a prolific author of books and articles on the old West (he even published a mystery, *The Wine Room Murder*, in 1935)—in the Oklahoma City *Daily Oklahoman* wrote sourly of Alan Lampe's *A Torch to Burn* (1935) that it was "another of the spicy novels for which the firm [Claude Kendall] is known. . . . of course the adventures are sad, gay and mad. Those who find night-clubs exciting will probably like this book." Similarly, Kenneth C. Kaufman—editor of the literary page of the *Daily Oklahoman*, a

courts. See Catherine Turner, *Marketing Modernism between the Two World Wars* (Amherst: University of Massachusetts Press, 2003), 193-193 and Keri Walsh, ed., *The Letters of Sylvia Beach* (New York: Columbia University Press, 2011), 136. In his book *Trial and Error: A Key to the Secret of Writing and Selling* (New York: Carlyle House, 1933), pulp writer Jack Woodford expressed amazement that Claude Kendall was able to publish its "splendid" edition of Mirbeau's *Torture Garden*: "I don't see how it would be possible to write a more 'dangerous' book (from the standpoint of the censor) yet it was published."

professor in the University of Oklahoma foreign languages department and mentor of Oklahoma detective novelist Todd Downing—
primly noted that the protagonist of Frank Walford's *Twisted Clay*
was "a young girl, a homosexual, who . . . indulges in all sorts of
sexual experiments, of which the less said the better. . . . it just
happens that I am not interested in sexual abnormalities."[13]

On the other hand, some reviewers savored the spice in Claude
Kendall books. The esteemed California novelist Gertrude Atherton
said of Lionel Houser's *Lake of Fire*, for example, that it had "ex-
cellence, brilliance, distinction, originality and high imaginative
fire." In his syndicated "A Book a Day" column, the future Pulitzer
Prize winning narrative historian Bruce Catton deemed *Twisted
Clay* "a creepy tale about the collapse of a mind" that was certain
"to make you shudder," while a reviewer for the *New York Daily
Mirror* proclaimed the novel "a prose nightmare, tinged with Poe

---

13 F. Scott Fitzgerald, *The Crack-Up* (1945; rpnt, New York: New Directions,
1993), 78; *Greensburg Daily Review*, 6 June 1930, 24; *Salt Lake City Deseret
News*, 27 June 1936, 6; *Lawrence Journal-World*, 10 June 1933, 5; *Okla-
homa City Daily Oklahoman*, 22 July 1934, 45, 23 June 1935, 49. Kenneth
Kaufman allowed, however, that sexual abnormalities "may, with proper han-
dling, become legitimate material for a work of art." Like Kenneth Kaufman,
Todd Downing taught in the OU foreign languages department. For more on
Todd Downing and his OU colleagues, see Curtis Evans, *Clues and Corpses:
The Detective Fiction and Mystery Criticism of Todd Downing* (Greenville,
OH: Coachwhip, 2013). F. Scott Fitzgerald's scornful reference to Thayer
appeared in his 1936 "Crack-Up" essays, when Fitzgerald was at a personal
low point and must have found the slick success of someone like Thayer
especially disheartening. "I saw that the novel, which at my maturity was the
strongest and supplest medium for conveying thought and emotion from one
human being to another, was becoming subordinated to a mechanical and
communal art that...was capable of reflecting only the tritest thought, the
most obvious emotion," Fitzgerald bitterly reflected of literary culture in the
1930s. Fitzgerald, *Crack-Up*, 78. The writer Dorothy Parker concurred in
Fitzgerald's dismissive assessment of Thayer, writing satirically in her 1933
New Yorker review of Thayer's *An American Girl*: "[Tiffany Thayer] is beyond
question a writer of power; and his power lies in his ability to make sex so
thoroughly, graphically, and aggressively unattractive that one is fairly shaken
to ponder how little one has been missing." Bendan Gill, ed., *The Portable
Dorothy Parker* (1944; rev. ed., New York, Penguin Books, 1976), 549.

and Baudelaire substance." A reviewer for the *Providence Journal* deemed *Thirteen Men* "a masterpiece of our time."[14]

For his part, Claude Kendall remained cheerfully sanguine about the stones hostile critics cast at the books his firm published. Of the Kendall novel *Tangled Wives* (written by divorced journalist Peggy Shane), for example, Kendall bluntly pronounced: "It is not the great American novel; it is, however, swell entertainment." In those rental libraries dotting America that F. Scott Fitzgerald so witheringly disparaged, people crowded to borrow Claude Kendall books. With all the money rolling into the Claude Kendall coffers, the publisher was able to take up residence in a luxurious Manhattan penthouse apartment—one formerly occupied, newspapers were wont to note, by the actress Ethel Barrymore.[15]

In comparison with Claude Kendall's more risqué and attention-grabbing mainstream books, the detective and mystery fiction that the firm published offered subtler attractions. Besides the detective novels of Willoughby Sharp, books on the Claude Kendall mystery list included Andrew Soutar's *Secret Ways*, J. R. Wilmot's *Death in the Theater*, David Whitelaw's *Murder Calling* and Willam Sutherland's *Death Rides the Air Line*. All these titles seem originally to have appeared in England and were published by Claude Kendall in the fall and winter of 1934. All are competent pieces of mystery fiction, though only the Sutherland novel, with its unique plot structure and somewhat unsavory subject matter, departs from traditional Golden Age mystery norms.[16]

---

[14] *Berkeley Daily Gazette*, 15 April 1933, 4; *Spartanburg Herald*, 22 June 1934, 4. See also the review blurbs found on the dust jackets of the Claude Kendall editions of *Death Rides the Air Line* and *Murder Calling*.

[15] *Milwaukee Journal*, 19 November 1932, 4; *Watertown Daily Times*, 27 December 1932.

[16] William Sutherland's previous detective novel, *Behind the Head-lines* (1933), was published in England but not the United States. The name was the pseudonym of John Murray Cooper, who may have been the John Murray Cooper (1908-1991) who was an American war correspondent during World War Two. "William Sutherland" also published in England a third detective novel, *The Proverbial Murder Case* (1935). My thanks for this information go to Alexander Inglis and Douglas G. Greene.

Willoughby Sharp did not formally enter into Claude Kendall & Willoughby Sharp, Inc., his publishing partnership with Claude Kendall, until November 1934, yet he likely influenced Kendall's selection of mystery titles during the latter half of that year. Additionally, Sharp was scheduled to publish with Kendall & Sharp a third detective novel, *The Mystery of the Multiplying Mules*, in 1935. However, this novel never appeared, nor does Kendall & Sharp seem to have published any additional true mysteries over the scant sixteen months of its existence, despite the company's intriguing announcement in March 1936 that it was planning a monthly series of detective novels, to be released under a new imprint, the Clue Chasers Club, presumably under Sharp's supervision.[17]

In point of fact, Sharp apparently sundered his relationship with Kendall & Sharp mere weeks after the March 1936 announcement about the formation of the Clue Chasers Club; and the company, now styled Claude Kendall, Inc., went bankrupt before the end of the year. This was a bad blow for Kendall, but he stayed on his feet and accepted a position with the publisher James T. White

---

17 *New York Times Book Review*, 22 November, 2 December 1934. A possible exception to this generalization might be *The Second Mrs. Lynton* (1935), a tale by Wilson Collison (1893-1941), a prolific writer of novels, plays and film scripts, yet the book seems to be more a romantic melodrama than a true detective novel. "It is fairly apparent that the guilt for Dexter's unmourned death rests upon either Carla or Beth, her hysterical stepdaughter," pronounced the reviewer of the book in the *New York Times Book Review*, "and it does not require any very brilliant deduction feats for Channing to conclusively prove and correctly pick which lady actually fired the fatal shot." *New York Times Book Review*, 28 July 1935. In the publisher's blurb Kendall & Sharp avowed that *The Second Mrs. Lynton* "is a love story, not a mystery, yet it combines the elements of both types of novels." The Clue Chasers Club recalls Doubleday, Doran's highly successful Crime Club imprint. Another small publisher, Hillman-Curl, launched a "Clue Club" in 1937. See Bill Pronzini, "Hillman-Curl [1936-1939]," in William F. Deeck, ed., *Murder at 3 Cents a Day: An Annotated Crime Fiction Bibliography of the Lending Library Publishers, 1936 to 1937*, at http://www.lendinglibmystery.com/HCurl/Covers.html.

& Co. Sadly, however, the ex-publisher was not destined to long survive his defunct business.[18]

By 1937, Claude Kendall had vacated the Manhattan penthouse apartment once occupied by Ethel Barrymore and moved into a $7-a-week room at the Madison Hotel, located at 21 East Twenty-Seventh Street, just off Madison Avenue. On the morning of November 25, 1937, a hotel maid entering Kendall's room found the ex-publisher dead on the floor, a bed sheet wrapped around his neck. The medical examiner's report concluded that Kendall had been the victim of a "homicidal assault," dying from "shock and hemorrhages caused by repeated blows on the face and neck." Kendall's killer almost certainly was a "slightly built youthful white man" whom Kendall took up to his room at about 3:30 in the morning on Thanksgiving Day. Richard Barry, a fiction writer who with his wife resided in the room directly above Kendall, told police that beginning around 4:30 a.m. he and his wife had heard loud "thumping noises" in Kendall's room. These noises continued for half an hour.[19]

[18] *FOB: Firms out of Business*, Harry Ransom Center, The University of Texas at Austin, at http://norman.hrc.utexas.edu/Watch/fob_search_results_next.cfm?FOBFirmName=C&FOBNote=&locSTARTROW=101; *New York Times Book Review*, 1, 22 March 1936; *Watertown Daily Times*, 26 November 1937. The announcement that Claude Kendall was forming "a publishing firm to be known as Claude Kendall, Inc." was made in the *New York Times Book Review* on March 22, 1936. That month the Kendall & Sharp offices were relinquished and Kendall hired a new editor-in-chief, Geoffrey Marks, a graduate of Trinity College, Oxford, as well as a new agency to handle advertising. *New York Times Book Review*, 20, 22, 30 March 1936. Many years later Willoughby Sharp's son stated in an interview that "Kendall absconded with hundreds of thousands of dollars," causing Kendall & Sharp to go under, but this claim does not seem in accord with the information reported in the *New York Times*, or the fact that Kendall was living in New York, reputably employed, a year later and apparently on decent terms with Sharp. However, it does seem quite possible that Kendall lived over lavishly off the firm's profits, alienating his new partner. Montano, "Interview," 308.

[19] *New York Times*, 26, 27 November 1937; *Reading Eagle*, 27 November 1937, 2, *Watertown Daily Times*, 26 November 1937. Richard Barry, the fiction writer who lived above Kendall and heard those suggestive early morning thumps, probably is the Richard Barry who wrote the lost race novel *Fruit of the Desert* (1920), as well as several adventure serials for the pulp magazine *Argosy*.

Despite having this clearly marked trail to follow, the police apparently failed to find Kendall's killer. Of course, in the stereotypical 1930s detective novel, Kendall's murder would have been solved not by some invariably bumbling police inspector but rather by the murder victim's dapper, sophisticated and oh-so wealthy dilettante friend, Willoughby Sharp (the man even came supplied with a simply smashin' amateur gentleman detective moniker, don't you know). And, to be sure, when he was interviewed by the press, Sharp did have some advice to offer investigators. The detective novelist opined that the murder "undoubtedly" was the result of a robbery committed by the slim young man who accompanied Kendall back to his hotel room; and he suggested that to find this man the police should make "a close check of the bars Claude frequented." Sharp explained that his ex-partner "was a gregarious person, liked to talk, and he was friendly and could make acquaintances easily."[20]

Willoughby Sharp may have missed his chance to solve a real-life mystery (a fictionalized version of the Claude Kendall case might well have been called *Murder of My Ex-Partner*), yet with *Murder in Bermuda* and *Murder of the Honest Broker* Sharp gifted fans of classical mystery fiction with two top-drawer 1930s mysteries, both delightful examples of the Golden Age puzzle-oriented detective novel. The two appealing tales also were excellent sellers for Claude Kendall, and were published not just in the United States but also in England and Germany—though there was a financial hitch with Germany in 1935, when Nazi authorities refused to export monies due Kendall & Sharp on the first three printings of Sharp's *Murder in Bermuda*; it finally was agreed that the German publishers would remit to Kendall & Sharp "in kind—kind being 100 cases of the finest Rhine wines."[21]

[20] *Watertown Daily Times*, 27 November 1937. The available facts concerning Claude Kendall's murder strongly suggest to me that the killer was a male hustler whom Kendall picked up at a bar. On hustling in New York in the 1930s see George Chauncey, *Gay New York: Gender, Urban Culture and the Making of the Gay Male World, 1890-1940* (New York: Basic Books, 1994), 191-192.
[21] *New York Times Book Review*, 24 February 1935.

After eight decades, Willoughby Sharp's excellent tales of detection are finally in print again, courtesy of the industrious Coachwhip Publications. So what makes these mysteries appealing to fans of Golden Age crime fiction? *Murder in Bermuda* naturally benefits from the fact that Willoughby Sharp had been living in Bermuda for two years when he wrote the novel. Over the course of the first third of the twentieth century the beautiful island increasingly attracted moneyed American tourists. "As elite tourism gave way to mass tourism," notes one scholar, "America's wealthy went further afield. In addition to its sandy beaches and temperate year-round climate, Bermuda had the distinct advantage of being an island colony. Ordinary Americans could not hop into their cars and drive there." Ordinary, homebound Americans, however, could read about Bermuda in Willoughby Sharp's novel.[22]

One of the most surprising things about Bermuda that non-Bermudans would have learned from perusing *Murder in Bermuda* is that motor cars were prohibited on the island in the 1930s. At the behest of writer Mark Twain, future United States president Woodrow Wilson had drawn up a petition of prominent American tourists of Bermuda, requesting that automobiles be banned from the island, on the grounds that auto traffic on the island was offensive "to persons of taste and cultivation." Knowing who buttered their bread, so to speak, Bermudans with the 1908 Motor Car Bill banned all motorized vehicles on the island. This prohibition was not repealed until 1946. During the years the Motor Car Bill held sway, Bermudans were limited for transportation either to horse and buggy or bicycle until 1931, when a single line railway running from St. George's to Somerset by way of Hamilton was completed. All these forms of transport, including the recently completed railway, make their appearances in *Murder in Bermuda*.[23]

In addition to the appealing local color Sharp provides in *Murder in Bermuda*, readers also will discover in the book's pages an

[22] Steven High, *Base Colonies in the Western Hemisphere, 1940-1967* (New York: Palgrave Macmillan, 2009), 45-46.

[23] High, *Base Colonies*, 45-46; "The Years of Change 1930-1979," *Bermuda Police History*, at http://www.bermudapoliceservice.bm/node/102.

interesting puzzle and a pleasingly realistic depiction of police procedure. *Bermuda* details the police investigation that occurs after Constable Simmons, on the morning before Easter, discovers a woman's lifeless body on Snake Road. The woman has been stabbed to death. Incongruously, a bouquet of lilies lies by her side. From the slender clue of the Easter lilies an intricately interlaced murder problem quickly blossoms. The Bermuda police are shocked to find that a murder has occurred on their peaceful isle. "Damn it, Simmons!" laments Inspector McNear. "What's this island coming to when a girl's not safe on the highway?" Today the inspector's plaint seems rather quaint, no doubt, but in fact Bermuda was known in the 1930s for its paucity of violent crime (bootlegging was not counted as such, of course). "There has never been a murder in Bermuda in my time—not among our white people at least," reflects a worried Chief of Police Masters. "I ask you to think of the most unpleasant publicity if we admitted it to be murder! Think how the interests of the island would suffer!" Yet murder it inarguably proves, much to the mortification of Masters. Soon another person is found dead, a man this time. He has been polished off in Hamilton, the territorial capital, by means of a favored 1920s poison, mercury bichloride. "If there's another crime in Hamilton I'm going to move to Chicago," announces one islander.[24]

It becomes apparent that the rash of criminal mayhem in Bermuda may be connected to the abduction of a young child in the United States. Surely Willoughby Sharp was influenced to include this plot element in his novel by the notorious Lindbergh kidnapping case of 1932, which also famously inspired Agatha Christie's

---

[24] Willoughby Sharp, *Murder in Bermuda* (1933; rept., Greenville, OH: Coachwhip, 2013), p. 122. On mercury bichloride deaths in the 1920s see "Popular Poisons Part II: Mercury Bichloride," *Mary Miley's Roaring Twenties: A Unique Decade in American History*, at http://marymiley.wordpress.com/2009/08/15/popular-poisons-part-ii-mercury-bichloride/. "It is said that there has never been a murder in Bermuda," the notice for *Murder in Bermuda* in the *New York Times Book Review* noted sardonically, "but since the island has become a favorite resort of Americans, a people notoriously addicted to homicide, there is no telling what may happen in days to come." *New York Times Book Review*, 27 August 1933.

Murder on the Orient Express (1934). Interestingly, Sharp, a scion of American wealth and privilege with young children of his own, allowed himself a bit of acid social commentary concerning the markedly unequal attention afforded by the American press in a depression-wracked decade to the tragedies of the rich and the poor. "Quite typical of a rich, individualistic nation in which fifteen million men, with their wives and children, were undergoing various stages of starvation," he wrote caustically, "the kidnapping of little Marcia Marsden from the Fifth Avenue home of her fabulously wealthy parents had filled the front sheets of America's daily newspapers until even the stirring foreign political news was crowded to an inside page."[25]

Happily, in Sharp's fictional mystery tale the dark tragedy that enshrouded the Lindbergh family is averted and his puzzle, which involves some clever authorial sleights-of-hand, is solved—not by some preternaturally gifted amateur detective who happens to be visiting Bermuda, it should be added, but by the dogged local police force. *Murder in Bermuda* actually is an early police procedural crime novel, in that the book focuses on the investigatory activities not of one Great Detective, but rather an entire police force. To be sure, three men predominate: Chief of Police Masters, Superintendent Welch and Inspector McNear. It is Welch who has the keenest insights into the crimes, yet several men have their moments to shine, including Constable Simmons, the only black cop we get to see in action in the tale.[26]

The reviewer in the Book of the Week column of *The Harvard Crimson* perceptively noted the unusual emphasis on police detail

---

[25] Sharp, *Bermuda*, p. 62.

[26] Constable Simmons appears to have been partly inspired by Charles Edward Simons, who had been appointed Bermuda's first Detective Officer in 1919 and "soon became a familiar figure to one and all as he pedal cycled around the island investigating crime." See "The Early Years 1609-1929," *Bermuda Police History*, at http://www.bermudapoliceservice.bm/node/101. By 1933, Bermuda had a police force that numbered seventy-five individuals, "two-thirds of whom were expatriate Englishmen." See "The Years of Change 1930-1979," *Bermuda Police History*, at http://www.bermudapolice service.bm/node/102.

in *Murder in Bermuda*: "The pleasant variation from the general mystery story is the manner in which the various police officers working upon the case help each other and together see the thing through, so that in this story, instead of the one stereotyped super sleuth very nobly carrying on, we have the small group solve their problem by their cooperative efforts." The reviewer also highly praised the novel more generally, noting especially its "welcome freshness and originality" and the technical assurance of its author: "[Sharp] utilizes all the long-accepted conventions of the mystery story, but he does so with such ingenuity and creates such a welter of involved circumstances that we are almost entirely unaware of his technical trickery."[27]

A chorus of American reviewers echoed this *Crimson* laudation. "Willoughby Sharp has produced an entertaining yarn with enough legitimately misleading clues scattered through it to keep the reader guessing wrong most of the time," declared the notice in the *New York Times Book Review*. Joining in the hymn of praise, the reviewer for the Albany, New York, *Knickerbocker Press* avowed that the novel was "as complicated and satisfying a mystery as one could hope to find." On the other side of the United States in California, the *Sacramento Bee* reviewer concurred, confidently asserting that any reader would be "loath to lay down [*Murder in Bermuda*] until the final page is completed."[28]

Willoughby Sharp's second detective novel, *Murder of the Honest Broker*, maintains the standard of *Murder in Bermuda*, again offering readers an interesting, authentically depicted setting for violent death, as well as an intriguing fair play puzzle. *Broker* takes us back to the United States, to a very different locale from *Bermuda*, yet, withal, one with which Willoughby Sharp was quite familiar: the New York Stock Exchange. In his review of the novel in the *Daily Oklahoman*, Todd Downing suggested that Sharp had caught the temper of the times: "It's axiomatic with mystery

---

[27] "In Bermuda," *The Harvard Crimson*, 28 October 1933.
[28] These reviews snippets are drawn from the back panel of the Claude Kendall edition of *Murder of the Honest Broker*.

writers that readers like to vent spleen vicariously upon the corpse, so what's more welcome these days than a nice, well-fed financier?"[29]

In *Murder of the Honest Broker*, the generous Willoughby Sharp actually provided, for the delighted Depression-era reader's delectation, the corpses of not one, but two, well-fed financiers. Continuing the streak of originality he had exhibited in *Murder in Bermuda*, he also introduced a new lead detective: Inspector Bullock, an acerbic, tough guy New York cop who is amusingly endowed with an abiding aversion to the great cloud of fictional gentleman amateur sleuths, such as Philo Vance, Ellery Queen and Drury Lane, that plagues the New York police force, snapping up every last clue like hungry locusts. "I'd like to run up against one of those mincing, namby-pamby, know-it-alls just once," cries Bullock. "Detectives! Bah! They and their Egyptian mummies and stuffed fish and their underground passages and their slant-eyed Chinese hatchet men. They give me a great big pain and I'll give you one guess where!"[30]

The "honest broker" of the title is the prominent New York stockbroker Philip Torrent. He dramatically dies on the floor of the Stock Exchange, from some form of poison. Another broker, Sandy Harrison, expires in his office at the Exchange only a few minutes later. Bizarrely, he too has been poisoned. "Don't tell me it's a strange, oriental poison known only to the high priests of an obscure tribe in the upper Himalayas," Inspector Bullock sarcastically advises the Medical Examiner. "Don't tell me that, 'cause I'm way behind on my Fu-Manchu stories."[31]

---

[29] Evans, *Clues and Corpses*, p. 258.

[30] Willoughby Sharp, *Murder of the Honest Broker* (1934; rept, Greenville, OH: Coachwhip Publications, 2013), p. 52. Bullock's comments reference S. S. Van Dine's Philo Vance detective novels, *The Scarab Murder Case* (1930) and *The Dragon Murder Case* (1933), as well as the Dr. Fu Manchu mystery thrillers written by Sax Rohmer and possibly Alexandra David-Neel's *Magic and Mystery in Tibet* (1932), perhaps the most successful non-fiction book published by Claude Kendall. This latter book was also referenced in two highly praised 1938 mysteries by Clyde B. Clason and Clayton Rawson, *The Man from Tibet* and *Death from a Top Hat*.

[31] Sharp, *Broker*, p. 59.

Just *how* the two men were poisoned is as a tricky question as *who* was behind it. Certainly there is no shortage of murder suspects in the case of Philip Torrent. At least a half-dozen people had motives for his murder: the brokerage partner, who has been defrauding Torrent; the unfaithful wife, who has been carrying on an affair; the unfaithful wife's broker boyfriend, who is angry that Torrent will not give her a divorce; the debauched nephew, who wants the money that Torrent holds in trust for him; the discarded mistress, who still carries a torch for Torrent; and the speakeasy partner, who finds it extremely inconvenient at the moment to return Torrent's investment funds. But who had a motive to kill Sandy Harrison as well? It adds up to a tricky problem for Inspector Bullock, who at no point in his investigation spares tears for the stockbroker murder victims. This is Bullock's response when he first hears of the deaths of the two men:

> "Two members of the Stock exchange have been poisoned."
>
> "Whee!" whistled the inspector. "Ain't that what they call the perfect crime? Somebody beat me to it! I've had my eye on that job myself ever since the time I lost five hundred dollars in Anaconda Copper back in '29."[32]

Inspector Bullock emphatically is no respecter of persons, be they of high or low social station. On one occasion he makes his class resentment clear to Mr. Barton, an assistant secretary of the Stock Exchange:

---

[32] Ibid, p. 53. Inspector Bullock refers to a late 1920s boom and bust cycle in the values of Anaconda Copper shares, which wiped out the savings of many small investors. The losses were blamed on a share pushing scheme by Percy Rockefeller and other tycoons. See Lucy Moore, *Anything Goes: A Biography of the Roaring Twenties* (New York: The Overlook Press, 2010). Obviously Sharp, who was on the New York Stock Exchange at the time, would have been well aware of what was going on behind the financial curtain, so to speak.

"Will the head waiter be there [at the Luncheon Club] now?" asked Bullock. "It's 5 o'clock."

"Yes," smiled Barton. "It's another one the blessings of Repeal [of Prohibition]. This time two years ago the Club was deserted after three o'clock but now the members like to linger in our new bar and lately they've even taken to ordering their dinners there."

"That's a funny thing," said Inspector Bullock. "The exact same thing happened in my club, the McGillogolly Social Association of Brooklyn. Lately we've had to throw the boys out on their pants at the closing hour."

Mr. Barton's face lost its affable smile. "Oh, yes, quite," he finally managed to reply.[33]

Bullock is similarly *direct* with his subordinates:

"That you, Mulligan? Your troubles aren't over. Go back to the Alden Apartments, sit downstairs in the lobby and if that girl goes out tonight you stick to her tighter than a chorus girl's brassiere."[34]

Love him or hate him, Willoughby Sharp's Inspector Bullock is, as they used to say, *a real live wire* (and he does in fact solve what turns out to be for him a frustratingly bookish case, though only after consulting the *Encyclopedia Britannica*). Admittedly, the other characters in *Broker* are more in the nature of stock, although it is gratifying to see that Philip Torrent's speakeasy partner, Chipo Marinelli, is one of the rarest of things in Golden Age Anglo-American mystery, an Italian male who does not spend all his time speaking in painfully exaggerated dialect, gesticulating wildly and threatening people with death by stiletto. In both *Bermuda* and *Broker* Sharp commendably refrains from crudely

[33] Sharp, *Broker*, p. 77.
[34] Ibid, pp. 96-97.

caricaturing individuals belonging to racial/ethnic groups that stand outside the WASP charmed circle.

Like *Bermuda, Broker* garnered good critical notices. The take in *Kirkus Reviews*—"Good reading and an ingenious solution"— was echoed in the *New York Times Book Review*, which pronounced: "An amusing yarn and a puzzling one." For fans of classical detection, a delighted Todd Downing avowed, reading *Murder of an Honest Broker* was "like meeting a long lost friend."[35]

For 1935 Willoughby Sharp had promised detective fiction devotees that he would deliver another Inspector Bullock adventure, *The Mystery of the Multiplying Mules*, yet it never appeared, despite being advertised by Claude Kendall as a soon-to-be-published book. Certainly the title is intriguing, as is the brief description of the plot given in Claude Kendall promotional material: "Inspector Bullock is called in by the Logans not because something has been stolen, but because something has been added to their household. On three successive Friday mornings they have found in their locked barn, mingling with their own animals, two strange mules. Before the reason for the multiplying mules is found, three deaths follow in rapid order." Sadly, crime fiction fans up to this day have never yet been able to learn how Inspector Bullock mastered the mystifying matter of those multiplying mules. Perhaps one day Sharp's manuscript will suddenly appear (assuming it ever in fact existed).

After retiring from the crime fiction field and his publishing venture with Claude Kendall in 1936, Willoughby Sharp lived for two more decades. In 1943 he joined the Research Institute of America as an account executive. When, after a long illness, he passed away in New York City in 1956, he was a member of the Research institute's executive staff. Sharp's best-known contribution to posterity, however, surely is his son, also named William Willoughby Sharp, who was born in 1936, the same year that his

---

[35] *Kirkus Reviews*, 10 August 1934; *New York Times Review*, 19 August 1934; Evans, *Clues and Corpses*, p. 258.

father left Kendall & Sharp. The younger Willoughby Sharp, who died in 2008, was an internationally renowned conceptual artist.[36]

The elder Sharp's two murder mysteries were never reprinted in paperback after their initial appearances in the United States in 1933 and 1934, respectively, and, as we have seen, Sharp's publisher, Claude Kendall, met his own violent demise at malign hands in 1937. If ever an author had seemed to have dropped into the pit of artistic annihilation, surely it was Willoughby Sharp. But seasoned mystery fans know to expect surprise endings and here, happily, they now have one. The delightfully devious detective fiction of Willoughby Sharp has returned from the dead, to entertain a new generation of discriminating classical mystery fans.

---

[36] See "Willoughby Sharp, 72, Versatile Avant-Gardist, Is Dead," *New York Times*, 30 December 2008.

MURDER IN BERMUDA

1
DEATH ON A HIGHWAY

Saturday Morning, April 10th.

To Constable Simmons that morning before Easter began as serenely as every other morning of his twenty years' service with the Bermuda Police Force. And half an hour after a peaceful breakfast found him pedaling sedately from his home in Khyber Pass across the limestone surface of Middle Highway to await the ferry which touched at Darrel's Wharf.

The tranquil sunlight was like a steady golden shower. There was a shimmer of green from the carefully tended fields, the glitter of blue from the surrounding sea; and Constable Simmons as a native Bermudian enjoyed the scene with all the ardour of an American tourist seeing the island for the first time.

One of those muscular West Indian negroes, Constable Simmons had a straight, fastidious nose on which a pair of large horn-rimmed spectacles set with appropriate gravity. His skin was a fine old copper and his grey, frizzy moustache gave him an expression of severe dignity.

As he pedaled down Snake Road he smiled benignly, for he saw the ferry, the old *Laconia*, still far enough from shore to assure a leisurely meeting at Darrel's Wharf. And besides, the road dipped so that he had a long stretch of effortless coasting.

Setting his coaster-brake and letting the bicycle wheels spin freely, Constable Simmons, comfortably relaxed, turned an approving eye on the flowering hibiscus which hedged the roadside. Farther on grew oleander, soon to be in bud.

"Eek!" The healthy copper of his skin turned to a sickish blue. Constable Simmons hastily swerved his handle bars to avoid running over a lifeless object by the edge of the road. He had meant to bellow his dismay, and it was no fault of his that the noise he made was like the squeak of a mouse. He filled his lungs for a lusty shout, but terror again contracted the muscles in his throat. "Eek! eek!" he choked desperately.

Constable Simmons had seen a dead body where he knew it shouldn't be. It suggested violent death. He had studied the little blue book of police regulations till he had learned it by heart. For twenty years he had been an exemplary officer of the law. But now, with such an unexpectedly appalling sight before him, he began to pedal wildly, as if King Voodoo and all the malignant spirits of the night were howling at his back.

It would have been a long, weary ride to Police Headquarters in Hamilton, but, luckily for Constable Simmons' legs and his reputation as a dependable man, when he saw the painted front of an A-1 Grocery his reason reasserted itself. Riding up to the steps, he jumped off the bicycle and ran inside past the astonished clerk to the telephone.

While the clerk gaped, he called Headquarters in a shaky voice. The Chief of Police answered coolly, "Hello. Masters speaking."

Constable Simmons tremblingly gasped his report, shattering the police chief's calm. "A body, sare. A lady, I should say. I very nearly ran over it on Snake Road."

"What, what?" Masters snapped. "A lady's body?" His voice sounded incredulous. "Come, come, Simmons, is that what you're telling me?"

"Y-yes, sare!" Simmons answered in his tensely sibilant tone.

"Well." Masters seemed to be at a loss for a moment. Then he suddenly recovered and became sharply executive. "Go back there instantly. Don't leave until somebody arrives from here. You should never have left in the first place. I'll send McNear—he lives closest, and if he's still at home he'll get there before anyone else."

Hearing the Chief's receiver click, Simmons backed away from the telephone and wiped his sweaty forehead. "Whoo-ee!" he muttered unhappily.

"I say," the amazed clerk asked dubiously, "what's this about a body?"

Simmons' thin, dark lips tightened determinedly. He glanced proudly down at the silver service chevrons on the sleeve of his neat serge jacket and went out to his bicycle.

Under the all-pervasive sunlight the island lay bright and placid as before. There were fields of shiny Bermuda grass and scattered patches of freshly flowering Easter lilies. Far out in Grassy Bay, beyond a score of tiny islands, lay six recently anchored cruise ships filled to the gunwales with holiday tourists from the States. And steaming to meet them across the shallow water ran a hooting shoal of tenders to fetch the passengers back to the streets of Hamilton. The fields, the seldom-failing sun, the ships, the coral reefs, the calm—each feature of the scene was a familiar sight. But to Constable Simmons, with his memory of that horribly lax body by Snake Road, the bright Bermuda quiet was like the drums and cymbals of a tragedy.

Still shaky from dismay, he pedaled on up the Middle Highway hill past the budding oleander shrubs to the scented hibiscus hedge. There he climbed off his bicycle and respectfully approached on foot. Nearing the top of the hill he saw a white slipper and a silk stocking ending at the hem of a summer dress. The body was lying upturned on the grass, the slipper extending into the limestone road, the head half-hidden by the flowering hedge. But the girl's bosom was in plain sight and on the white cloth blood showed both wet and bright. Simmons grimaced and looked hastily away.

Laying his bicycle on its side, Simmons gingerly sat down on the edge of the road and awaited the arrival of Inspector McNear.

2

THE BOUQUET OF LILIES

Saturday Morning, April 10th.

Horse's hoofbeats and the creak of swift carriage wheels sounded on the highway, and Simmons, vainly mustering his lost dignity, stood up and assumed an air of efficiency with which to impress Inspector McNear.

Burly, red-headed and usually jovial, the Inspector rode up full of unconcealed concern. He climbed out of the carriage and nodded abruptly, first at Simmons and then at the body. He twisted his broad, freckled face into an expression of repugnance and said, "Whew! Rotten business, Simmons."

"Yes, sare," Simmons answered promptly.

Inspector McNear bent over the body. "This just the way you found it?" As the Constable nodded the Inspector frowned thoughtfully down at the small, lifeless figure. The girl was extremely pretty—about twenty-two, with black hair and pert, attractive features. Her arms were stretched out at her sides, as though she had tried to fling something away from her when she fell. She wore a white linen sports dress and a gay knitted beret which had slipped forward so that it partly obscured one heavily fringed eye. Since the bloodstain on her bosom was still widening, it was evident that she had been struck only a short time before. It was also clear from her untroubled attitude that death must have come without a struggle and almost instantaneously. By her left hand lay a huge bunch of lilies bound together by a wide, green ribbon.

McNear stood up and rubbed the dust from his hands. "You'd think she'd have had a handbag, now wouldn't you?" he said a little reproachfully.

Simmons asked anxiously, "Does it look like robbery?"

McNear took out his pipe and bit at the end of it. "You'd think she'd have had a bag," he repeated doggedly, "and if there's no bag here—well, maybe somebody stole it."

"But who?" Simmons demanded. "Nobody from this neighbourhood, sare!"

McNear slowly crammed tobacco into his pipe bowl. "No jewellery either," he observed. "No necklace, bracelet or rings—but then, if she had on a sports dress you wouldn't expect her to wear jewellery, would you?"

To this question Constable Simmons spread out his dark hands in a gesture of such abject helplessness that McNear began quietly to swear at his own ineptitude.

"We don't know much," McNear said finally, "and that's the truth. Here's the body of a strange girl, and by the looks of that wound I'd say she had been murdered. But we don't know that much, for certain. We don't know what she was doing here or where she came from—at least, I don't." He looked at Simmons hopefully. "You've never seen her before, have you?"

Simmons shook his head. "I'd have remembered it if I had."

McNear looked down at the girl again. A little timidly he knelt beside her. "Simmons," he said soberly, more as if to reassure himself than to seek the Constable's co-operation, "we've got to find out about this." And as he spoke he gingerly drew one of the girl's slippers off her stockinged foot.

He frowned. "Thought I could tell where she bought it," he explained, "but the trade mark's worn off."

Simmons leaned forward with bated eagerness. "Perhaps there would be a label on the dress, Mr. McNear."

McNear flushed and mopped his face. "Damn it, Simmons," he said uncomfortably, "why did you have to think of that?" But being a conscientious Inspector, he began to investigate. And on the collar of the dress he found the label he was looking for. Neatly stitched on a piece of rectangular silk were the words, "The Sports Shop. Hamilton, Bermuda."

That the label placed the girl as coming from Hamilton made the tragedy so much closer and all the more ghastly. McNear's stirred emotion showed in his shaking hand. "Damn it, Simmons! What's this island coming to when a girl's not safe on the highway?"

Simmons looked wretched and hopeless. McNear's glance fell on the bunch of lilies. He said sympathetically, "It's clear enough now what she was doing out here. She was gathering lilies for Easter Sunday, poor kid!"

"Yes, sare," Simmons agreed, "and she was carrying them when the foul scoundrel struck her." He stooped and picked up the large bouquet. "Look, Mr. McNear," he said, lowering his voice to a hoarse, hushed whisper, "you can see the heads of the blossoms covered with blood!"

The Inspector reached carefully for the bouquet, but suddenly drew back his hand and gave a warning exclamation. "Good God, Simmons. Look there!"

Too flustered to speak, Simmons stared in silent amazement to where McNear's finger pointed.

There, between the stems of the tall, white lilies, its hilt buried deep in the green leaves, and with the blade pointing upward like an adder's tongue among the flowers, was a fine, razor-edged stiletto.

3
THE WRONG LABEL

Saturday Afternoon, April 10th.

That afternoon Bermuda's small but painfully disturbed group of police officials sat in the Chief of Police's office at Headquarters listening to Dr. Jenkins, who had just completed a brief post-mortem upon the body of the dead girl.

The Chief of Police, with a thin, straight back which made him look like a major, which indeed he had formerly been, turned once more to Dr. Jenkins. "How long had the girl been dead?"

"Dead, I should say"—Dr. Jenkins' pinched grey eyes and pursed lips squeezed and inspected each word as he uttered it—"about an hour when found—perhaps slightly less. The blood, as you could see for yourselves, had just begun to coagulate."

"Would you say, sir," Superintendent Welch inquired deferentially, "that death was instantaneous?" He was a dapper little man with sharply inquisitive eyes and keen, regular features. A quirk of sardonic humour was never far from Welch's incisive lips; this alone made him distinctly dissimilar to the red-faced, more stolid Inspector McNear. But in spite of their differences in temperament there was a lasting friendship between the two men which had not even been threatened when Welch had been promoted over McNear's head to his present rank.

"Instantaneous?" Dr. Jenkins repeated Welch's question. "Practically, yes. Though the girl may have lived a few moments."

"But you said the knife penetrated the heart," Inspector McNear interrupted.

"The left side," Dr. Jenkins said, nodding. "But there have been cases of a similar nature in which the victim lived for several minutes. In fact, I read recently, in a medical journal, of a man who, wounded in the late war, still carries the bullet in his heart."

"In any case," questioned the Coroner, whose jury had been adjourned until the following Monday, "if the blade entered the left side of the heart, that rules out suicide, doesn't it, Doctor?"

Dr. Jenkins considered the question in his scrupulous way and announced, "Not necessarily. The knife was thin and long, and as the girl was of so slight a build the blade could very easily have touched the heart and have been drawn out by her afterward."

"Exactly." Masters gave a satisfied nod. "Or it might have been dislodged when her body struck the ground. We have absolutely no reason to suspect murder. Absolutely none!"

Superintendent Welch's shrewd eyes penetrated those of his Chief, and he remarked laconically, "Only a dead girl with a knife wound in her heart."

Masters compressed his lips. "I refuse to entertain the thought. As you, and as men in service older than you, know, Welch, there has never been a murder in Bermuda in my time—not among our white people, at least. Now, apart from the fact that it would break our enviable record, I ask you to think of the most unpleasant publicity that would result if we admitted it to be murder! Think how the interests of the island would suffer!"

"Quite so," Dr. Jenkins agreed. "Quite so. But while, in answer to the Coroner's question, I admitted suicide as a possibility, I must say, frankly, that I can't personally subscribe to that theory. On the contrary, I most emphatically believe it was—murder!"

Superintendent Welch and Inspector McNear, who had both been listening attentively to Dr. Jenkins, now looked at each other and nodded.

Masters frowned at Welch and persisted stubbornly, "Yet Dr. Jenkins admits that it could be suicide."

Welch grinned embarrassedly and proceeded to undermine his Chief's contention. "Isn't a main highway a rather unusual place to choose for a suicide? And why should she try to hide the stiletto, which McNear found in the bunch of lilies, from herself? And what about the missing bag?"

"Exactly," the Coroner a little pompously agreed. "Although I am no policeman and make no pretence to detective talent, I would suggest that even a young woman intent on taking her life would carry a handbag containing those small articles of repair which women of today so slavishly depend on for their appearance."

McNear rubbed his square chin. "I don't know much about that," he said bluntly, "but I know how odd it seemed not to find a bag around. And, as the Superintendent said, why would a lady go out on a dusty, bare road if she wanted to kill herself?" Masters brought his hand down loudly on the top of his desk. "Theories! Questions! But what have you done about the most important step—discovery of the girl's identity?"

"Not much yet," Welch admitted modestly. "None of our constables had ever seen her before—and that seems odd because the police know nearly all Bermudians by sight."

'But why should they recognize her?" Masters demanded. "You've no reason to believe she had been on the islands any length of time."

Welch smiled. "There's her dress, Chief."

Masters shook his head. "Nonsense. You mean because she bought it in Hamilton? Why, man, she could have come off a cruise ship yesterday morning and bought it in the afternoon."

"But she didn't," Welch answered quietly. "I've had it tested and it's been laundered half a dozen times."

"Excellent, Superintendent," the Coroner nodded approvingly. "Excellent reasoning. And by the same token we will be able to find out who the poor creature was. I'm sure the Sports Shop people know their local customers well enough to recognize them."

"That is what I thought, sir, when Inspector McNear mentioned the label he'd found. And I sent it away with Detective-Constable Steele a good half-hour ago to be identified." Welch peeped at his wristwatch. "I'm waiting for him now. And I'm hoping he'll bring the information we need. If he doesn't," Welch confessed, "I'm afraid we're up against it for information till after Easter."

"The *Gazette* ought to have a Sunday edition," McNear said injuredly. "Then the story'd be all over the islands."

Welch gave him a crooked smile. "Better speak to the editor about it."

There was a discreet tapping on the frosted glass door.

"Come," the Chief of Police called.

Detective-Constable Steele, long-lipped, grey and rangy, saluted stiffly and waited for permission to speak.

"Now, Constable," Masters rapped out, "I trust you've brought the information you were sent for."

"No, sir," Steele said flatly. Then, as gloom settled over the group, he added self-righteously, "but I made what you might call a very peculiar discovery, sir!"

Masters said irritably, "Come, come, man. Don't keep us in suspense. What did you find? It *was* the Sports Shop label, wasn't it?"

"Oh yes, sir," Steele answered quickly, "it was theirs, right enough. Mr. Outerbridge—he's the manager—identified it straight off. And then he took the dress up to the ladies' department, and I waited while he went through a stack of old sales slips. It was when he came down that the funny business started; I could tell it was coming from the strange way he looked. 'Officer,' says he, 'this isn't one of our dresses.' 'What,' says I, 'you just told me it was!' 'My mistake,' says he; 'we not only didn't sell this particular dress, but the label here is not the kind we put in dresses we do sell!'" Pausing for breath and dramatic effect, Constable Steele reached into his pocket and carefully brought out a small piece of cloth. He laid it on the Chief's table, a blue silk bit about three inches long and one inch wide. Beside it he placed the label that had been taken from the dead girl. It was of white silk and of four inches square. "You see, sir," he explained, pointing to the longer piece of silk, "that's the kind they put in dresses!"

"Yes, yes," Masters prodded him, "but what of this other one? There's the name—Sports Shop—plain on it. What is it, counterfeit?"

"Oh no, sir," Constable Steele answered in surprise. "Mr. Outerbridge said the label was theirs, right enough. But he couldn't understand how it came to be on a dress because it was one of the sort they always put in the lining of their hats."

4
A QUESTION OF HORTICULTURE

Saturday Afternoon, April 10th.

Constable Steele's revelation was a triumph for Masters. When all but Welch and McNear had departed for a long overdue luncheon, Masters looked at the Superintendent with crinkly eyes which gave out a gleam of satisfaction and said, "So much for your theorizing, Welch!"

Welch was disconcerted, but only mildly. "Yes, sir?" he inquired politely.

"I should say," his superior continued smoothly, "that young woman was a sly little minx."

McNear regarded his Chief with curious expectancy.

Over the end of his long cigar the Chief of Police slowly and tolerantly explained, "The Sports Shop has a certain reputation, hasn't it? I mean, it's expensive, exclusive, what?"

Welch nodded. "I've heard so."

"Well, it would be, in a manner of speaking, a feather in a girl's cap to have a dress from there, you'll agree?"

"It might," Welch agreed.

"And if you," the Chief proceeded, "a girl, I mean, were too poor to patronize the Sports Shop, but wanted to pretend you could, what would you do?"

McNear smote his thick leg in sudden comprehension. "You mean she sewed the label on, herself, sir?"

Masters smiled complacently. "Exactly. And now, Gentlemen"—he turned to Welch, who was casually lighting a cigarette—"you'd better get a bite of lunch and set to work on the identity of this girl. Establish that and I think you'll find the mystery will solve itself." He paused. "There are half a dozen cruise ships out in the harbour. The pursers will have a list of the passengers, and you can check with the stewards on anyone who may be missing—that should give you the girl's name if she's a tourist. If she's of Bermuda we ought to know soon, for we instructed every constable to make the closest investigation in his district. Moreover, we'll have photographs of the victim in an hour or so."

McNear took his hat and stood up. Masters' assurance had made him more confident. He said as he and Welch started for the door, "At least, we've something to go on now, sir."

"Exactly," Masters replied.

"Exactly," Welch muttered through quirked lips, as he and McNear went down Headquarters steps into the street.

McNear was painfully surprised. "Don't you think we ought to investigate the cruise ships?"

Welch frowned thoughtfully, ignoring his question. "McNear, what's the antithesis of being on the islands a long time?"

"What?" McNear asked blankly.

Welch patiently elaborated his cryptic remark. "Let's put it another way. Who would most likely want to give the impression of having been in Bermuda a long time? The answer is, somebody who had just arrived."

McNear nodded. "Sounds sensible. And that, as the Chief said, points to the cruise ships. Now let's have a spot of lunch and take a tender."

Welch laid his hand on McNear's burly shoulder. "I'm sorry, Mac, but you'll have to go out alone. I've got to wait till after Clemson has fingerprinted those lilies."

McNear stared at him. "And what do you think you'll find out from fingerprints?"

"I don't know," Welch admitted casually; "it's the lilies themselves that interest me."

McNear's honest face looked worried, as if he feared his friend and superior had become slightly mad. "Oh," he protested, "come on and have a spot of lunch. You can look at those lilies any time."

Welch laughed and waved his hand. "You can try it, but you won't find any stewards or pursers aboard this afternoon. They're all ashore. I'll meet you at Headquarters when you get back."

After watching him swing back up the steps, McNear walked slowly toward Reid Street and turned west to his favourite tavern. The morning had been the most trying of his police career, and he felt that three fingers of Johnny Haig would be a Godsend. Therefore with a quick, businesslike step, he marched toward Queen Street and bowled his way through the easy, laughing crowds that filled the narrow sidewalk. Undoubtedly Welch was right in saying the ships would be deserted. For the Easter tourist rush was in full blare, and it seemed as if every one of the passengers and crew from the six gaudy cruise ships in the harbour were all thronging the streets of Hamilton.

Passing rows of tourist-filled "Eastern Bazaars," where sleek Armenians forsook their fathers' God and posed as Hindoos for their pockets' sake, McNear turned in the door of the Windsor's private bar and walked to the farther end, where he posed one heavy foot on the shiny brass rail and rested an elbow on the polished mahogany surface.

Jack, the bartender, blandly sleek and genial, was busy serving a customer, but strolled toward McNear as soon as he was free.

"Well," Jack inquired amiably, "been any murders today?" He burst out laughing at his own joke.

McNear winced at the blithely spoken jest. It was as if the dead girl's face were mirrored in his whiskey glass. "Guess you haven't heard," he said quietly.

Jack ceased his circular motions with the bar-rag in surprise. "You don't mean there *has* been a murder?" he asked earnestly.

McNear took a deep breath. There was no use keeping it secret that the girl's body had been found. "I can't rightly say it was a murder," he admitted slowly, "but we found a girl stabbed to death over in Paget early this morning."

Jack gaped. "God bless my soul!"

Near the entrance a customer spun a coin significantly, and Jack left, saying to McNear, "I'll be with you in a minute."

But the minute lengthened. Torn between the urge to learn more and the desire to tell what he already knew, Jack yielded to garrulity and stayed up at the farther end of the counter, the centre of an astonished group of topers.

Finally, he returned for further information. "Fair takes your breath away, don't it?" he said to McNear in a hushed, scandalized voice. "Wasn't a Bermuda girl, was she?"

"Don't know yet," McNear muttered. "But if she's off one of those cruise ships we'll have a hell of a time finding out who she was—there must be three thousand passengers and all of them ashore!" Moodily he drained his whiskey glass.

"Here," Jack recklessly lifted the dimpled bottle of whiskey, "have one on the house, Inspector." He leaned nearer. "See that man sitting over there in the corner. Purser of the *Baledonia*—John McKnight by name. I don't know but what you might find out something from him. Shall I ask him over?"

McNear nodded. It was a stroke of luck to find a purser in so huge a crowd, and the *Baledonia* was the largest of the cruise ships.

Jack ambled along behind the bar and returned with the Purser, a squat, weather-beaten seaman, with colourless grey eyes, a listing gait and a deep bass voice.

"Inspector, your health," the Purser proposed as they clinked their glasses, "and may you never be after me!" he added, chuckling with good humour.

"Be that as it may," McNear, whose job always came ahead of little pleasantries, answered soberly, "there *is* a party I want to know about, and she may have been on one of your whoopee cruisers."

Jack and the Purser exchanged glances. Jack said confidentially to the seaman, "It's that girl I was telling you about. The girl whose body was found this morning."

The *Baledonia's* Purser nodded, closing his fingers around the whiskey glass. "Help you out all I can, Inspector," he said. "But it's going to be a devil of a job to find out whether the poor girl was a passenger on one of the cruise ships. In port, like we are now, half our people stay ashore. Of course, we run tenders every hour till after midnight, but they come to enjoy themselves, and they like the hotels."

McNear was discouraged. "I knew it wasn't much use checking up during the day, but I'd counted on most of the passengers being where they belonged for the night. Sort of makes it seem foolish for me to go out there at all," he ended gloomily.

"Oh, I wouldn't say that," the Purser answered. "But I do say you can't make an accurate check till all the ships are on the high seas. Not many, but some of the tourists took their baggage ashore as soon as we landed, and they'll stay in Hamilton till the afternoon we sail."

"So that's the way it is," McNear said, glumly sipping his whiskey.

He was so dispirited that the bartender apologized for him to his friend, the Purser. "You see, Mr. McKnight," Jack said sympathetically, "until this happened we hardly knew what it was to have a violent crime. Now, in the States, with all those gangster murders, the police are used to it, but down here—"

"I know," McKnight agreed understandingly. "A dirty business. Well, Inspector," he said, extending his hand, "don't hesitate to call on me if you think I can be of any help."

McNear thanked him and went out into the street again. Plodding through the bright, light-hearted crowd, he felt like a dull schoolboy in for a reprimand from his teacher. For he would have to go back to Headquarters and inform his Chief that unless he was prepared to canvass not only the six cruise ships, but every inn and hotel on the island, there was no point in trying to check the passenger lists of the tourists. And he knew Masters well enough to realize that if his orders, impossible or otherwise, were not carried out, it was the subordinate that always got the blame.

Slowly he walked on up Reid and Parliament Streets and turned south to the familiar steps of Headquarters. But as he drew level with the door to the left of the main entrance the constable on duty behind the grilled desk called out to him, "Superintendent Welch said to tell you, Inspector, that he's in Masters' office."

That cheered McNear a little; pleased that he would not have to face the Chief alone, his step became more brisk.

Welch was sitting comfortably in a large leather chair when McNear entered. On the Chief's desk lay the fateful bunch of lilies. Beside it a book had been turned upside down, open in the middle.

Welch, who was visibly excited, smiled quickly and asked, "Any luck?"

"Didn't go out," McNear answered morosely. "There was nobody on board, but by luck I met up with the Purser of the *Baledonia*. When did you get here?"

"Just came," Welch said, enjoying himself.

At that moment the Chief came in through a side door.

"Well, Superintendent, I hear you have something to tell me."

"I have," Welch said promptly. "Will you have a look at those lilies, sir?"

Masters a little hesitantly took up the bunch of flowers. "You don't expect them to give us a clue, do you?"

"They gave me one," Welch answered quietly.

"So?" His superior was incredulous.

"Just look at 'em," Welch directed enthusiastically. "Remember, I said they weren't regular lilies? Of course, I don't mean they're not regular *lilies*, but they're not regular *Bermuda* lilies."

"Here," objected McNear in a baffled tone, "say that over again, will you?"

Welch laughed. "The point is, there are so many lilies on the islands and you're so used to them that you take it for granted that all lilies are alike. So would I," he added modestly, "if I didn't help my sister with the garden sometimes of an evening. At any rate, I knew these weren't Bermuda lilies, but Madonna lilies. And now if you'll let me read a passage from Miss Harriet Keeler, an authoritative source, I think I can make clear what I'm getting at."

"Go on," Masters said resignedly.

Welch picked up the little book, *Our Garden Flowers*, and turned the leaves. "'The Madonna lily, or *Lilium candidum*,'" he began, "'is the oldest and loveliest of lilies—'"

"Never mind that," Masters said in a discouraging tone.

"'Unlike the Bermuda Easter lily,'" Welch continued blithely, "'it blooms in June, not in April, unless forced in hot-houses.'" He looked up. "There are no forced lilies grown in Bermuda—point one!"

The Chief of Police sniffed dubiously.

"'When a lily,'" Welch went on, ignoring his Chief's disdain, "'is sold in shops the flowers are usually mutilated, frequently not only the anthers, but all the stamens are removed. There are two reasons for this; one, the abundant pollen which would soon be scattered over the inner surface of the flower and so mar its exquisite whiteness; the other, that if fertilization is prevented the life of the flower is extended; the florist knows that the flower lasts longer even if he does not know the reason why.'" Welch paused to close the book. "Bermuda lilies are never mutilated by our local florists, but the lilies in the bouquet are—point two!"

"Ah!" Masters threw back his head and opened his jaws in surprise. "I see! Then the lilies were grown in a hot-house—"

Welch nodded decidedly. "And not in a Bermuda hot-house, but probably one in the States. So the answer is, they came off one of the cruise ships!"

5
IDENTIFIED AND WANTED!

Saturday Evening, April 10th.

"Those lilies," Masters said, laying down the bouquet with a gesture of repugnance, "point directly to the cruise ships. Is that what you're getting at, Welch?"

The Superintendent nodded. "Seems like it, sir." McNear gloomily shook his head. "I was afraid of it. And we might as well try to find a pin in a haystack, sir! As the Purser of the *Baledonia* said, there's no way to make a check on the passengers till they're all aboard and ready to sail back to the States."

"But that's not true any more," Welch interposed confidently. "At least, it's only partly true. We're no longer looking merely for the identity of the dead girl. We're also looking for a cabin that contained a bunch of lilies on the way down—and unless all the stewards are blind we'll find out which cabin it was!"

Masters decisively tapped his long fingers on the top of his desk. "Welch, I believe you're right." He pressed a button and the sergeant on duty answered by appearing swiftly at the door. "Sergeant, I want four men to report for service tonight. They will receive their instructions from Superintendent Welch."

"Yes, sir." The sergeant saluted and disappeared.

"That," Masters said to Welch, "will give you a man for each of the smaller ships in the harbour. The big ones, the *Cedric* and the *Baledonia*, can be investigated by yourself and McNear. And by that time the photographs of the dead girl will be printed—that ought to help you with your identification. Right?"

"Right," Welch answered. He looked at his watch and turned to McNear with a smile. "Mac, it's time that lunch you suggested had grown into a full-sized dinner. What about it?"

McNear beamed his willingness.

As they left, Masters advised them, "Unless it's too late when you get back I'll be here if you've anything to report."

Going downstairs, Welch said, "That 'if' of the Chief's sounded a little sceptical, didn't you think?"

McNear rubbed his chin. "I'm not any too optimistic myself."

But a good steak and a pint of beer cheered him immensely. And after they had returned to Welch's office, where the Superintendent instructed the constables who were to search the smaller ships, McNear felt as if there might be some solution to the deepening mystery after all.

It was dusk when, after waiting for prints of the dead girl's photograph, one of which was given to each of the constables, they went down to Transportation Wharf.

"There's the *Baledonia's* tender," Welch said. "You take it, since you've met the Purser. I'll go out to the *Cedric*."

Saluting, McNear walked over the gangplank.

A number of *Baledonia* passengers were already waiting to be taken back to their staterooms, and in a short time the tender began steaming across the harbour, past the fashionable Princess Hotel and out into the bay.

As the little tender chugged farther and farther from Transportation Wharf, Inspector McNear cast a professional eye over his fellow passengers. It might easily be that the murderer was among them. But was that possible when there was so much hilarity between them all? They were so eager-eyed and cheerful; it did not seem that it could be possible. Yet there was the cold, stark truth—a pretty, young girl lay fearfully and dreadfully murdered and doubtless she, too, had been as lively and gay as these fellow holiday-makers on the *Baledonia's* tender.

The shrill tooting of the whistle interrupted his gloomy thoughts. The boat was drawing near the liner. Stepping outside on the miniature deck, McNear waited impatiently while the smaller vessel manoeuvred fussily back and forth in a calm sea, until finally it was safely hugging the *Baledonia's* side.

Climbing the accommodation ladder, McNear made his way quickly to the Purser's office, and there he found his acquaintance busily meditating over a great stack of papers.

McKnight's barroom joviality had receded like the effects of too much liquor and he had the harassed air of a man beset by a thousand troubles. But except for a certain weariness his greeting was cordial enough, and as he took McNear's arm and led him into an alcove adjoining his cubby-hole of an office he asked solicitously:

"And what can I do for you, Inspector? I didn't fancy I'd see you again so soon. Anything new turned up?"

McNear scratched his cheek a little dubiously. "I can't say about that till I've asked a few questions—but I won't bother you. If you'll just tell me the best way to get hold of the ship's stewards."

"Not at all," McKnight interrupted hastily. "No bother. What questions, Inspector?"

"I want to ask your stewards if any of them noticed a bunch of lilies in one of the *Baledonia's* cabins," McNear answered.

"Lilies?" McKnight leaned forward perplexedly. "Lilies?" he repeated, as if he must have been mistaken in what the Inspector had said. "My good man, why are you looking for lilies?"

McNear leaned forward confidentially. "You see, Mr. Purser, the weapon that killed that poor girl was hidden in a bouquet of them."

"I—I see," McKnight faltered. "But why should you think they came from this ship? Your island is chock full of lilies, isn't it?"

McNear nodded. "We've plenty of lilies in Bermuda, Mr. Purser. But these were a different kind. And since Chief of Police Masters gave orders to search all the ships—or to inquire on all the ships— why, the questioning of the *Baledonia* is simply part of the routine."

McKnight laughed. "That's ridiculous, Inspector. Nobody would carry lilies to Bermuda—however," he shrugged and led the way to the main lounge, where he gave orders for the stewards to assemble.

The stewards, in their neat white jackets, arrived with ship-shape efficiency. They formed in line as if for inspection, and, except for a discreet buzzing of curious whispering, stood waiting attentively.

With a brief nod, the Purser turned them over to McNear.

Quietly McNear took out the photograph and handed it to the Purser.

McKnight studied it under the glittering candelabra of the main lounge.

"Recognize her?" McNear asked.

The Purser shook his head and passed it back.

"Men," McNear said heavily as the dead girl's picture began to travel from hand to hand, "look at that face carefully! That poor girl was found murdered—stabbed to death—this morning in Bermuda!"

There was a startled gasp, and the picture was studied with feverish excitement. Slowly it passed from one steward to another. Meanwhile McNear watched the men with shrewd scrutiny. But from the head of the line to the bottom there was not even a hint of recognition.

Finally the photograph was given back to him. McNear put it in his pocket. "Sorry," he said, "but one more question and I'm through bothering you."

The men waited expectantly.

"Think carefully now!" McNear adjured them. "Did any of you see a bunch of lilies brought aboard from New York?"

The response to that was immediate. A pale, thin young man with carefully brushed sparse hair answered, "Yes, sir! I did!"

"You did!" McNear purred his satisfaction. Now at last he felt he was getting somewhere. "One of the passengers had them?"

"Yes, sir," the thin young steward answered promptly. "The gentleman in 72-D. When I put them in his stateroom I thought, Well if that's not 'Coals to Newcastle!' That's how I happened to remember it—seemed so funny, sendin' lilies to Bermuda when that's where they grow 'em!"

McNear turned to the Purser. "Who's in 72-D?"

McKnight sent for the passenger chart. When it was brought he glanced cursorily over the pages and then said, "a man named George Collins." He raised his eyes from the book and addressed the steward who had given the information. "Have you seen Mr. Collins today, Lawson?"

The steward was thoughtfully silent. At last he answered, "No, sir, can't say as I have. But I'll step down and take a look if you wish."

"Never mind," Inspector McNear ordered hastily. "But you can show me the way, if you will."

Disbanding the others, the Purser went along with McNear and the steward down the corridor to the companionway, where they descended to the lower deck. They stopped before one of the many doors and the steward stood respectfully aside, saying, "Here you are, sir."

McNear rapped on the mahogany panel.

There was no answer.

The steward stepped forward and flung open the door.

McNear saw an empty cabin. He looked quickly for the lilies, but found only an empty vase on the dresser. In one corner stood a small steamer trunk. This, the Inspector observed, was locked, fastened by two staunch brass catches and bound securely round with four strong leather straps. In the absence of the lilies the trunk absorbed his interest. Four stout straps! A man who would take such lengths to gain security must, he thought, have something to conceal. He wished he had the legal right to open the trunk. But he hadn't.

In the opposite corner was the partly open door of a closet, revealing several neatly pressed suits hanging inside. On a shelf below lay a pile of shirts and underclothes. A row of brightly polished shoes interspersed with white sports oxfords was ranged along the floor. About the whole cabin was such an air of sober neatness that McNear concluded its occupant—Mr. George Collins—was a man of the most methodical and orderly turn of mind.

McNear looked wistfully at the heavily fastened trunk. "I don't know but what I'm exceeding my authority if I go any farther," he said regretfully. "But I suppose I might have a look around, eh, Mr. Purser?"

The Purser hesitated, but finally said, "Oh, go ahead, Inspector."

McNear stepped to the door of the bath. The glass shelf above the washbowl was bare of any of those articles usually found in a cabin occupied by a man—there was no toothbrush or paste, no razor, brush or soap. He bent down and looked beneath the narrow bed. There was no suitcase or traveling bag to be seen.

Without a search warrant he had, he knew, seen all there was to be seen. He stepped back to the threshold. "The man must have gone ashore for the night," he said.

"I think so, sir," Lawson said.

"But what about the lilies?" the Purser asked. "No sign of them!"

"They were standing on that dressing chest," the steward answered. "I brought that big green vase up special to put 'em in."

"You saw them last—when?" McNear demanded.

"Yesterday, sir, when I was straightening up the room."

"They weren't here this morning?"

The steward looked embarrassed. "Well, you see, sir, when I came in this morning I saw the bed hadn't been slept in, and since the cabin was in good order I went on about my work."

Inspector McNear frowned, not at the steward, but at the slowness of his thoughts moving toward light in the distance. Evidently George Collins had spent the night ashore before the murder. Obviously he had taken the lilies with him. And the next time the lilies had been seen they were lying, dipped in blood, beside the body of the murdered girl! Clearly a search of the islands for George Collins was one order of the day.

"What sort of man was this Collins?" he asked the steward.

Lawson thought a moment. "Well, sir, he looked like one of those college men—Yale or Princeton; you know what I mean?"

The Inspector showed his bafflement.

But the steward knew what was in his mind, and he struggled to express it. "Sure you do," he said. "Good-lookin'—kind of full around the jaws, round bright eyes always lookin' out at you, but sort of as if he was thinkin' of what a good dinner he'd had and not seein' you at all—hair a little thin, but brushed so that it seemed like a lot. You know, sir—a regular bond salesman type!"

McNear dubiously scratched his chin. "But what did he *look* like? Now, his hair—what colour was it?"

"Black, sir. Bound to be. And brown eyes. And a lot of colour in his face—sort of flushed. And his neck a little big and the collar tight around it. A man about forty years old."

Taking out his well-worn notebook and the stub of a pencil, McNear hastily jotted the description on a page. In spite of the fact that the steward had mentioned no peculiar characteristics, he suddenly realized that from the description already given he should recognize Collins if he was ever fortunate enough to meet him.

"You can, perhaps, tell me where he was from?" McNear asked the Purser.

The Purser investigated his passenger chart. "He registered from New York, Mr. Inspector."

McNear turned back to the steward. "Did he seem to be with a party, or was he alone?"

The steward thought deeply. "Alone, sir," he finally announced, "now that I come to think of it. I don't believe I saw him talking to a soul."

"Thank you, steward," he said with a smile. "This may be very valuable information you've given me." Nodding dismissal, McNear turned to McKnight "And now, Mr. Purser, if you will go to your office and fetch the keys to this room I will wait till you come back."

McKnight glanced up quizzically. "Then you've found something, Inspector?"

McNear answered gravely, "Mr. Purser, I want this stateroom locked. I want it kept locked till George Collins returns. At that time you must notify me immediately, be it night or day."

The Purser whistled with surprise. Turning, he ambled down the corridor to the companionway.

McNear waited till he had returned from his office with the key.

In silence the ship's officer locked the door. "And now what's to be done with the key, Inspector? Shall I put it in the safe?"

McNear nodded. "That's the best place for it," he said weightily.

"I think so," the Purser agreed. "And if Collins comes back—"

"He won't come back," the Inspector interrupted grimly, "if we get our hands on him before he reaches the tender!"

They walked together to the accommodation ladder.

Pointing across the water to a small vessel approaching from the next ship at anchor, the Purser said, "Here comes the tender from the *Cedric*. It picks up passengers from our ship, too. So now, unless there's something further you want of me, I'll go on about my business."

"I'll trouble you no more today, and thank you," McNear said gravely. As the Purser left he leaned eagerly against the rail, anxiously waiting for the boat which would take him ashore to begin his search for George Collins.

As the tender slowly sidled toward the accommodation ladder the watchful McNear discerned through the dusk the uniform of a Bermuda police officer on the deck, and a moment later he saw that it was Superintendent Welch.

When the ladder was made fast, McNear climbed briskly down.

The two men greeted each other with nods of secret import and silently retired to a corner of the tender.

It was obvious that Welch had information of his own, but it was McNear that spoke first. Carefully but briefly he recounted his various discoveries, and ended, saying, "As soon as we get our hands on Collins it'll be all over but the confession."

But, to McNear's astonishment, Welch frowned and shook his head. "I wish I thought so."

"But," McNear protested, "it was you that made the bouquet of lilies such an important link. And now that I've traced them to Collins you shake your head!"

"That's right," Welch admitted with forced cheerfulness. "Not that I don't think the lilies are important. They may turn out to be our most important clue. But, while I admit that they implicate Collins, we're still a long distance from proof."

"But," McNear objected, scowling painfully.

"Oh, by the way," Welch said in an off-hand manner, as if the matter was of little importance after all, "the body has been identified."

McNear stared at his superior in bewilderment. "But that's fine, man. Why aren't you more pleased about it? Who is she? Where's she from?"

"She was a passenger on the *Cedric*, sailing last Wednesday from New York," Welch answered unenthusiastically. "One of the stewards recognized her from the photograph. I sent him ashore to the morgue to make identification sure. Just before I left the *Cedric* I had a message saying there was no doubt of it. Her name's Pamela Hawkins. And now"—his lips twitched sardonically— "where does that get us?"

"Of course, you searched her baggage?" McNear said.

"I not only searched it, I also had it put on the tender with me. But there was nothing in it but clothes—no letters, not even a picture."

"Pamela Hawkins," McNear mused. "Seems to me I've heard that name before."

Welch smiled slyly. "In those motion picture magazines you're always reading, I suppose?"

McNear squirmed at the good-natured taunt which showed up his principal weakness. But his answer was sober. "No, it wasn't in a movie magazine that I've seen her name. It was somewhere else."

The bow of the tender bumped gently against Transportation Wharf and there was the noise of rattling chains as the gangplank went down. McNear pushed forward, staring eagerly into the city where thousands of tourists were jostling gaily in and out of shops, taverns and hotels. "And now to find Collins," he said grimly.

"Yes," Welch said. "We'll send out a general alarm straightaway."

They hailed a carriage and had the dead girl's baggage stowed aboard.

"Police Headquarters," Welch directed authoritatively.

But when the carriage had creaked to a dead standstill and they had gone up the wide stairs to Masters' office they were confronted by such astonishing information regarding Miss Pamela Hawkins that they were stunned.

"This cable came five minutes ago," the Chief of Police tersely greeted Welch and exasperatedly pushed a slip of blue paper across the desk toward him.

Taking it in his hands Welch read:

> Police Headquarters,
>   Hamilton,
>   Bermuda.
> Hold Pamela Hawkins passenger aboard *Cedric.*
> Wanted here in connection Marsden kidnapping.
> Details follow.
>   (Signed) Rafferty,
>   *Police Commissioner,*
>   *New York City.*

6

AN INOPPORTUNE SUICIDE

Saturday Night, April 10th.

Quite typical of a rich, individualistic nation in which fifteen million men, with their wives and children, were undergoing various stages of starvation, the kidnapping of little Marcia Marsden from the Fifth Avenue home of her fabulously plutocratic parents had filled the front sheets of America's daily newspapers until even the stirring foreign political news was crowded to an inside page.

Likewise typical of the same condition was the fact that in all of those countless columns of type there was scarcely a word of truth to a page of reportorial imaginings and sob-sisters' hysterical maunderings.

For, fearful of experiencing the horror which climaxed the Lindbergh case, Owen Young Marsden, the child's father, had entrusted the conduct of the entire investigation to the regular police of America and Canada and had steadily refused the aid of money-hungry private detective agencies and the irresponsible newsmongers of the daily press.

And the police, co-operating with the influential Marsden to the fullest extent, had denied the newspapers even the smallest hints of their progress or lack of progress as they searched feverishly to recover the missing child.

Meanwhile two rewards, of a hundred thousand dollars each, one for the return of the child, the other for the capture of her abductors, had been offered by the distraught family. These offers, however, in accordance with the Marsdens' determination to

62

work solely with the constituted authorities, were open only to the police.

Even in quiet Bermuda the few facts, including the reward, of the Marsden kidnapping were known and had been commented upon. In the recreation rooms at Police Headquarters a circular tacked to the bulletin board offered the two alluring prizes. Nevertheless both Welch and McNear, on reading the cablegram handed to them by Masters, experienced distinct sensations of profound annoyance. For the introduction of the kidnapping aspect was like a strong red herring drawn across a trail that was already tortuous and baffling enough without it.

"That's where I saw the girl's name—in a New York newspaper," McNear said. "She was Marcia Marsden's nurse. But why the devil should she come here—?" he muttered resentfully.

"She could, of course," Masters drily cut in, "have been implicated with the kidnappers and, growing afraid of discovery, have come here to escape. There"—he turned challengingly to Welch—"now, Superintendent, tell me that doesn't offer a motive for her suicide!"

Unimpressed, Welch smiled. "Sure," he agreed, "and she could have come, perfectly innocent, because the New York police had badgered her half to death! Also she might have come to enjoy the scenery and"—his lip curled bitterly as he reflected on the tragedy—"to smell the beautiful Bermuda lilies—poor kid." Suddenly he reached for the telephone. "Chief, we've got to find a man named George Collins, no matter if every constable and officer on the island has to work all night to do it!" While Welch hurriedly sent off instructions for all district constables to inquire and search at every inn, boarding-house and hotel in Bermuda for one George Collins, about forty, dark-haired, brown-eyed, full-faced, and expensively dressed, McNear reported the afternoon's discoveries to the Police Chief.

"However," Masters observed when the story had been told, "we shouldn't leap to conclusions. Collins has a perfect right to go ashore and stay as long as he chooses, providing he's on deck when the *Baledonia* sails. Moreover, from what you tell me about the condition of the cabin it would seem that he certainly expected to return."

McNear tried to look respectful and doubtful at the same time. Finally he blurted out, "But he took the lilies ashore, sir. And they were found by Miss Hawkins's body!"

"But by your own account," the Chief pointed out, "nobody saw him leave the ship with the flowers—they only saw him bring them aboard!"

Welch, who had been listening with one ear to the conversation between Masters and the Inspector, put his hand over the mouthpiece and interrupted his call long enough to interject thoughtfully, "That's a fact to be remembered."

McNear turned and stared at him again, but he had already began talking into the transmitter.

"Now," Welch said when he had finally finished, "we've got everybody at work on the island. Luckily for us, there's only nineteen square miles of territory in Bermuda, and I miss my guess if we don't put our hands on Collins, guilty or innocent, whichever he may be, before morning."

"All the same, Superintendent," McNear addressed Welch, "unless the Chief has other duties for us, I'd feel better about it if we did a little private investigating, too."

Masters smiled a little tolerantly at McNear's eagerness to prosecute the search. "By all means, go!" he said. "The sooner you discover a solution in this case, the better it will suit me!"

"And me!" Welch said emphatically. "Come on, Inspector."

As they walked toward the Windsor, where they both decided that a man of Collins' description was likely to be registered, Welch said broodingly:

"I'm afraid this Marsden angle is apt to make quite a difference in the verdict of the Coroner's jury when it meets Monday. As Masters suggested in advance, they'll probably hold that Pamela Hawkins, fearful of being implicated in the kidnapping or having knowledge that she was already wanted by the New York police, had made away with herself. And, of course, they'll take special note of the Police Surgeon's statement that, though he didn't believe the girl committed suicide, yet it was his opinion that she could have easily done so. Put those two things together, add them to Masters' bias and also the fact that it's better for Bermuda's reputation to have self-destruction instead of murder, and I think you'll get a verdict of suicide. Confound it!"

"Scandalous and nasty," McNear said, "that's what a murder is."

"So is a suicide," Welch countered brusquely. They approached the trim facade of the hospitable Windsor Hotel and went inside. The lobby was even more crowded than usual, and though they used their eyes to as much advantage as possible, there was no way of choosing from the active, moving throngs a man to fit the *Baledonia* steward's description.

Welch went up to the desk and nodded to the suave-looking room clerk. "Has a Mr. George Collins registered here yesterday or today?"

Carefully adjusting his tie and moving his head as if his neck were stiff, the clerk called to a young woman sitting in a wicketed compartment, "Miss Noble, have we a Mr. George Collins with us?" Rapidly consulting her registry cards, Miss Noble answered with brisk efficiency, "No, sir. No Mr. George Collins."

As Welch turned back from the desk McNear murmured, "If he thinks he's wanted he'd probably be here under another name. Anyway, this is the tourist Mecca of the city. Let's sit down and watch." That suited Welch, and after telephoning Headquarters to inform them where he could be reached, he went with McNear to a small lounge from which they could watch the main entrance.

It had been a long day, and McNear sighed as he sat down. "If we don't get something out of this Collins I'll be willing to call it a suicide myself," he said half-earnestly.

Welch gave a harsh, humourless laugh and kept watching the mobile crowd. "Suicides don't bring lilies to their own funerals. Nor do they sew fake labels in their dresses."

McNear was mildly doubtful. "As the chief said—"

"Rot," the Superintendent interrupted. "Listen here. The *Cedric* arrived on Friday morning. On Saturday morning at about seven o'clock Constable Simmons found Miss Hawkins' body. In her dress was sewn a label from the Sports Shop. Now that we know that the girl was the Marsden nurse, it is unlikely that she had been here before, or at least not recently, for New York will have kept track of most of her movements these last two months since the kidnapping. How they let her slip out on the *Cedric* I don't know, but still, she managed it somehow. But if she came out here to kill herself—well, would she rush off and buy a hat from the Sports Shop as soon as she arrived, take out the label and sew it into her dress?"

"I don't know," McNear said timidly. "These modern girls will do anything to impress."

"What, to impress the policeman who finds your dead body?"

"I wouldn't put that past some of 'em," said McNear gloomily.

"Well, anyhow," Welch proceeded, "this one didn't. Think a minute! What day did she arrive in Hamilton?"

"Yesterday—Friday."

"Friday, precisely—Good Friday. And since all the shops were closed, how could she have bought a hat from the Sports Shop?"

McNear nodded, convinced. "She couldn't. And she couldn't have brought those lilies from Collins's cabin, either."

Welch sat back, drumming his thumbnail against his teeth and looking shrewdly thoughtful. "McNear," he said, "we've got to find that man before the inquest."

As he spoke a bell boy came darting through the crowd and directly approached Welch.

"Superintendent Welch? Telephone for you, sir."

"Must be Headquarters," Welch said, and followed the boy quickly.

McNear waited. Scarcely a minute elapsed, however, before Welch returned. And the Inspector, able from long years of close contact to read his superior's emotions, could see that Welch had received a nasty jolt. And his first words confirmed this surmise.

"Mac," Welch cried in a low, vexed voice, "we're stumped. That was Sergeant Harris from Somerset on the wire. He tells me he has found Collins, but that the man is dead!"

7

THE BANK ROBBER

Saturday Night, April 10th.

McNear was thunderstruck by the news of Collins' death. The mystery was becoming far too complex for his simple mind to grasp. "Deeper and deeper," he lamented, and looked helplessly for direction from his superior.

"And deeper," Welch muttered shortly. He gave a sudden jerk at his neat helmet. "Come on," he said. "We're on our way to Somerset—at least, I am."

McNear abruptly heaved his heavy bulk from the softly upholstered chair, and together they walked briskly through the lighted, crowded lobby of the Windsor.

"On a time like this," Welch grumbled, as they stood waiting in the darkness for the Somerset train, "when an aeroplane is what we need, it seems a shame that the Government bans motor-cars from the Island. Instead of zipping along at sixty miles an hour straight to Somerset, we have the choice of crawling along in a carriage or waiting for the train! Damn!"

McNear, loyal Bermudian that he was, rebuked his superior in a shocked tone. "Hush, man! Don't blame Bermuda if criminals from the States make us dash about a bit." He peered at his illuminated wrist-watch. "Besides, the train comes along in five minutes."

Even then the rails began to sing with the approach of the railway car.

It came up slowly, stopped still more slowly to let them aboard, and rolled leisurely on into the night.

67

An hour later they met Sergeant Harris in the local police station at Somerset. He was a tall, cadaverous officer with sunken cheekbones and a prominent gold tooth which shone fascinatingly when he talked. Touching his cap respectfully, he said, "I presume you'll want to see the body, sir?"

"Right, Harris," Welch assured him briskly, "and you can tell me your story as we walk along." He set out at a swift pace through the tropic darkness, and Harris, striding between the Superintendent and McNear, began his story:

"As instructed, sir, I made a round of the hotels and boarding-houses here in Sandys Parish as soon as I got your message. We haven't many such places out on our little tip, but what we have are rather far apart from each other. After inquiring without success at various places, I came to the Blazing Star—it's up here near Mangrove Bay, you know, sir?"

"I know," Welch assented. "Proprietor is old Mr. Eldridge, and a finer old codger I've never met."

"Mr. Eldridge is my friend of long standing," Sergeant Harris resumed in his slow, deliberate way. "And when I explained my mission he replied, 'Harris, you'll need to look no further, my boy! The man is here—been staying in this house for the past two days. Has he done anything wrong now?'

"'That I don't know, Mr. Eldridge, I'm sure,' I said to him. 'But I have orders from Superintendent Welch to locate a Mr. George Collins and, on finding him, to report at once to Headquarters.'

"'I hope it's nothing serious,' Mr. Eldridge said to me, concerned like. 'Mr. Collins is a very pleasant gentleman, although a shade on the moody side. All yesterday he sat in his room—brooding, sort of.'"

"All day yesterday?" McNear interrupted.

"That's what Mr. Eldridge told me, sir," Sergeant Harris answered gravely. "Beautiful weather though it was, he stayed indoors."

Welch made an impatient sound. But slow and verbose as Harris' story undoubtedly was, the Superintendent hesitated to interrupt or cut it short for fear of missing some important clue.

"'I've a problem to solve, Mr. Eldridge,' Collins said to him sad-like when he first arrived, 'and I must have peace.' With that he went up to his room, and the only living soul that spoke to him all day was Lester, the waiter, who gave him his breakfast and lunch.

"Well, sir," Harris resumed. "Since Collins had asked for quiet, Mr. Eldridge was reluctant to disturb him, but I made a point of it, and a few minutes later he came clattering down those old wooden stairs and burst into the tap-room where I was waiting. I saw at once that something was up because the veins stood out in big purple welts all over the proprietor's forehead.

"'Dead!' Mr. Eldridge gasped. 'Lyin' there dead on the floor!' Sir, it hurt Mr. Eldridge dreadful-like to have a guest of his dead in the Blazing Star.

"'And me about to go down on my knees on Easter morn to thank God for a prosperous and happy season!' he said."

"So you went upstairs," Welch gently urged him.

"I went upstairs," Harris repeated, "and sure enough, Collins was stretched out stark and cold."

McNear sniffed suspiciously. "When you say cold do you mean cold or are you just saying it to make it sound better?"

"Sir," Harris answered stiffly, "I mean *cold*. Collins had been dead for hours."

They approached the Blazing Star, an ancient, snug little tavern. There was a light from the taproom window, and inside old Mr. Eldridge, the grizzled proprietor, was waiting.

Without a word, as if the shock had been too much for him, Eldridge led the officers up the aged cedar stairs to Collins' room. There, in the lamp light, Sergeant Harris took a huge key from his pocket and handed it to Welch.

"I locked it as soon as I discovered the body, sir," he said.

"Right," Welch commended him and swung open the door. It grated sharply on its rusty hinges as the three men stepped inside.

Doubled up on the floor in a hideously cramped position lay the body of the late George Collins. As the *Baledonia's* steward had described him to McNear, he had that indefinable but unmistakable air of the college man who had graduated into a bond salesman or the vice presidency of a large bank. Underneath the ghastly distortion of his features there was still the remnant of a well-fed, well cared-for expression, as if he had found life good and easy for him.

McNear held the lamp for his chief, and Welch bent close to the dead man. The hands interested him. They were clenched with agony more stiffly than *rigor mortis* could give. The nails had cut into the soft flesh of the palms.

Welch stood up grimly and called in Mr. Eldridge.

"Mr. Eldridge, you said this man has been alone all day?"

"Since luncheon," the proprietor said.

Welch sighed. "Suicide. Suicide by poison, no doubt of that."

From the circumstances, no other possibility existed.

With a glance at his chief, McNear lifted the lamp so that he could see about the room. On the nightstand beside the undisturbed bed stood a squat green bottle. Reaching for it, McNear spelled the word "Poison," which was lettered in red on the label.

"Bichloride of mercury," he said. "No wonder he is all twisted up with pain like that."

Welch was sadly quiet. He looked slowly about the room. "Nothing has been disturbed here?"

"Not a soul has crossed the threshold since Sergeant Harris locked the door," Eldridge answered.

The proprietor went downstairs and Welch, assisted by McNear and the Sergeant, began a careful investigation of the room.

As McNear had surmised from the lack of luggage in Collins' cabin, the dead man had taken a traveling bag ashore with him. It stood empty on a chair beside the bureau. On top of the bureau was ranged a row of the usual toilet articles, and in the upper drawer McNear found a small, neat pile of shirts and underclothing.

Near Collins' stiffly outstretched left arm Welch picked up the glass in which the bichloride of mercury tablets had been dissolved. This he carefully handled for fear of obliterating the fingerprints, which, even in the lamplight, were plainly visible at its rim. Not that he had the vaguest belief in murder having been done—it was no more than an additional bit to the irrefutable evidence he had already discovered.

Meanwhile McNear had begun to search the dead man's clothing. Piece by piece the contents of his pockets were disclosed—a thin, gold watch, a handful of coins, seventy-five dollars in American bills. Reaching his hand inside Collins' coat pocket, McNear felt the crinkle of paper. He withdrew an envelope and held it toward the light. On it had been written in a heavy, painstaking hand, "To the Police."

McNear gave the letter to Welch and waited with an expression of grim expectancy.

Welch carefully slit the envelope and read the letter slowly. Then he read it again, frowning more deeply with each perusal.

"Doesn't it clear up everything?" McNear demanded.

Welch gave a sardonic, exasperated smile. "It clears up—precisely nothing!"

"Oh, come," McNear protested.

Welch carelessly handed him the letter. He read it swiftly to himself, then read it slowly aloud:

"I am taking my life because the weight of my crimes no longer permits me to live. This is the end."

"But, Welch!" McNear protested, "there's the whole solution. It's practically a confession that he killed Pamela Hawkins! And with our evidence of the lilies—remember the steward aboard the *Baledonia* saw them in his cabin and I, myself, saw them, with the dagger inside, by Miss Hawkins' body—"

Welch shook his head. "That, I'm afraid, is what the Chief of Police, the Coroner and the Coroner's jury will conclude. Meanwhile, the murderer of that poor girl—well," he muttered, "give me a hand here. Let's get this body up off the floor."

Gently the three men carried the inert form to the bed, where Harris drew a sheet over the hideously convulsed features.

Shepherding the others out of the bedchamber, Welch locked the door and followed down the stairs to the tap-room. While McNear and Harris joined Mr. Eldridge in a glass of toddy, Welch stepped to the telephone and called Headquarters.

Masters, the sergeant on duty informed him, had gone home hours ago. "No wonder," Welch muttered to himself as he looked at his watch, for it was after midnight. He made his report and rejoined the others in the tap-room.

"Well, Mac," he said genially, "the last train's gone. Shall we hire a carriage or wait for the first train in the morning?"

Old Mr. Eldridge set down a bottle and boomed hospitably, "I've got plenty of beds for you here, Superintendent Welch; and you're welcome to the best in the house!"

They thanked him, but as neither felt like going to sleep, McNear, after exchanging glances with Welch, said, "We can sit. Be good for us."

So Harris went home—to his "good lady" as he put it—and the other two officers waited till dawn in the taproom of the Blazing Star. Then, after a leisurely breakfast, they tramped along the bay to Somerset, where they took the train back to Hamilton.

"First of all," Welch said as they marched along the bright, deserted streets, "we'll want to get hold of what baggage Collins left in his cabin, and I propose we do it ourselves so as to miss as little as possible. You had a look at it yesterday, didn't you?"

"I did," McNear said. "There was a trunk in a corner, heavily locked and strapped. But, having no warrant, I couldn't search it, much as I'd have liked to."

"Of course not," Welch, who was a meticulous stickler for correct procedure, agreed readily.

That bright Easter morning was still fresh when they reached Headquarters, but as they went inside they saw the Chief of Police stalking about the corridor.

"Well," McNear said jovially, "you're early this morning, sir!"

But Masters was too perturbed to answer pleasantries.

"Welch," he said, "I've read your report. And I have some news myself." Brusquely tapping the cablegram he held in one hand, he continued: "A few minutes ago I received word from Boston. This man Collins—though that is not his name—was the cashier of the Third National Bank in that city. He has been missing for two weeks, and with him went half a million dollars of the bank's trust securities!"

8
FORESTALLED

Easter Morning, April 11th.

"A thief as well as a murderer," Master observed with asperity. "All of which further complicates matters, though in no essential point, I'm happy to say. The girl must have been mixed up in the bank robbery in some fashion—doubtless the Boston police will discover the connection. However, the main fact is clear—Pamela Hawkins was murdered by this man. Now we must find the bonds."

"But," Welch expostulated, ignoring his chief's interest in the stolen funds, "according to Mr. Eldridge, the owner of the Blazing Star, Collins was in his room all day, sir."

"I've read your report," Masters answered caustically, "and permit me to contradict you. It says he was there when the servant brought up breakfast and again at lunch and that he wasn't seen again until his body was found. It does not state that he was in his room earlier in the morning—say at the time Miss Hawkins was murdered."

"That's true," Welch admitted. "And I'll admit it was physically possible for him to bicycle the ten miles between Somerset and Snake Road and get back unseen by Mr. Eldridge."

"Exactly!" Masters said. "Besides, he confessed to it, man. You found the confession yourself!"

"Begging your pardon," Welch said with mock humbleness, "but he didn't confess."

Both Masters and Welch's trusted friend, McNear, regarded the Superintendent impatiently, somewhat as if they felt that Welch had suddenly lost his mind.

"Explain yourself," the Chief demanded. "I suppose you must have some reason for making such a fantastic statement."

Deliberately Welch withdrew the letter from the pocket of his tunic and opened it "These are the words left by Collins," he said. "I will read them:

> "'I am taking my life because the weight of my crimes no longer permits me to live. This is the end.'"

"Well? Well?" Masters said huffily. "That's what I thought it said. Isn't that a confession?"

"A confession," Welch agreed, "but not a confession of murder—least of all, not a confession of having murdered Miss Hawkins. On the contrary, it's an admission of guilt in connection with that bank embezzlement—that and nothing else."

"Superintendent," his superior charged him with an exasperated smile, "first you were so sure that Miss Hawkins was murdered and now you're so sure that Collins was not the murderer, I'm almost tempted to believe you committed the crime yourself!"

Welch grinned.

"You are simply turning a supposition into a statement of fact," his Chief accused him. "Now that we've discovered the man to be a thief you want us to believe he wasn't capable of committing murder, too. Why, man, from time immemorial a killing has frequently followed robbery. Now," he paused weightily, "in addition to this I think you have overlooked that little letter 's' in that confession to the police. The man admits to crimes, not just one crime."

"Granted," Welch agreed, "but that doesn't really mean anything. People often write in that theatrical sort of way when they're desperate. Probably we'll find out that he deserted his family, or something like that."

McNear, who had been listening worriedly to the protracted wrangle between his two superiors, interrupted quietly, "But, Superintendent—when he committed suicide within a few hours and not more than ten miles from where the girl's body was found! After all, as the Chief of Police said, the man confessed to more than one crime."

"At any rate," Masters cut in, "I'm sure the Superintendent doesn't seriously propose that we make a public announcement to the effect that Collins is innocent of making away with that poor girl!"

Welch grinned again. "Not in advance of the jury's verdict, sir."

"Therefore," Masters went on gravely, "we will proceed to the next important item—which is the missing securities. Now, first of all, I had a talk over the telephone with Boston this morning. These stolen securities consist solely of United States Treasury Notes and Certificates of Indebtedness, and the President of the Bank gave me a list of them.

"Ordinarily, so the police in Boston informed me, these bonds are as negotiable as gold or paper money. It so happens, however, that among the stolen certificates there were ten of them in five thousand dollar denomination, and each of them had been registered at the Treasury Department in Washington in the names of their owners.

"Now Collins himself," the Chief continued, stressing the importance of his words, "didn't know that ten of these certificates were registered in their owners' names. And that is the only hope the Boston authorities have of recovering them. Their hope is further strengthened by the fact that as yet none of the numbered securities have been reported. And this leads them to believe that Collins probably had the full amount, still intact, when he arrived here. Therefore it is our duty to give as much help as possible toward recovering them."

"That trunk!" McNear blurted.

"What trunk?" Masters demanded.

"The trunk in his stateroom, sir," McNear said, with a gleam of satisfaction in his eyes. "When I went aboard the *Baledonia* yesterday to investigate I noticed a small steamer trunk all locked and trussed up like the vaults of the Bank of England. I wondered then what was in it, but as I had no warrant to search—"

"Quite right," his Chief commended him, "but you can go there now, man! And the sooner, the better!" He paused, then said as they stood up and swung their helmets on their heads, "You'd both better make note of the description of these ten bonds that have been registered."

McNear and Welch sat down with their notebooks on their knees and their pencils poised.

"They are of the 3½ per cent, series due this coming December fifteenth, and their numbers are as follows:

        AH—641—642—643
        LP—702—703—704
        BBA—1020
        HAL—1425—1426—1430

"Got it," Welch said. He arose and buttoned the notebook inside his tunic. "Off to the *Baledonia*, Inspector."

As they turned off Parliament Street the mellow far-carrying bells from the cathedral on the hill began to ring, and McNear became gloomy. He had never missed an Easter service since his childhood. Easter services in Bermuda have a very special appeal, and long before the hour of eleven the massive grey cathedral is filled to the chancel with closely packed rows of devotees. The bright sun glowing through the stained-glass windows makes rainbow tapestries on the finely carved altar, so heavily laden with the Easter flower.

And there was more to the pageant than that, McNear reflected sadly. He thought regretfully of the Governor in his brilliant uniform of silver and crimson, followed by his aides as he arrived with a fanfare of ceremony. He thought of the Admiral flanked by his gold-braided staff mounting the outer steps and making stately passage between the wide portals of the church. He thought of the officers of the garrison, resplendent in green full dress, their busbies tucked under their stiffened elbows as they marched down the aisle.

Welch, on the contrary, seemed in the best of spirits. "If we don't find the bonds," he said with a chuckle, "I pity the poor unfortunate tourists who try to smuggle a bottle of whiskey or rum into New York on this trip! They'll be due for a sad awakening when the American Customs men start to go through their belongings!"

McNear listened glumly. "But there's one thing to remember, and that is—they can't search the clothing of all these people. As a matter of fact, I saw a United States Government Certificate once, and it wasn't a bulky bit like the ordinary bond with pages of future coupons; it was not much bigger than the regular American currency. Five hundred thousand dollars worth of them wouldn't take up much room if they're in big denominations. Why, the whole lot wouldn't be too big for a man to carry in his inside coat pocket!"

They reached Transportation Wharf and went aboard the *Baledonia's* tender which, some fifteen minutes later, chugged out into the bay with a few scattered passengers.

"We'll get hold of McKnight, my friend the Purser," McNear said after they had swung up the accommodation ladder to the main deck. "He was very helpful the other time I came out here."

They went on down to the Purser's office. It was empty, but there was a brisk little page boy in the offing, and when they stopped him he became alert to their question.

"If you'll follow me, sirs," he assured them, "I'll see if I can find Mr. McKnight. But he's a hard man to catch, sometimes. Fairly hops all over the ship, he does."

Up around the promenade deck, through the public rooms and deserted bars, Welch and McNear followed their diminutive guide. And, after peeping into almost every corner of the ship, they at last found the Purser sitting in the wireless roam, chatting amiably with the operator on duty.

"Well, gentlemen!" McKnight jumped up to greet them.

After introductions had been made McKnight offered the policemen the only two chairs of which the small cabin boasted. As for himself, he perched a-top a nearby table with the air of a man completely at home.

"We looked for you all over the ship, McKnight," McNear said as he wearily sat down. "Never thought we'd find you up here."

The Purser laughed easily. "Oh! I often come up here to pass the time of day. All these valves, sparks, condensers and that maze of wires gives me a feeling of wonder and fascination just to be up here. To think"—he dropped his voice ruminatively—"that years ago when I was a lad before the mast we never dreamed of anything like it. Air—why air was something you looked through! I still have to pinch myself to realize that you can pull sounds out of it."

Regarding him with amused tolerance, the operator said, "You certainly like to putter around up here." He turned to Welch. "Not that I blame him, you understand. For my part, I wouldn't trade my job with any purser in the world."

"It must be an interesting life," Superintendent Welch agreed hastily, anxious to begin his investigations.

"Yes," McNear added, appreciatively eyeing the wireless set, "and you've got a magnificent contraption to work with!"

"Brand new," the operator boasted. "Just installed in New York. The last word in wireless equipment, I'll say that much for the owners. Every tested improvement that they could buy, they bought."

McNear restlessly signaled to the Purser, who jumped to the floor, saying, "But you Gentlemen have business with me."

"If you don't mind," Welch observed, "we'll go down to your quarters. There are a few things we'd like to talk over with you."

Soon they were seated in the Purser's private cabin, where McKnight set three glasses and a bottle before them.

"Now, gentlemen," he said, and waited expectantly. "Something about Collins, I presume?"

McNear nodded. "It's no secret, so I may tell you that you no longer need watch for him. He swallowed bichloride of mercury yesterday morning, and by now he's in the morgue at Hamilton."

"Good God!" McKnight cried. He was thoughtful a moment. "The murderer of that girl, eh? To think I had a man on my ship like that!"

Impatient to begin his search, Welch forestalled any futile discussions of a moral, fatal or mysterious nature, and remarked drily, "If you'll take us to his stateroom we'll collect his belongings and send them ashore on the next tender."

"Of course, Superintendent." The Purser arose. He knelt before his safe and spun the knob. Taking out the key, he handed it to Welch.

They went down the companionway to the lower deck and tramped along the corridor till they stood before the door marked 72-D.

"The room has not been entered since I locked it?"

"No, Inspector," the Purser answered McNear. "Not unless somebody crawled through the key-hole. This little key has been in our safe since you handed it to me yesterday."

McNear opened the door and the three men stepped inside.

As soon as McNear entered he had a feeling that something had been changed. There was some detail, some little correlation of objects that was not now as it had been when he had closed the room the day before. He racked his memory to catch the elusive difference, but it remained tantalizingly outside his mental reach.

Something in the room was different from what it had been— but what could it be? The row of suits in the small closet hung ready as before. The shoes stood in the same straight line. The shirts and underclothes remained folded as before. And the steamer trunk still stood in its corner of the cabin. And yet—?

Superintendent Welch moved directly toward the trunk. "This the trunk that was in here yesterday, Inspector?" he asked McNear.

"Yes," McNear assented. As he spoke something clicked in his brain. Yesterday the trunk had been trussed securely by four leather straps. Now one of the straps, though buckled as before, was slack.

Kneeling beside the trunk, Welch said, "If it's locked, as it probably is, I'll have to break it open."

McNear spoke, his voice anxious and mistrustful. "It was locked, but it's probably not locked *now!*"

Welch gave him a hasty stare and looked suspiciously at the trunk fastenings. "Right!" he muttered disappointedly.

For, plainly to be seen around the brass key-hole were deep, criss-crossed scratches. At the touch of his hand, the hinged lock fell back.

Hurriedly, Welch unfastened the straps and raised the lid.

Packed in beside a pile of rumpled clothing lay a large tin box. It took up nearly half the space of the trunk. The cover of the box was twisted back and it was completely empty of contents!

"Damn!" Welch exploded. He began rummaging among the clothing in the bottom of the trunk.

Meanwhile McNear had gone to the door and was investigating the stateroom lock. It was of a flimsy sort, but it, too, had been tampered with, for there were scratches on the plate around the key-hole.

"Mr. Purser," McNear said angrily, "you've got a thief on board!"

Still bending over the trunk while he investigated the clothing, Welch checked an exclamation of utter astonishment. "Well, I'll be—" he began, then covered his surprise by turning it to McNear's discovery.

"So the door has been forced, eh, Mac?" The Purser looked from one to the other with puzzled eyes. Finally, his gaze rested on Welch. He said, "But what was the thief after, Superintendent?"

9
A LEAK AT HEADQUARTERS?

Easter Midday, April 11th.

Rummaging the clothing back into place, Welch pointed toward the empty box with a sardonic smile. "Plenty," he said.

The Purser looked wonderingly at the trunk. "Something that was in that box, I presume?"

Welch nodded. "Stolen bonds."

"Worth half a million dollars," McNear added.

"Good God!" the ship's officer exclaimed, "is there that much money in the world!"

Welch heard the Purser's remark in silent abstractedness.

But McNear stated grimly, "There is. And I'm afraid, McKnight, that you've a thief aboard the *Baledonia*."

"Come," McKnight protested, "you don't think he's still aboard?"

"I don't know," McNear admitted. "Even if the thief is aboard I hardly think he'd dare to run the gauntlet of the New York Customs officers."

"Ah!" McKnight pointed out. "Now Collins, I take it, must have stolen the bonds himself! But supposing the second thief doesn't know that Collins had been discovered? In that case he would have no reason to think that the ship would be searched when it landed at New York!"

"That's a fact," McNear said slowly.

"On the other hand"—the Purser resumed his reasoning—"you have no reason to suppose that the thief was a passenger of the

Baledonia or of any other of the cruise ships. During our time in port there are hundreds of Bermuda visitors who come out here—native Bermudians—people who have taken houses for the season—all kinds. I shouldn't be surprised if the thief was a Bermudian who got wind of Collins' death and went through the things in here without any idea of the haul that awaited him."

Welch looked up and spoke emphatically. "Whoever broke into that trunk knew exactly what he was after!"

"In that case," the Purser said, "he must have been an accomplice of Collins. Who else would know that the bonds were hidden there?"

Welch sat on the top of the trunk and frowned. "McKnight, we need facts more than theories. Do you recollect any suspicious actions on the part of any of the passengers or crew?"

"As for the passengers," McKnight said slowly, "that's a rather large order, Superintendent. But I think I can answer for the crew. And I'm glad to say I haven't noticed anything out of the way here on this trip. The ship's crew have been behaving themselves like good seamen. It's true that one of our stewards got drunk last night and stayed ashore without leave. But that's no more than a nuisance, for I anticipate no trouble in bringing him back."

"You're going ashore after him, then?" McNear inquired.

"I was getting ready to start when you gentlemen arrived," the Purser answered.

"In that case," Welch said, "we'll go along and give you a hand if you need it."

The Purser nodded. "I'm going ashore in one of the ship's motor-launches, and I'll be glad to take you with me. But I think," he ended a little grimly, "that my roistering steward will be quiet enough when I've caught up with him."

"As you like," Welch said.

With McNear he began to pack up every available belonging of the dead man's and to get the things ready for transportation to Headquarters.

"I'll meet you near the aft accommodation ladder in five minutes," the Purser said as he withdrew.

"Hurry up," Welch directed when they were alone; "let's get this stuff together, Mac."

They worked swiftly and silently till they had finished. Then Welch, calling two stewards, had the baggage carried below decks to the water-line where he followed it, remaining standing there after Collins' effects had been put down.

"Come on," McNear said.

Welch shook his head. What he had seen in the trunk had made him determined not to lose sight of the luggage until it was safely delivered at Headquarters. "You go on up," he directed. "I'll get aboard from here."

McNear looked at him curiously, but obeyed. Waiting in the baggage hold, Welch saw the ship's motor-launch swung down from the side and steered up to the aft accommodation ladder. He saw the neat, efficient-looking boatswain stand at the helm and look expectantly upward. But it seemed more like half an hour, than the five minutes in which the Purser had promised to return, before McKnight and McNear descended the ladder to the launch.

Slipping along the hull in the motionless sea, they picked up Welch and his baggage. Then, with an "All ready, sir?" the launch swung away, and, beginning a smooth put-put-put, streamed toward the narrow jaws of Two Rock passage which led to the harbour and the new Corporation's Steps.

When they landed, Welch hailed a carriage and had the baggage piled aboard. With his hand on the trunk, he turned to McNear and the Purser, who were standing by.

"Inspector," he said, "I'm going on to Headquarters. I suggest that you go along with McKnight in search of that missing steward of his."

"Yes, sir," McNear accepted promptly.

"Very well, gentlemen," McKnight said. "Of course, I'll be very glad of your help."

Welch touched his helmet and climbed into the carriage. "Police Headquarters," he directed the startled cabby, who whipped up his horse with a sense of great importance.

As Welch disappeared down the street, the Purser dropped his hand on McNear's arm and spoke amiably, "I'm much obliged to have you along, Mr. Inspector. Not that our steward Davis is likely to be ugly—but you never can tell about a man with too much liquor under his belt."

McNear agreed a little vaguely. "Maybe it will work out well for both of us, Mr. Purser." Obviously, he thought, Welch wanted him to pursue the missing steward, and it was a project that he was glad to undertake. For there was the possibility of some connection, and perhaps a very close one, between the missing sailor on a spree and the stolen bonds.

"It was reported last night," the Purser explained, as they walked into the city, "that Davis was hanging out at a place on Burnaby Street—a place called Jack's."

McNear's face became grim. "Jack's!" he repeated, for Jack's, on Burnaby Street, was notorious, the only saloon really noted for disobeying the regulations governing hours of opening. And here it was Easter Sunday! "If he's not sleeping off the effects of his liquor, and if he's in a place where he can be served more," McNear reasoned aloud, "then Jack's is the place. And," he added threateningly, "if we find him there, we'll close that bar down for good!"

So it was with a minatory tread that boded no good to Davis, the steward, nor to Jack, the proprietor, that Inspector McNear led the way toward the suspected establishment. Finally, they stopped before a building whose one lone, dingy window displayed a crudely lettered sign, "Jack's Bar."

Descending the steps, Inspector McNear paused to peer through the murky window. He saw a figure standing at the rail and heard a maudlinly-rendered snatch of an old sea song.

"The door's locked," called the Purser, who had gone on down ahead of him.

"Never mind," McNear counseled. He was fully at home in dealing with such offenders against the law as Jack and he rapped authoritatively.

The door was opened by the proprietor himself, a slouchy, unkempt man in a soiled white jacket. He had evidently tried to get Davis into hiding and had failed, for through the open door Davis could be seen, disheveled but triumphant at the bar.

"My man!" McNear upbraided the proprietor. "I'm ashamed of you. Easter Sunday it is, and you serving drinks like a heathen. It's your last warning!"

"Now, Inspector," Jack pleaded, "and what could I do with him? Here he come and here he stayed—and how was I to get him out?"

McNear silenced his hypocritical apologies with a scornful look and turned toward McKnight. Nodding toward the man at the bar, he said, "This is your affair now, Mr. Purser."

The Purser had stood beside McNear, evidently sizing Davis up. He said, "The man's pretty far gone. Looks to me as if he might be a handful. I'm glad you're beside me, Mr. McNear, because I may need your help."

The Inspector was silent, for McKnight's burly shoulders and rolling, confident gait as he walked up to the bar gave evidence of his ability to handle the situation without outside aid.

"Come on now, Davis"—McKnight grasped the steward's arm in his huge fist—"let's not have any fuss about this. You're absent without leave—the ship's under sailing orders, and I'm sure you don't want to spend the way back in the brig!"

Davis lurched unsteadily and turned his bloodshot eyes till they rested belligerently on the Purser's face.

"Whatcha think I care about yer stinkin' ol' tub! Take yer bloody fingers offa my arm. You make me sick!"

Thinking that he had thus disposed of the matter, Davis returned to the contemplation of his half-full tumbler of strong Jamaica rum.

Scandalized by such procedure on an Easter Sunday, Inspector McNear felt it high time for the voice of authority to ring out in the wilderness.

"My man," he said in a determine tone, and stepping forward where he could lay a heavy hand upon the steward's shoulder, "although I can take no official action until your ship has sailed and you are left behind, I must warn you now for your own good that you had better do as your superior has commanded and step lively about it! If not, I shall make it my business to see that things go especially hard for you when you arrive, as you certainly will, in gaol this night!"

These sobering words and the dignity of the Inspector's uniform seemed to penetrate the man's befuddled mind. After staring
fixedly and without comment at the clock which hung over the bar,
Davis lurched toward the door.

But when he reached the sidewalk his docility unexpectedly
changed and he became belligerent again. "Wher're you takin' me?"
he muttered suspiciously.

"Never mind that," the Purser said. "Come along, now."

Davis squared off. "To hell with you! I gotta date. Ain't no law
that says a man can't have a few minutes to himself! I gotta go to
St. George's!"

"My man!" Inspector McNear told him sternly, "your engagement in St. George's will have to keep. Obey your officer or you'll
live to regret it!"

But Davis drew back and uttered his war cry. "To hell with the
both of you!"

McKnight and McNear exchanged hasty glances. Propelled by
the same motive, they closed in on Davis and pinioned his arms.

He submitted as if in a daze. The manoeuvre so auspiciously
begun seemed certain to be crowned with complete success. Once
having been headed in the proper direction, Davis appeared to have
lost all his pugilistic desires, and except for an occasional muttering of inarticulate oaths went along meekly enough in the hardy
grip of his two stalwart captors.

But not for long. Approaching Front Street, Davis slowly realized that his feet were carrying him in a direction of which his mind
disapproved. With a lusty bellow and a strenuous jerk he dragged
himself free and charged down the street with tremendous strides
which at every step put him a little farther ahead of his pursuers.

But at this moment the benevolent god who protects fools and
drunkards foully deserted his galloping charge. With a crash that
could be heard in the next street, Davis rushed headlong into a
pile of packing-cases standing outside a shop and sprawled in a
heap beneath them on the pavement.

McNear and the Purser reached him simultaneously, and
McNear bent unwarily down to pull the steward to his feet.

But Davis, in spite of the buffeting he had received from the collision, was still in fighting mood. He started an upswing as he got to his knees, and his fist caught Inspector McNear above the bridge of the nose.

"Oh, you will, will you!" McNear muttered, gently rubbing that distressed member. "We'll see about this!"

He dived in, and in a moment all three of them were rolling in the gutter with grunts and jabbing fists. But at last McNear got a firm grip on Davis' collar, and the fighting steward was jerked to his feet.

"A joke's a joke," McNear panted grimly, "but, Mr. Purser, this fellow goes to gaol!"

The effects of twenty-four hours' indulgence in alcohol had at last worn off, and Davis was an abject sight. His knees sagged so that the Purser had to put his arm around his waist to keep him from falling.

"I know how you feel about it, Mr. Inspector," McKnight pleaded a little, "but the fight's all out of him now, and I know he'll repent if you let me take him back aboard."

McNear shook his head. "He'll repent, man—but on ten days' bread and water in a cell!" He signaled to a constable, who came springing up the street to investigate the rumpus. "Here's your prisoner, Hodgson!"

"Yes, sir." Hodgson saluted with one hand and grasped Davis with the other. "Now, my man," he commanded ominously.

The Purser wiped his forehead and tried vainly to rearrange his disorganized apparel. "I'm sorry, Inspector. I hope the next time we meet it will be in pleasanter circumstances."

"Pshaw, man," McNear said, "'twas nothing but a little rumpus."

"Well." McKnight paused uncertainly, anxious to leave, but seeming to feel that he must make amends for having drawn the Inspector into so unprofitable a brawl.

"Go along, Mr. Purser," McNear instructed him genially. "You can do as much for me some time."

"That I will," McKnight promised, and set off lamely for the motor-launch.

McNear saw him hurrying down the street, and smiled to himself. He didn't blame the Purser for his hasty retreat. The ship's officer had surely gotten more than he had reckoned for. Turning at last, McNear caught up with the constable who had collared Davis, and together they carried the half-conscious man up the steep hill to Headquarters.

Gently rubbing his nose, McNear informed the desk sergeant, "Drunk and incapable is the charge." The sergeant, regarding McNear's nose, grinned in spite of himself at the word "incapable."

McNear grinned too, slightly ruefully. "Drunk and," he repeated, surveying Davis' mauled person, "incapable. Also, resisting arrest. Also, assaulting a police officer. I think that will do for the present."

The prisoner was led off to the detention quarters to be searched and locked up.

Leaving the sergeant to write down the charges, McNear walked up the steps to his room, threw his helmet on the table, slipped off his tunic, and settled himself in a chair. He filled and lighted his great churchwarden pipe, and through the gratifying fumes of good tobacco was looking on the shelf for a bottle of iodine when there was a sharp tapping at the door.

Welch stepped inside and closed the door. He was so preoccupied he barely noticed the Inspector's temporary disfigurement or his efforts to heal it.

"Mac," he said, "I've something to tell you."

McNear laid down his pipe and waited soberly.

"There was a scabbard in Collins' trunk," Welch continued in a slow, reflective voice. "I found it among the loose clothing when we first opened it up and I was looking for the bonds. Mac, the scabbard fits the stiletto that killed Pamela Hawkins!"

McNear gaped at him. When he had recovered from his surprise he said, "Now that is what you might call luck!"

"I might," Welch morosely agreed.

"But surely, man," McNear exclaimed disbelievingly, "after this you can't doubt that it was Collins who killed her! Next to the confession, that scabbard is the biggest piece of evidence we've got!"

Welch nodded, but not in agreement. "I had it fingerprinted, Mac. Haddersly had already taken Collins' fingerprints, and I hoped the scabbard would settle the matter."

"And didn't it?" McNear asked, as if he were sure it must have.

"There was not the sign of a fingerprint on that scabbard!" Welch emphatically answered.

Still, McNear was not overly impressed. "Maybe he wiped the fingerprints off. I've heard of criminals doing just that."

Welch shook his head. "In some cases that could be expected. In this case—well—it doesn't sound reasonable to me. Think, man— Collins takes the stiletto from the scabbard some time Friday. At least twelve hours before the murder he wipes the scabbard off to prevent it being proved that he had touched it, then he not only replaces it in his own trunk, but in a trunk that contains half a million in bonds which he has taken the trouble to steal! No!!"

"Ah!" McNear said tolerantly, and reached for the iodine. "You're trying to make it hard for yourself. Why, man, it's only the criminals in the storybooks that don't do foolish things. Now you take that case of Jerry McCoy in New York. He had it all arranged in his mind to plant a knife in McGovern's hands after he had shot him and then claim self-defence. And what did he do? He shot him, right enough, but then he got the wind up so bad he left the pistol by the dead man and went running out into the hall with the *knife* in his hand!"

Finding no ready answer to this, Welch changed the subject. "You collared that missing steward, didn't you?"

McNear rubbed his nose and nodded.

"Anything out of the way occur in that connection?"

"Nothing," McNear answered severely, "except that the proprietor of Jack's in Burnaby Street was serving liquor of an Easter Sunday!"

There came a rap at the door.

McNear regarded it dourly. He was weary and he had hoped nothing further would be required of him that day. "Come in," he said.

A constable stood in the doorway.

"The Chief of Police's compliments, and he would like to see you, Inspector McNear—and you too, sir," he added, seeing Welch.

Buttoning their tunics, the two officers followed the messenger.

Masters had an unusually stern expression on his sharp, military-looking face.

"Sit down, gentlemen," he directed.

As the two men found chairs Masters turned to McNear. "This morning you arrested a steward from the *Baledonia*?"

"Yes, sir," McNear answered. "Drunk—resisting an officer—I had plenty of cause, sir."

Masters nodded. "He was searched, as usual. Do you know what was found?"

"No, sir," McNear said. "I've no idea, sir. I instructed the constable in charge to go through his belongings, as we do to anyone we arrest, but I myself was not present."

Masters surveyed the Inspector with troubled eyes. "McNear," he said, "in that man's pocket we found United States Treasury Certificates!"

McNear noticed the displeasure on his superior's face, but was unable to comprehend the cause of it. Also, the news was astonishing. "Must be the ones that were stolen, sir!"

"Part of them, yes." It was acknowledged grimly.

"Well, sir," McNear demanded triumphantly, "then why haven't we got our thief?—for surely he knows where the rest of the bonds are, this Davis."

"Perhaps so," admitted his superior sombrely, "but there's a much more serious matter which has come up, gentlemen. There is a traitor here at Police Headquarters—some man who is in touch with the person or persons responsible for this robbery!"

McNear's face became indignantly red.

Welch, too, was outraged at the charge, but he covered his feelings with a fine, sardonic smile.

Both men demanded, but in different tones:

"What do you mean, sir!"

Masters gave his attention to the Superintendent. "I mean this, Welch. That man Davis had Treasury Certificates in his pocket—

fifty thousand dollars worth of them. But do you know what fifty thousand they represented? They were the registered bonds, the numbers of which I gave you and McNear this very morning—the only part of the loot that could not be disposed of—and therefore worthless to the thief!"

Welch was astounded. "But that is impossible, sir," he said incredulously.

"Quite right!" Masters charged grimly. "Impossible! That is what makes the situation all the more critical. Nobody but the police—not even Collins, the man who embezzled the bonds, not even the man who stole them from the trunk—knew the numbers of these ten certificates. They were known only to us! Now, how then do we find these ten certificates, and no others, in this man Davis' coat pocket?"

10

THE BLACKMAILER

Easter Sunday Afternoon, April 11th.

That afternoon Henry Hastings, junior partner in the well-known firm of wine and liquor merchants, Hastings and West, pushed open the swinging doors of the Bermudiana tap-room and, placing a brightly polished shoe on the gleaming brass rail, simultaneously rested his elbow on the equally shining cedar bar.

"Hel-lo, Bill!" Hastings' greeting to the bartender was a smooth, beneficent blessing. That caressing voice of his, coupled with his sympathetic eye, was one of his chief stocks-in-trade.

Bill the bartender welcomed him as an amiable but highly respected friend. "Glad to see you, Mr. Hastings. Haven't been around lately, sir! Where've you been?"

"Too much business, Bill," Hastings sighed. "And then I was in Montreal for ten days."

"Too much business!" Bill grinned enviously. Hastings, he knew, made a great deal of money, but there was no indication that the man could be accused of keeping his nose unduly to the grindstone. His naturally happy disposition and debonair appearance made him popular with all his customers, especially with the American coterie, and in the cultivation of those friendships he found a mere application to routine in Hastings and West's shops was insufficient. Hastings was a staunch believer in the efficacy of the great glad hand; and since his affairs had prospered till they had been greatly expanded since his father's death, the value of his theory had been more than borne out

There were, however, those of the older and straitlaced element among his fellow-Bermudians who did not quite approve of his well-practised formula of mixing business so thoroughly with pleasure. There were those, indeed, who hinted that the hours Hastings spent in the various thirst-quenching establishments of Hamilton were more for the purpose of selling himself to the ladies than for selling his liquor to the hotel keepers.

But this, of course, might have been base calumny—possibly inspired by rival wine merchants who perceived in the prosperous young man an adversary who was taking too much of their business. Indeed, the firm of Hastings and West had been so successful with their aggressive tactics that some of the more conservative liquor dealers of late had actually veered a little from their time-honoured take-it-or-leave-it policy and had begun timidly to adopt Hastings' more effective methods.

"That's a terrible complaint—too much business!" Bill laughed. "You're not going to let it get you down, are you?"

Hastings smiled genially, and gave Bill a confidential nod. "I'm not. You know my motto, Bill—when business interferes with pleasure, give up business!"

With a broad grin Bill reached beneath the bar and selected a pint bottle of champagne, which was the chief ingredient in Hastings' favourite cocktail.

Watching him approvingly, Hastings directed, "Make a whole shaker full, Bill. I've got a thirst this morning."

"Morning?" Bill laughed. "Where've you been all night? It's afternoon!"

Hastings waited avidly and was silent till his fingers had closed appreciatively around the thin stem of the tall, cool glass. As he was about to lift it to his lips a hearty slap descended on his shoulder-blades and a hilarious voice boomed, "Well, if there's not Henry Hastings—Hank, you old son-of-a-gun, you!"

Hastings turned, discovering a sporty New York friend who was beaming in a haze of alcohol and good nature.

"Been looking for you ever since I landed," the new arrival proclaimed, "and now the sky's the limit. Here—gotta introduce you

to the best little scout that ever stepped foot on a gangplank—
Henry, I want you to meet Ianthe Brown!"

Dragged, but not unwillingly, down the length of the bar toward a corner table, Henry Hastings found himself looking into
the recklessly challenging eyes of an extremely pretty girl, and he
forthwith blessed the thought that had brought him to his favourite
bar at just that moment.

The idea that his New York acquaintance might have established a prior claim to Miss Brown didn't for an instant enter
Hastings' determined mind. And when the three were tucked away
at a cosy corner table, he at once displayed the tactics of his cus-
tomary plan of campaign.

Hastings' unconcealed eagerness to attract the girl might have
led an unprejudiced observer to remark that the aforementioned
straitlaced tabbies who had charged Hastings with an excessive
fondness for pretty girls had not been mewing up the wrong drain-
pipe. But that was Henry Hastings, and there were no two ways
about it. You liked him or you didn't like him. And if you were one
of those that disapproved of him, he, as a broadminded egoist,
laughed the matter away with a shrug of his well-clad shoulders
and was the first to sing your praises. A sensible fellow, Hastings—
sensible in larger matters, insensible to smaller ones—and therefore successful.

As the afternoon wore on, the drinks continued to flow over
the bar toward the corner table where the hilarity had become so
infectious that new chairs were continually being pulled up to it
by new arrivals. In the midst of shrill laughter of girls and the deep,
complacent bass of the men, Hastings and Miss Ianthe Brown were
fast approaching a tacit understanding when the bartender himself came up and signaled urgently to the wine dealer.

"Mr. Hastings," the bartender said when he had drawn him
aside a little, "there's a lad up at the other end of the bar that says
he's got to see you in private. Lad named Henderson. I tried to
talk him out of it—told you you wouldn't want to be interrupted,
but he kept insisting on it."

"Insists, eh?" Hastings' face was flushed. He frowned. "That's a pretty strong word, Bill. What does the fellow want?"

"I don't know, that's a fact," Bill said. "But he says it's for your own good. Says you'll regret it if you don't talk to him."

Hastings irritably excused himself and scowled his way toward the heavy beamed doorway.

Arriving near the entrance, Hastings found an undersized, shifty-eyed individual who made a furtive gesture toward him and stepped out into the hotel lobby.

"Well, my man!" Hastings demanded angrily. To the best of his knowledge he had never seen the fellow before. "What have you to say that's so important?"

Henderson, the undesired caller, looked suspiciously up and down the corridor. "What I've got to say had better be said in private, Mr. Hastings!"

"Nonsense!" Hastings sternly answered; "say it, man. Out with it. Let's make short work of this."

Henderson shot him a crafty look. "It's not me that'd be the loser, Mr. Hastings, if anybody heard what I've got to say!"

Hastings frowned. There was such secret knowledge in the man's eyes! He had a guilty feeling that all his actions were not above reproach. "Come on," he said abruptly, sneering a little. "Will my private office be private enough for you?"

"Your private office! Sure it will!" Henderson said cockily.

The offices of Hastings and West were but a short distance from the Bermudiana.

As Hastings, unlocking the door, opened the way to his private room, Henderson pushed ahead of him and impudently seated himself in the most comfortable chair, from which he continued to watch the wine dealer through his crafty eyes.

"Well, out with it!" Hastings demanded grimly. "Now what is it you've got to say?"

"Now, now," Henderson complained in a cringing, conciliatory tone. "You don't want to get mad about it, Mr. Hastings. You jist listen—and then say whether I ain't done you a favour."

Hastings controlled his annoyance. "I intend to listen. That's what I came back here for. But I'm in a hurry and you'd best make haste!"

The shifty-eyed Henderson cast a wandering look along the wall and focused his gaze on a calendar which hung above Hastings' head. He said in a quiet, knowing tone, "I've heard it said there was a girl named Pamela Hawkins murdered yesterday morning."

"What sort of bloody nonsense is this?" Hastings burst out angrily. He had been drinking heavily and the veins came out and throbbed in his temples. "What interest have I in the affair?"

Henderson kept looking at the calendar. "I've heard it said the police are looking for anyone that talked to her on Friday."

Hastings glared furiously at his crafty tormentor, but kept his voice modulated as he answered, "And what if they are?"

In a falsely casual tone Henderson inquired, "You don't ever drop in at the Royal Palm Hotel, do you, Mr. Hastings?"

"Occasionally."

"One of them occasions wasn't last Friday, was it?"

Hastings clenched his fists. "I was there one day last week. What difference does it make?"

"Ah!" Henderson said with mock sadness, "that's jist the pity of it, sir! Any other day would make no difference at all. But it was Friday, Mr. Hastings. Yes, sir, it was Friday afternoon that I seen you sittin' in the ship's bar at the Royal Palm, and you and that Pamela Hawkins, sir, was a-goin' it pretty hot and heavy!"

Hastings' eyes bulged as if with a sudden shock. His fists relaxed into limp, open fingers. He made a great effort to rally himself and maintain his superior attitude. "I recall being in the ship's bar at the Royal Palm with a young lady. Maybe you're right—it may have been on a Friday. But I'm not prepared to admit that the young lady was the person you mention!"

"But you're not prepared to swear it wasn't the Hawkins girl, are you?" Henderson inquired softly.

"Look here!" Hastings blurted, getting a firmer grip on himself. "What do you want from me? What is your game, my man?"

"Game, sir?" Henderson's shifty eyes assumed a hurt, reproach-ful expression. "I don't know what you mean. I'm an honest, law-abiding man, I am. You can ask any man in Hamilton and he won't tell you to the contrary. Now when I heard the police were on the look-out for them as had seen poor Miss Hawkins on that fatal Friday, sir, I says to myself, 'See here, Tom Henderson, you saw that murdered girl! Now where did you see her? 'Twas in the ship's bar of the Royal Palm, wasn't it? And who was she with, Tom Henderson? Why, she was with Mr. Henry Hastings, that's who she was with!'"

Henderson paused and regarded Hastings with an injured look. "That's how it was, sir," he explained. "And then I says to myself, 'Tom Henderson, the police are lookin' for the man that was talkin' to Miss Hawkins. Now are you sure, Tom Henderson, that Mr. Hastings was the man you saw her with? Well, maybe I was wrong, I says, back to myself. Anyhow, before I go to the police and maybe cause Mr. Hastings a bit of annoyance, I says, it's only fair to come to Mr. Hastings first and ask him about it, 'cause maybe I was wrong!'"

And Henderson sat back, the picture of misunderstood virtue.

"Very kind of you, I'm sure," Hastings answered grimly. "And now that you have done me this great favour, what next?"

Henderson was unabashed. "Nothing, sir," he lied brazenly. "I said to myself, 'Tom Henderson, you're a poor, hard-working man, that's God's truth. And Mr. Hastings is a rich and generous man. Now if Mr. Hastings was to recognize how you looked out for his interests by comin' to him first, and if he was to give you some little token of his gratitude, would you, Tom Henderson, risk offending Mr. Hastings with your pride in refusing it? No, I says, I would not!'"

"I understand," Hastings muttered. "How much?"

"Well, sir." Henderson resumed his role of virtuous well-wisher toward his patron, the generous Mr. Hastings. "If my eyes were at fault, sir, which they must have been, it means money for the eye-doctor, sir. Yes, sir, that's likely to run into money. I don't see how I could bear the expense for less than a hundred pounds!"

"Pretty stiff," Hastings commented.

"Yes, sir," Henderson agreed; "everything's high these days, sir. Of course, Mrs. Hastings, if I was to tell her my troubles, might help a little with the expense, since it was a young lady I thought I saw you with—"

"Never mind," Hastings hurriedly interrupted. He had been to the bank the day before and there was a large sum of money in the safe. He stalked angrily over to it and withdrew the amount of the blackmail while Henderson peered interestedly at his back.

"Now," Hastings said, as he gave Henderson the crisp bills, "get out!"

Henderson wadded the money deeply in his left-hand trouser pocket and continued to occupy Hastings' most comfortable chair. "There's one other little matter, sir. A matter of my hearing."

"What do you mean?" cut in Hastings ominously. "There's a limit to my patience, and I've told you to go!"

"Yes, sir." Henderson was unperturbed. "It's my hearing, sir. A man can't go through life as deaf as I am. It wouldn't be fair to ask it—"

A black, murderous look on the wine merchant's face caused the blackmailer to drop his whining tone and to face Hastings with a determined and menacing expression.

"Another hundred pounds, Hastings! You've got it in there! Or do you want me to go to the police and tell 'em I heard you and Miss Hawkins in that booth of the ship's bar and you makin' a date with her for half-past six the next morning—the morning she was found murdered!"

11

THE CORONER'S INQUEST

Monday Morning, April 12th.

Proceedings in the case of Pamela Hawkins, spinster, aged twenty-three, found dead the morning of April 10th on Snake Road, Paget, were about to begin before the Coroner. The little courtroom had quickly overflowed with interested and curious listeners, and its small number of seats had long since been filled by an early rush of spectators.

Even the Coroner's jury had been obtained with dispatch; and for the inquest the constable had experienced no difficulty in serving warrants which demanded the presence of prospective jurymen. For the first time in the history of the Islands the townspeople had been so concerned with a criminal affair that they had rejected their usual practice, which was to evade unrelished duty by going in hiding till the constable had left.

In a short row of chairs opposite the jury sat the three principal officers of the Bermuda Police—the Chief of Police, Superintendent Welch, and Inspector McNear. In their uniform tunics and with helmets resting on their knees, they made a formidable-looking block of official opinion for the onlookers to gape at, but, as a matter of fact, their low-voiced discussion among themselves, if the spectators could have heard it, would have shown them as far at sea in the mystery as anybody in the courtroom.

Masters, waiting for the Coroner's arrival, muttered to Welch, "I still can't account for it, that we should have found those bonds on Davis. I myself took the telephone message from Boston. It was a secret which only you gentlemen shared. And yet within a few hours we found the registered bonds on Davis!"

Welch was also puzzled. Davis had disclaimed any knowledge of the bonds. He had claimed he had been so drunk since the night before that he was unable to remember where he had been or what he had done. And the Captain of the *Baledonia*, who had searched Davis' bunk and sea-bag, had reported that not only had he found nothing, but that Davis had been aboard from the time the ship anchored until late that Saturday afternoon.

"Order, please!"

Their talk was interrupted by the Coroner, a grey-faced, long-lipped man who stalked in gravely and, after a nod to the members of his jury, climbed up on his raised dais where he began shuffling a pile of papers. These having been arranged to his solemn satisfaction, he rapped for order and the inquest began.

Called as the first witness, Constable Simmons a little hurriedly described his discovery of the body, how it lay between the hedge and the roadside, and how Inspector McNear, being sent from Headquarters, had made the strange and gruesome find of the stiletto concealed inside the bouquet of lilies.

"Superintendent Welch!"

Welch arose. In answer to the Coroner's questions, he told of his visit to the *Cedric*, described how the victim had been identified, and mentioned the cablegram received from the New York police.

This resulted in the wire being read and passed to the jury, after which the Coroner stroked his long upper lip and observed, "I presume that the New York authorities have been notified of the death of this young woman?"

"Yes, sir," Welch said, and sat down.

The Chief of Police, called as witness, was asked, "You were informed by the New York police of their reasons for asking that Miss Hawkins be detained?"

"Indeed, yes," Masters answered. "Moreover, I was in telephone communication with the New York authorities this morning and was told that they had got some new evidence in the Marsden kidnapping case that pointed to the deceased as being actively implicated in the crime. As you know, this girl was the Marsden child's nurse at the time it disappeared."

The Coroner nodded. "Had the New York police been searching long for this young woman?"

"I believe not," Masters answered. "I am informed that this new evidence was uncovered four days ago. They had made efforts to find her before she sailed for Bermuda, and, because of recent developments, they now believe that she left to avoid further questioning."

The Coroner nodded toward his papers. Raising his eyes, he addressed the jury. "Of course, gentlemen, the question of whether or not this young woman was concerned with the kidnapping of the Marsden child is not the reason for these proceedings. However, this point may have a very substantial bearing upon the mystery of her death. As I think the moment appropriate, I shall ask Dr. Jenkins to give us the benefit of his medical knowledge."

Dr. Jenkins, after being duly sworn, fussily seated himself in the witness chair and faced the Coroner.

"Now, Dr. Jenkins," the Coroner began in his weightiest of manners, "I would first like to have your opinion as to whether Pamela Hawkins was a suicide or was murdered."

"In my opinion," the Police Surgeon began in his brisk, tripping way of speaking, "that is, in my medical opinion, it could have been—either! From the nature of the wound, also from the position of the weapon near the body, one would say—suicide. Yet, from the disappearance of the handbag, likewise from the concealed position of the knife, the alternative is equally possible!"

"But," the Coroner urged, "you must have a personal opinion, Dr. Jenkins!"

"Ah!" Dr. Jenkins exploded tolerantly, "a different matter—indeed! Medically, I say, the girl could have been murdered; she could have been a suicide. Personally, I must confess, I have inclined from one theory to the other. Yesterday, had you asked me that question, I would have said—murder. Since then, I have heard the testimony of Superintendent Welch. Miss Hawkins was being sought by the American police. She must have known the authorities were searching for her. In this event, fearful of escape, burdened with perhaps a guilty knowledge, she may have done away with herself!"

"Quite so," the Coroner said in a doubting tone. "But that possibility gives rise to another interpretation. If Miss Hawkins was implicated in the kidnapping of the Marsden child, she may have been murdered because she knew too much for her fellow-criminals' good!"

To this the spectators, whose attention had been strained by the confusion of opinion, suddenly became tense and looked expectantly about as if the criminal would be produced instanter.

Welch leaned toward McNear and said in a bored, surreptitious whisper, "Here's where they fasten the guilt on poor Collins!" He sat back in his chair again, reflecting gloomily that, by the irony which dogs well-meaning mortals, it would be his testimony which would convincingly track the guilt to Collins, and that, nevertheless, Collins could not possibly have been the murderer.

Reflectively, the Coroner glanced at the written material before him, and at last, after taking up a penciled notation from his desk, excused the witness and called the proprietor of the Blazing Star.

"Gentlemen," the Coroner informed the jury while old Mr. Eldridge was comfortably settling himself in his chair, "though I have no precedent for an inquest upon two deaths, they seem so closely related that I have taken the liberty of hearing testimony regarding both of them. It is to be understood, of course, that the duly accredited Coroner in Somerset will hold the actual inquest over the body of George Collins. Had it been feasible, I should have preferred that the two investigations be held simultaneously. This being impossible, we have done the next best thing and have called Mr. Eldridge, since it appears that his testimony will have a direct bearing on the decision which the jury will make as to the death of Miss Pamela Hawkins."

The Coroner paused. The jurors stared at him as if fascinated. Spectators shifted in their seats to assume firm positions from which they could lean tensely forward.

"We will now," the Coroner continued, "take up the case of George Collins, deceased."

"Mr. Eldridge"—the Coroner rubbed his nose glasses with a snowy handkerchief—"George Collins was a guest in your establishment at the time of his death, was he not?"

"He was."

"Where was he at the approximate hours of from six till eight o'clock on Saturday morning, April 10th?"

"Well"—old Mr. Eldridge turned up the palm of his hand and studied his life-line with desultory interest—"I expect he was in his room."

"You expect?" the Coroner prodded tardy.

"Well," old Mr. Eldridge responded, "I can't say I seen him there. I didn't go up, as he'd asked for quiet and I thought he was in his bed. But to the best of my belief, he was in his room till he come downstairs for his breakfast."

"That was at what time?" the Coroner demanded.

"Eight o'clock," Mr. Eldridge answered. "I heard him comin' down the stairs and served his breakfast in the tap-room. He sat around awhile and then went out for a walk—toward Watford Bridge."

"But it would have been possible for Collins to have been away from the Blazing Star earlier in the morning, Mr. Eldridge?"

Eldridge rubbed his cheek. "I wouldn't like to say he *couldn't* have been," Mr. Eldridge admitted.

The Coroner leaned forward. "Say, at six o'clock that morning?"

Mr. Eldridge nodded. "Yes, he could have been gone then. I wouldn't have noticed it any time before seven o'clock, because I was asleep."

"So!" The Coroner inclined his head toward the jury and spoke impressively, "Gentlemen, six o'clock was the approximate hour of Miss Hawkins' death!" He paused, wiping his spectacles while the jurors digested this fact. Then he resumed: "Mr. Eldridge, I have failed to bring out one important point. The main stairs is not the only way by which Collins could have left and returned to the Blazing Star, I understand?"

"That's right," Mr. Eldridge affirmed. "There's a side entrance and staircase near the room he had. But," he added as an after-thought, "I never saw him use it."

"However, he could have?" the Coroner inquired.

"He could have," Mr. Eldridge agreed.

"Thank you, Mr. Eldridge." The Coroner twisted about in his seat and addressed his next words directly to the jury. "I will now read," he announced, "the letter which Collins left for the police."

There was a crackling of paper in the Coroner's hands. He cleared his throat importantly and glanced about the crowded courtroom, delaying his voice till there should be complete quiet among his listeners.

Finally he dropped his eyes to the note and dramatically in-toned the fatal words:

> "'I am taking my life because the weight of my crimes
> no longer permits me to live. This is the end.'"

Having read this confession, the Coroner made the words the more effective by adding no comment of his own. Silent while he replaced the note among his other papers, he at last turned toward the row of chairs in which the police officials sat and said drily, "Inspector McNear."

McNear arose and took Mr. Eldridge's place on the witness stand. Welch's keen gaze inspected the jurors, and he knew from their expressions that the reading of Collins' suicide confession was having its full effect. It only needed the tracing of the dagger to the sheath in Collins' trunk, and, had the man been not already dead, the jurors would have been ready to lynch him. Welch passed his hand over his lips to conceal his sardonic, mirthless smile.

"Inspector McNear, you were sent yesterday to search the cabin which George Collins occupied aboard the S.S. *Baledonia*?"

"Yes, sir."

"Will you tell the jury, in your own words, what you found?"

"Yes, sir," McNear agreed. "But perhaps I'd best start with the day before, sir—when I first went aboard the *Baledonia*."

The Coroner nodded. "Tell it in your own way, Inspector."

McNear scowled thoughtfully. "The first time I went aboard the *Baledonia* I was looking for a cabin in which lilies had been carried from New York, sir." The Coroner nodded. Crowd and jury sat back with puzzled stares.

"You see," McNear continued, "the lilies that hid the stiletto found beside Miss Hawkins, as Superintendent Welch discovered, were not Bermuda lilies; they were Madonna lilies, which are not grown on the Island and which don't bloom till June unless raised in a hot-house. Well, with the help of Purser McKnight I found a steward who had seen such a bouquet in cabin 72-D aboard the *Baledonia*. I then went down to the cabin and investigated it. There was a trunk which struck me as peculiar, as it was not only locked, but fastened with four stout straps. But as I could not exceed my authority, I only had the cabin locked and requested Purser McKnight, who put the key in his safe, to let me know, night or day, when Collins returned."

McNear stopped, and the Coroner quickly prompted him, "Go on!"

"The next time I saw the cabin," McNear proceeded, "was after we had found Collins' body with the bottle of bichloride of mercury and the note. Superintendent Welch and I went out to the *Baledonia* to fetch Collins' belongings. As we went into the cabin I saw that the trunk, which had been securely fastened the day before, had been disturbed—one of the straps was loose on it, sir."

The crowd murmured excitedly.

"First, myself, then Purser McKnight, and finally Superintendent Welch examined the door to the cabin. The lock had been tampered with. Stateroom locks are of a flimsy sort, as perhaps you know, sir, but it was plain that this lock had been tried with a skeleton key and had finally been forced."

"The trunk"—put in the Coroner—"it, too, had been tried by a pass key?"

"No, sir," McNear answered promptly. "From where I stood when Superintendent Welch lifted the lid of the trunk, I could see that the lock had been ripped out of its socket, and the tin box inside—well, the cover was jerked and twisted off—"

"We'll come to the tin box in a moment, Inspector," the Coroner interrupted. "Just now let's concentrate on the trunk. I gather from your description that the person responsible for breaking into the cabin took great pains to unlock the door to the corridor without leaving signs of breakage such as would be detected by the ship's officers."

"Yes, sir," McNear said.

"But once having entered the cabin," the Coroner asked, "the intruder began in haste to break the lock off the trunk? This would imply, would it not, that the person responsible for this outrage, being pressed for time, pried the trunk lock hurriedly and escaped from the ship with whatever he was after?"

"It might, sir," McNear agreed. "There were scratches on the lock of the trunk, but still—"

"The ship, I believe," the Coroner interrupted, "is free of access to anyone who chooses to visit it?"

"Unfortunately in this case," McNear answered, "that's the way it is."

The Coroner nodded. "As I understand it, tourists have the use of their vessel as an hotel while in port, and consequently passengers who have met friends in Hamilton often invite them aboard as guests. I understand also that the hours of closing the bar are not so strictly observed as those of the city of Hamilton; consequently there is much entertainment aboard after our local places have long been closed?"

"I guess that's right," McNear said.

The Coroner nodded, evidently pleased with his own thoughts. "And now," he said agreeably, "when you opened the trunk, Inspector, what did you find?"

But as that was as far as McNear's first-hand testimony went, he explained that it was Superintendent Welch who had made the actual find.

Welch was recalled to the stand.

"Superintendent, you will please describe the trunk and its contents."

"It was a small trunk," Welch said easily, "about four feet long and two feet deep, but very strong. Half the space was filled by a large tin box, the cover of which had been twisted off. The box was empty. In the rest of the trunk was a lot of clothing—"

"And now," the Coroner directed, with the air of a conjuring ventriloquist about to draw a rabbit out of his dummy's hat, "tell the jury what other object you found inside the trunk, Superintendent!"

"In the bottom of the trunk," Welch answered drily, "hidden beneath the pile of clothing, I found the leather scabbard of a long, thin knife."

Even among the grave-faced jurors this revelation caused such excited whispering that the Coroner had to rap loudly for order before the inquest could proceed.

Finally, the Coroner asked, "You have fitted this sheath to the blade with which Pamela Hawkins was stabbed?"

"I have," Welch answered.

"And blade and sheath go together, as if the one were the cover of the other?"

"They do," Welch said, and stepped down from the stand amidst the murmuring of astonishment from the crowd.

At that moment the constable in charge at the entrance walked up between the rows of chairs to the Coroner's bench and spoke in a low voice.

The Coroner frowned. He had attained a dramatic climax and had been about to deliver the case to the jury for a verdict, but now he leaned toward the constable and asked in a tone of annoyance, "What did you say his name was?"

"James Martin, sir," the constable repeated.

"Material evidence, eh?" the Coroner murmured; then called, "James Martin will please take the witness stand!"

For the first time since the inquest began, Superintendent Welch was as interested as the crowd. He closely watched the tall young man with gangling legs in knickers who strode embarrassedly toward the Coroner's bench.

Sworn and subjected to the usual ritual, James Martin was asked by the Coroner, "And now, what is the testimony you desire to give?"

Martin gulped. "Well, sir, I read the story in the *Gazette* this morning about that murdered girl. The report said one funny thing about it that mystified the police was that she hadn't any handbag. Well, sir, I believe I know where that bag is!"

"Ah?" The Coroner was mildly inquisitive. "Where?"

"Here, sir," James Martin answered promptly, and withdrew a small, reddish knitted bag from his coat pocket. He handed it up to the Coroner, who inspected it thoughtfully.

"When did you find this?"

"Saturday morning."

"Where?"

"I was bicycling along about a hundred feet beyond the Aquarium Railway Station when I saw it lying in the weeds at the edge of the road."

"At what hour was that?"

"About nine o'clock, Mr. Coroner."

"Humpf," the Coroner said, and turned the bag over in his hands. "What makes you think it belonged to Miss Hawkins?" He opened it up. "No marks of identification that I can see."

"No, sir," James Martin agreed. "There was no more in it then than there is now—fourteen dollars, a box of face powder and some lipstick. But when I read about it in the paper I thought I'd better come down and hand it in."

"Very proper, Mr. Martin," the Coroner commended the new witness. But he spoke in a tone that implied doubt as to the value of his discovery. "Thank you."

James Martin stepped down.

The Coroner turned to the jury. He summed up the various testimony which had been presented. And the jurors, convinced already in their minds without debate, filed out to the room in which they were supposed to cogitate.

Five minutes later the eight men filed back to their seats, and the foreman coughed apologetically.

"Gentlemen," the Coroner inquired, "you have reached a verdict?"

"We have," the foreman replied. "We find that the deceased, Pamela Hawkins, was stabbed to death by the dagger whose shield was found in the man Collins' trunk aboard the *Baledonia*. And it is our opinion that the deceased was murdered by this man Collins, who later committed suicide at the Blazing Star in Somerset!"

"Thank you, Gentlemen." The Coroner was gravely pleased. He began folding up his papers and prepared to return to his place of business. Avidly chattering, the crowd drifted toward the door.

"Well," McNear said, as he went out with Welch, "thank God that's over!"

"Yes," Welch agreed grimly, "now we can go quietly about our job of looking for the murderer!"

McNear stared at him. "Man, you've got a streak of stubbornness a mile wide. Now just why, after that chain of evidence we've piled up against Collins, do you still say it wasn't Collins who killed her?"

"Oh!" Welch said carelessly, "there are several baffling little reasons."

"Give me one," McNear demanded.

"All right," Welch said. "I'll give you the latest one." He paused. "You listening?"

"Now, Welch," McNear protested, "you know I am."

"All right," Welch said. "It's pretty well established that Pamela Hawkins was killed about halfpast six Saturday morning. Now it's entirely possible that Collins could have found a bicycle, pedaled the ten miles to the scene of the murder and pedaled back again to the Blazing Star in time to come down from his room at eight o'clock for breakfast in the tap-room."

"That's what I thought," McNear said. "That's how he did it."

Welch grimaced. "Very well, then. How did he get to the Aquarium Railway Station, which is far off on the North Shore, and get rid of that bag and still return by eight o'clock? Hey?"

McNear rubbed his chin perplexedly, and a dawning light as he realized the physical impossibility of so much traveling in so short a time came into his eyes. Then his doubts came back again.

"Maybe, Welch, that bag didn't belong to Miss Hawkins—maybe somebody else lost it—"

But Welch didn't answer. He was already swinging down the street, bound nobody save himself knew where.

12
MORE NEEDLES AND MORE HAYSTACKS

Monday Midday, April 12th.

While the other members of the Bermuda constabulary were congratulating themselves upon the neatness and despatch with which the murderer of Pamela Hawkins had been discovered, Superintendent Welch marched purposefully to the terminal offices of the slow little railway system which, with carriages, bicycles and shanks's mare, rounded out the only means of the Islanders' locomotion.

Welch had often condemned the Bermuda railway in the past, especially when, after coming back from London or New York, where he went for infrequent vacations, he got aboard one of the cars and crawled along at a rate of speed no more than double that of a good horse trot and had his ticket taken by a conductor whose manner suggested that he had all day for the matter, and there was therefore no need to hurry.

But now Welch blessed these same picturesque quirks in the Island's transportation service. For, as his talk with McNear implied, he had seized firmly upon the testimony of the last witness at the inquest. That bag was of the same shade of dull red wool as Pamela Hawkins' hat; and though he knew little of the ways of women, he knew enough to realize that hats and bags for sports wear were often made of the same material. And, assuming that the handbag belonged to Miss Hawkins, he reasoned that it must have been thrown from one of the railway carriages—and probably at a very early hour Saturday morning, since James Martin had found it at nine o'clock.

Welch swung into the building and began to gather information from the various clerks. From a tall, sun-burned Bermudian who invited him behind his wicket, he learned that the only train which could have passed Aquarium Station before nine in the morning was the one that left the Cenotaph at 7.12.

"And who was the conductor on that train?" Welch inquired.

"I'll try to find out for you, sir," the clerk answered deferentially, and took him to still another clerk who kept a record of the trains on which the different crews of trainmen worked.

"Frawley," the first clerk said, "I'm sure you can help the Superintendent. He wants to know the name of the conductor who was on the train that left the Cenotaph for St. George's at 7.12 Saturday morning."

"Name of the conductor, eh?" Frawley gave a knowing glance at the Superintendent. "Any hanky-panky on our line, sir?"

"No, no," Welch hastily reassured him, "nothing of the sort. I'm looking for him only to get information. But it may be pretty valuable, so if you can help me—"

"That I can," Frawley said firmly, and began to con the weekly payroll sheet of the train crews. Pausing with his finger on a certain name, he looked up and announced, "Name of Hedgelock, sir. William Hedgelock."

"Fine." Welch thanked him. "And where can I find Hedgelock now?"

Frawley reached promptly for another sheet of neatly charted paper. After studying it for some time, he replied, "Well, sir; it's about half-past eleven now. You're bound to find him at twelve o'clock waiting at the yards."

Again Welch thanked him, and went out of the building.

With such succinct directions it would be easier to find the conductor than he had dared hope.

He walked through the streets to the Cenotaph. Near the tall stone shaft which honoured Bermuda's heroes killed in the war of

1914-1918, he saw a train standing, and he went up and began to inquire for Hedgelock.

"Conductor Hedgelock? Sure, sir," one of the trainmen said; "you'll find him down yonder on that first car near the repair shops." Soon Welch climbed aboard the empty train. He walked through to the first-class compartment forward.

As his fellow-trainman had predicted, Hedgelock sat in the end seat, a newspaper on his knees. He was nibbling at a sandwich, and as he saw Welch he said through a mouthful of what must have been rather dry food, "Train doesn't go for half an hour, sir."

"I know," Welch said. "And it's so much the better. You're Mr. Hedgelock?"

"That's my name, sir."

"I'm Superintendent Welch."

"Are you, sir?" Hedgelock asked respectfully. "And you've gone to the trouble to come and talk to me? Well, sir, what can I do for you?"

"A great deal, I hope," Welch answered. "You were conductor on the train that left the Cenotaph at 7.12 Saturday morning?"

"I was that, sir," Hedgelock replied emphatically. "Every other week all the days of my life, it seems, I've gone up with the 7.12 from the Cenotaph."

"Train's not very crowded at that time of day, I expect?" Welch asked.

"You couldn't call it crowded at all, sir, unless you wanted to make a joke. Passengers on train Number 14 at that time of day are mighty few and far between."

Welch nodded. "Would you say there were more or less than usual last Saturday morning?"

Hedgelock was thoughtfully silent. "Well, sir, I remember two in the first-class compartment. There were more, as there always are, in the second-class. I couldn't say exactly how many, but maybe half a dozen."

"Two in the first-class," Welch repeated. "You can't remember anything about them, can you?"

"No, sir, I can't. Not if you put it that way, sir. But maybe if you was to tell me what it was you wanted, sir?" He waited expectantly.

"Glad to tell you, Hedgelock," Welch said soberly. "As you no doubt read in the morning Gazette, there was a young lady murdered on the Island Saturday morning. Any information regarding that murder is of great importance—"

"Glory be!" Hedgelock interjected. "You don't suspicion anybody on train Number 14, do you, Superintendent?"

"No," Welch answered, "I can't say that I do. But there was one curious circumstance which developed this morning at the inquest. You remember reading in the *Gazette* that the young lady's handbag was missing when she was found?"

Hedgelock nodded. "That I do, sir."

"Well, Hedgelock," Welch continued, "that bag was found at nine o'clock Saturday morning near the railway line—rather near the highway which goes beside the tracks, about thirty paces from the Aquarium Station!"

Hedgelock wrinkled his brows in thought till his forehead looked like a washboard. "A bag, you said? Found not more than thirty paces from the Aquarium Station? Hmm."

"That's right," Welch answered, waiting watchfully.

"Now that's peculiar," Hedgelock said after a silence. "That's what you might call very peculiar!"

Welch continued to wait hopefully, though he had no notion that there might be a direct connection between the bag and the recollection that had come to the conductor's mind.

"Well, sir," Hedgelock finally said, after still more thoughtful silence. "Maybe I can tell you something about that bag, after all!"

"Tell whatever you're thinking about, man," Welch urged him. "We'll decide on the value of it afterward, but remember, every bit of information is bound to be helpful."

"Yes, sir," Hedgelock mused, half to himself. "I knew there was something about that run I'd forgotten, but I couldn't think what it was—matter of fact, I'd forgotten there was anything peculiar about it—till you said that handbag had been found near the

Aquarium Station. Because that morning I was sure I saw some-body throw something out of the train window at just about that distance from the station!"

Controlling his eagerness at this news, Welch said evenly, "Now, Hedgelock, try to remember the circumstances."

"Oh, I remember now!" Hedgelock said unhesitatingly. "I was standing in the second-class compartment talking with one of the passengers, and the engineer was slowing down for the Aquarium stop when of a sudden I saw something fly past the window. My first thought was that one of the passengers in the first-class com-partment ahead had accidentally dropped something out, so I opened the door and glanced in."

"Yes?" Welch said, waiting.

"Well, sir, both the passengers were seated on the left of the aisle, whereas the object—the bag or whatever it was—had come out of a window on the right side. So I shut the door again and went on about my business."

"These two passengers were together, I take it?" Welch asked.

"No, sir. They occupied different seats. There was a man, and he sat up near the engineer's box. The woman sat near the other end of the compartment."

Welch frowned. "Can you remember what they were doing when you looked in?"

"Not on my oath, sir," Hedgelock answered, "but as I do re-member it they were both reading papers or magazines—or maybe a book."

"Hedgelock," Superintendent Welch urged him, "I wish you'd try to give me a description of these two people—any little charac-teristic might be of the greatest help."

Hedgelock struggled painfully, ransacking the limbo of forgot-ten sights. "I'm not sure whether I'd recognize them again even if I saw them, Superintendent. You see, at the next stop—that was the Aquarium—a crowd of people from the Frascati Hotel got on the train, and I was so busy selling tickets and changing money that I didn't think another thing about whatever it was that went out the window. And I expect I wouldn't ever have thought of it again if you hadn't told me that a handbag had been found right about in the same place."

Welch nodded. "Taken by itself, it wasn't a very notable incident," he admitted. "And it's entirely possible that it's not worth remembering. However, we can't neglect the slightest clue, Hedgelock." He paused. "Now, I wonder if you happen to remember where those two first-class passengers got off the train?"

"As it happens, sir," Hedgelock said directly, "I don't need to trust my memory for that; though I'll admit I can't remember a thing about it. But if you go to the offices of the Railway Company I'm sure you'll be able to find out. They keep records of the number of tickets and the destination of the passengers on each train, and, as there were only two first-class tickets sold on Number 14 that trip, it will be easy to find out where the fares were bound for."

Welch's eyes gleamed keenly. Information was coming along in fine style; in fact, he was learning more than he had expected. He said, "You wouldn't have noticed whether those two first-class passengers were Bermudians, would you, Hedgelock?"

Hedgelock gave a quiet little laugh. "Not from the way they looked, if that's what you mean, sir. But I don't think they were people of the Islands, at that. No Bermudian that I've ever met, unless he had a pass, would be riding first-class on Number 14, because it's a Non-Statutory train!"

Welch smiled. "You mean that the regular fare is high enough on a Non-Statutory train without it?"

"Yes, sir," Hedgelock agreed. "I don't mean any criticism of the company, sir, but a first-class ticket on a Non-Statutory train comes to a good bit of money, sir; and you're not likely to find many Bermudians with so little respect for what they've worked for as to throw it away so easily!"

Superintendent Welch nodded, though the prospect of finding two tourists even after he had learned their destination was, in an island overrun by trippers from all countries, rather appalling. "Thank you, Hedgelock. I think I'll step along to the Railway Company offices."

Hedgelock touched his cap. "Good luck, sir."

Welch grimly inclined his head. He needed all the good luck that could possibly come his way, and he realized it fully.

He went back to the railway building, where, regardless of his own uneaten lunch, he waited for the Chief Clerk to return from his midday meal.

A little after one the Chief Clerk returned.

"You found Hedgelock, sir?" the clerk inquired politely.

"I found him," Welch admitted, "and now the next thing is to find out something else. As I understand it, you keep a record of the tickets sold during each trip?"

"Yes, sir."

"And you'd know where the tickets were sold and the station to which the passenger was going?"

"That's right, sir. We've had some criticism about our method of selling tickets on the train, because it is claimed it takes too much time and slows up the service, but every conductor is required to write out on his work-sheet a list of the tickets sold each trip— and, of course, that gives the point of destination as well as the point of departure."

"Fine," Welch proclaimed. "There were two first-class tickets sold on train Number 14 Saturday morning. I believe the passengers got on at the Cenotaph. What I want to find out is where they got off."

"Come with me, sir," the Chief Clerk directed, and led him to the desk.

After Welch had stood impatiently watching for some minutes, the Chief Clerk found the work-sheet for which he had been looking and read aloud,

"Two tickets, first-class. Cenotaph to St. George's." He looked up. "I expect that's what you were looking for."

"It is," Welch said, with satisfaction, "and I thank you!"

He returned hastily to Headquarters, where he sent word to the captains of the six cruise ships still in harbour to notify him at the earliest possible moment if any of their passengers were not aboard when the ships put out to sea. Then he sat back in his chair for a few minutes' rest before continuing his investigation. "A woman, a woman," he kept repeating to himself, thinking of the scene in the railway car which Conductor Hedgelock had described. There, flashing before his mind's eye, he could see the man sitting up front, the woman purposely sitting in the rear end, watching her chance to dispose of the tell-tale bag without being discovered. "Find the woman," Superintendent Welch said to himself, "*cherchez la femme* and all the rest of it!"

13

DEATH STALKS THE SUPERINTENDENT

Monday Afternoon, April 12th.
Monday Night, April 12th.
And early Tuesday Morning, April 13th.
The more Superintendent Welch pondered the matter the more convinced he became that the murder of Pamela Hawkins would never be solved to his personal satisfaction until he had discovered the identity and something of the habits of the woman who rode on train Number 14 from the Cenotaph to St. George's that fatal Saturday morning. Who but a woman, he asked himself, would have thought to sew that false label on Miss Hawkins' dress? And what of the wide green silk ribbon with which the bouquet was bound; wasn't a woman's hand to be seen in that as well?

Thus, while awaiting a wireless from the cruise ships, which were to sail that evening, he set out for the Sports Shop to seek the manager, Mr. Outerbridge, from whom Detective-Constable Steele had learned the important fact that the label found on Miss Hawkins' dress was of the sort that properly belonged on the Sports Shop hats.

"It's the same old story," Welch announced a little apologetically, as he stepped inside the manager's private office, "I've come to bother you about that infernal hat label."

Outerbridge good-naturedly inspected his finely manicured nails and said, "Fire away, Superintendent. I told Steele all I knew about it and I don't know what else I can tell your department, but ask questions and I'll try to answer them."

119

"First of all," Welch began, "Do you put the same kind of label in all the women's hats you sell?"

Outerbridge shook his head. "No. We have two kinds. One is sewn in hats bought for us in America. Then there's another kind for our better quality hats. These hats are specially designed for us in London by the well-known firm of Tooker and Sons, and the labels in these hats are stamped 'Made in England.'"

"Now the label found in the murdered girl's dress," Welch inquired, "Do you remember what kind it was?"

"It was taken from one of our American hats," Outerbridge answered.

"And of course," Welch said gloomily, "you sell more of the American kind than the British, which would make it much harder to trace?"

"Infinitely harder—infinitely more American hats, at any rate," the manager replied. "You see, the American hats are much cheaper."

Welch ruefully rubbed his chin.

"Everything about this case goes out of its way to be difficult. I suppose now, there'd be hundreds of women round about here who've bought these hats some time or another."

"Our goods," said Mr. Outerbridge, with the right note of unction, "have a wide reputation for quality which the public has always appreciated."

"You don't sell ribbon, do you?" Welch asked suddenly.

"Ribbon? Not in a Sports Shop."

"Well." Welch looked at his watch and noticed it was after five. The last tenders would be coming back from the cruise ships, and the ships themselves, the *Baledonia* among the others, would be under full steam ahead. In an hour or more he could begin to expect the wireless messages from the ships' captains. Until then he could merely hope that the new pleasure cruisers, some of which had already dropped anchor in Grassy Bay, would bring a less troublesome sort of passenger than the last.

He stood up and jauntily swung his helmet to his head. "Thank you, Mr. Outerbridge."

"Not at all," Outerbridge answered and escorted him through the store to the street.

Stopping at a familiar tavern, Welch ate a composite meal that took the place of his skipped lunch and would do for dinner in case work interfered with his routine to the extent of keeping him from getting home to his cottage, where he knew his sister, Mrs. Howe, would be awaiting him with dinner. Then, as it was nearly six, he started for Headquarters.

The news there set him to work at once.

There was a pile of red and white wireless despatches on his desk.

Four of the six ships reported all passengers aboard. But the message from the Captain of the *Cedric* read:

> Arthur W. Turnbull missing. Age, forty-seven. Height, five feet nine. Hair, curly brown. Complexion ruddy. Clean shaven. Stocky and inclined to plumpness. Home is Montreal.

And the second wireless, which was from the Purser of the *Baledonia*, was even more engrossing:

> Absent, Henrietta Sinclair. Thirty-five. Tall, black-haired, sharp features. All Mrs. Sinclair's baggage also disappeared.

Welch pressed a button with one hand and picked up his desk telephone with the other.

To the burly stenographer who promptly answered, Welch directed, "Make copies of those two descriptions for every officer and constable under our jurisdiction. Get it out in a hurry."

Into the telephone he said, "Get busy on the switchboard. Call up every one of the twenty hotels listed in the phone book and inquire for Arthur Turnbull of Montreal and a Mrs. Henrietta Sinclair. You'll have a description of them in a minute. Phone it to the hotel clerks as soon as you get it. Turnbull and Mrs. Sinclair may be together or they may not—no, not arrested. But have a man watch them as soon as they're located."

The stenographer went out. Welch dropped the receiver on the telephone hook, then hastily reached for it again. "Get me Mr. Gardiner of Calloway, Gardiner and Co.—the estate agents' office."

He drummed impatiently on his desk, waiting for the connection to be put through.

Finally it came. "Mr. Gardiner's office doesn't answer, sir. Shall I try his home?"

"Yes," Welch snapped and again sat waiting.

The phone rang and a voice said, "Arthur Gardiner speaking."

"Gardiner," Welch said, "this is Superintendent Welch. Have you rented any houses to women in the last three or four days?"

Gardiner laughed. "I'd have to look at my list, Welch. But what's all the excitement? If there's another crime in Hamilton I'm going to move to Chicago."

There was a sobering seriousness in Welch's voice as he answered, "Look here, Gardiner, I want to get hold of a list with all the recent house rentals in Bermuda even if I have to sit at this phone till morning—"

"No need of that, Superintendent," Gardiner answered in a brisk but friendly tone, "I've got practically the whole list in my office. And if you'd care to meet me there I'll join you in ten minutes."

"Great!" Welch said tersely. Leaving a few last instructions to the suddenly harried police force, he left Headquarters and walked rapidly along Reid Street.

Turning north toward the waterfront, Welch wondered dizzily what else he could do or could have done to place Henrietta Sinclair and Turnbull under the ægis of the law. All constables would be on the lookout, all hotels would be informed, and he, himself, was on his way to investigate the possibility that the man or woman had taken a house on the Island. Of course, either of them could have used an assumed name and, mingling among the hundreds of other tourists, escape for a long while. But that, Welch decided, couldn't be helped. As a matter of fact, he realized as an afterthought when he stepped under the arched entrance of the new Bank of Bermuda building he was taking a good deal of authority unto himself in going as far as he had gone. And Masters, considering that the murder case was officially closed, might vigorously disapprove.

Welch shrugged and smiled a little grimly. The lift was waiting, and he was whisked up to the fifth floor, where, after striding down a long corridor, he stopped before a door on which several lines of gold lettering announced the presence of Calloway, Gardiner and Company.

Gardiner was waiting for him. He had a pile of papers which he had evidently just removed from their folder.

"As I told you, Welch, I can give you most of the details of our own leases and, in addition, since we make it our business to keep track of those houses which our competitors have rented, I can give you a more or less bald list of every house in Bermuda leased during the past few days."

Welch's harassed expression widened into a pleased smile. "I thought I was coming to the right man when I rang you up, Gardiner. This may be no end of a lift to us, I tell you that frankly!"

"Now here's the list," Gardiner said. "Draw up a chair and I'll point out as much as I can while we go along."

Welch sat close to Gardiner and waited intently.

"Now these first twelve houses," Gardiner explained, "are those that my firm has leased during the past ten days. Let's go through them first, because I can tell you more about the occupants."

Welch looked hastily down the column. "Only three of your tenants are women," he commented, thinking that that fact narrowed the search, if only by a little.

"So I believe," Gardiner responded.

"Now this house"—Welch pointed to the first woman's name— "can you describe the new tenant to me?"

"Yes," Gardiner answered. "I rented it to her myself. Mrs. Gildersleeve is a widow, I believe. She's been coming here for a good many years and has a very attractive daughter of about eighteen—"

Welch shook his head impatiently. "And this house—the one in West Paget with Mrs. Putney's name opposite it?" he questioned.

"Mrs. Putney?" Gardiner looked up with a smile. "I hardly think Mrs. Putney is the sort of woman the police would be interested in, Welch. She's almost seventy years old and she came with a companion."

Welch scowled and continued to the next house recently rented by a woman. "What about that place out on Richmond Road?" he asked. "The one you've got Mrs. Bigelow down for."

Gardiner looked abashed. "I'm sorry, Superintendent, but I'll have to admit that I overreached myself when I said I could tell you about all our new tenants. As a matter of fact, my partner, Jack Calloway, rented that the other day while I was arranging an auction sale in Smith's Parish."

"Well," Welch said, "perhaps I can see him about it."

"I'm afraid you won't be able to do that either," Gardiner said in an even more crestfallen tone. "He sailed yesterday on the *Lady Rodney* for Canada for a little vacation and he won't be home for a month or more."

Welch essayed a disappointed grin. "Well—maybe I'll get what I want in spite of that handicap. Can you tell me if you remember having seen the woman I'm looking for?" he asked and read off the description from a copy of the wireless message.

"No-o," Gardiner admitted slowly. "I'm sorry."

Welch tried again. "Do you know if this Mrs. Bigelow rented that house on Richmond Road before last Friday or since then?"

Gardiner brightened. "I can tell you that very well. She rented it Friday afternoon because that's the day I was in Smith's Parish."

"For how long did she take it?" Welch demanded.

Gardiner got up and went to a filing case. "For a month," he answered after a search.

Welch stood up. Fool's errand or not, he was going out to the house on Richmond Road and interview its tenant "Gardiner," he said, "I'm very much obliged for this information. I may be back after more, though—"

"Come any time you think I can be of help," Gardiner said warmly.

"By the way," Welch asked, "what's the name of the place Mrs. Bigelow rented?"

"Greenleaf," Gardiner answered. "It's a small house, really a cottage, but it's very attractive."

"I know," Welch nodded. "Greenleaf, eh? I remember it well."

They went downstairs together and out into the street. There they separated, and Welch made his way up Queen Street, past the imposing facade of the Hamilton Hotel, and on toward Greenleaf, which was only a short distance from there.

It was growing dark. Between Welch and his destination stood a newly built house of such recent construction that a couple of men were still working on it. The cottage was a low rangy dwelling with the gently pitched roof and wide eaves peculiar to Bermuda. On one end a trailing wing ended in a typical buttery surmounted by the sharp, triangular roof. Still in the foreground stood a pile of the limestone blocks which comprise the almost universal building material of the Island.

As Welch was about to pass he was hailed by Mr. Hollis, one of the Customs House officials. "Hello, Welch!" he called. "How do you like my new house?"

"It looks very fine," Welch said, having been mildly admiring it.

Hollis turned away from the negro foreman with whom he had been talking and crossed over toward the roadway where the Superintendent had stopped.

Hollis, who had recently come to Bermuda from England, was in a fine state of enthusiasm over his new home. "Going to be a nice little place, isn't it?" he demanded, as they stood together, surveying the building.

"And what gets me," Hollis went on with a chuckle, "is that in this country when you buy a plot of land you buy the material to build a house along with it!"

Anxious to get on, Welch was nevertheless a little puzzled by Hollis' statement. Then his face cleared. "Oh, you mean the stone! Yes, yes," he admitted; "digging away the few inches of soil that covers the limestone is a good deal cheaper and easier than buying thousands of bricks from a kiln or paying high prices at a lumber yard."

"What pleases me," Hollis went on, "is that while one is cutting the stone out to make a basement, one is getting the materials for his walls, and that while one is getting materials for his walls, he is making a place for a reservoir to catch the water as it comes off the roofs and down the pipes. So far," he went on triumphantly, "I've had to buy just one material—the copper for the pipes."

Welch smiled at the man's enthusiasm. Looking up, he could see the thin limestone slabs, which were used as shingling, already in place. And from the generous eaves he had a glimpse of the copper piping through which the rain would come pouring down into the large concrete reservoirs beneath the house. Great pains are taken with the construction, care and cleanliness of those roofs, for on their sloping sides is caught the sole water supply of the average Bermuda householder. Still, as the sight was so common in his eyes, there was no particular surprise or delight he could work up for Hollis' benefit.

"It will be a beautiful house, won't it?" Welch said a little lamely, he thought.

But Hollis beamed complete satisfaction. "Yes, I think it'll make a pretty place. I'm glad to have a home here in Bermuda. I've been enough of a rolling-stone in my days. Now it's time I gathered some moss."

"Right," Welch agreed, and looked through the gathering darkness toward Greenleaf. "I hear you've acquired a new neighbour."

"So I believe," Hollis answered; "but whoever she is, she keeps herself well indoors. Although I've been here for a week at odd hours during the day while I saw how things were coming on, I haven't laid eyes on the lady yet."

Welch turned to go.

"You must come and see me one of these days—I'll have moved in before the month is out," Hollis said.

Welch thanked him, and murmured that he would be glad to. Then he went on, walking the remaining few hundred feet to the garden gate of Greenleaf Cottage.

Arriving at the vine-entangled gate, he went up the path to the doorway. It was growing still darker, and he had to bend over and peer in order to find the bell. Turning the little knob, he rang it brusquely and stood expectantly waiting.

For a minute or more there was complete silence after the tiny pealing of the bell had died in the stillness.

Welch rang again.

After a moment a curtain rustled in a window above the porch. Whether or not the occupant of the house was taking stock of his appearance, Welch was unable to discover; he only knew that his uniform was a highly distinguishing mark of his profession, also that from where he stood he was unable to see anybody at all.

Further silence followed. Then came the sound of footsteps descending the stairs.

The door opened. In the semi-darkness Welch glimpsed a woman's face.

"Come in," she said in a flat, distasteful voice.

Welch, removing his helmet with a polite little flourish, stepped over the threshold.

The door closed behind him, and he noticed that the room was even darker than he had expected it would be. The long shutters to all the windows had been tightly closed. In that crepuscular light he was unable to discern the features of the woman, but he had an impression that she was tall, with tight, dark hair and wore a dark costume.

"Mrs. Bigelow?" Welch asked inquiringly.

"Step into the living-room," the woman answered.

Welch turned obligingly and started down the dark passageway.

And suddenly he began to fall, falling with that slow, sickening heave and roll of a man gripped by a nightmare. He wanted to cry out, but his voice was mute. Then everything for him became a vast, soundless darkness.

It was not till his body was plunged into frigid water that Welch regained consciousness. And his first reaction was to strike out in swimming strokes, gulping, choking and blowing the water out of his mouth and nostrils. Everywhere about him there was nothing but darkness, but his hand, reaching out, struck smooth, wet limestone, and he realized with a shock where he had been thrown. He was in the water-filled reservoir beneath Greenleaf Cottage.

Then he remembered Mrs. Bigelow, and he realized what had happened to him. From the ache in his head he knew she had struck

him a murderous blow. And after he had been knocked unconscious, she had dragged him through the house to the kitchen,
where there was a concrete trap in the floor which opened to the
reservoir!

Welch looked up. The heavy trap had now been shoved back
into place. He reached out again, and his hand touched the side of
the reservoir. It was smooth and wet, with not even a chance of a
finger-hold. He lay on his back and began to float, inhaling deeply
and rhythmically, trying to keep his body warm and to conserve
his energy.

For some time he lay in the water with his face upturned, not
daring to let his feet down toward the bottom. When he did gather
courage to explore the depths of the reservoir, he found himself
standing in water that was no higher than his chest. His hands held
out in front of him, he waded blindly toward a corner of the tank
and stood there, trying to regain his thoughts and to make some
use of them.

It was lucky, he knew, that he was not dead. Everything else
that had happened was therefore sheer gain. His position, he hopefully told himself, was far from desperate. It was only a matter of
time until his disappearance would cause an investigation. Gardiner, who must have surmised where he had gone, would report
the conversation over the rental lists. And Mr. Hollis, seeing him
go on in the direction of Greenleaf, remembering the talk they had
had about the new occupant, would go immediately to the police
with his information.

Thus urging himself into a more cheerful state of mind, Welch
tried grimly to remember any detail of the adventure which might
lead to the capture of his assailant He was sorry to discover that
he could recall very little of what Mrs. Bigelow had looked like.
She was a tall, thin, sharp woman, and fitted the description of the
missing Henrietta Sinclair, but there were many such women even
in Bermuda. And her voice, he had an impression, had been dis-
guised, perhaps not so much intentionally as by the cold, vicious
determination of her plan to dispose of him.

The minutes passed slowly for Welch; and the longer markings of time which he assumed were hours crawled by like snails inching their way along the tedious road of infinity. He felt in his pocket for matches, but found the wet heads crumbled as he tried to strike them. He took out his watch and listened, but its immersion had stopped the works and it was as silent as a door-knob. A watch would have been useless, anyway, he took consolation in observing, since he would have been unable to see the hands without a light.

Save for his soaked clothing, he was not yet particularly uncomfortable. He still stood against a corner of the tank, leaning his back on the concrete wall, and except when his feet slipped and he had to struggle to regain his position, he was not required to expend much effort.

Well, he thought philosophically, morning would soon come. And long before that Mrs. Howe, his rather fussy sister, would have anxiously called the Chief of Police and the hunt for him would have begun.

Unexpectedly, Welch's optimism was shattered.

From up above his head, six feet or more, there came a scraping, grating noise. He knew at once it was caused by the concrete cover being pushed away from the reservoir trap. But long as the time had been since he was dropped below, he feared it was still too early to hope for rescuers on the scene. And the chance that it was Mrs. Bigelow was too great for him to risk crying out.

Quick-thinking at all times, Welch stepped forward into the water and lay on his chest, his face buried and his arms floating beside him like those of a drowned man.

In that way he remained till the blood began pounding in his ears and his head sang for want of air. He had a feeling that the trap had opened and that the tank was lighted by a flashlight, but he couldn't be sure because his eyes were under water.

At last, when he felt he could stand it no longer, he believed he heard the concrete cover scrape back into place. Whether he had or not, he raised his almost suffocated head and gulped for breath. The reservoir was dark again, black and silent as before.

Welch waded back to his position in the corner on weak legs. At every breath there was a rasping sound as the air rushed in and out of his tortured lungs.

He waited, panting.

A few drops of water splashed into the pool from the pipe above.

Now, Welch's gasping breath was due to sheer terror.

The fall of raindrops merged into a tiny trickle, then swelled into a stream.

Welch could feel his heart jump up and stop as if it had stuck in his throat. The one danger he had failed to reckon with had overtaken him. Rain! It might be only an April freshet, but it would pour down through the copper roof-pipes from the eaves in a steady flow till it had raised the water in the reservoir far above his head. He had an overpowering feeling that Mrs. Bigelow was Mrs. Sinclair, and that Mrs. Sinclair, whether he was to be her first victim or not, had the heart of a cold-blooded murderess.

Welch prayed. And as he prayed the water in seeming mockery crept up from his shoulders to his chin. Fifteen minutes later, the downpour still unabated, he stripped off his clothing and, with a despairing gasp, began slowly swimming in desperate, narrow circles.

14

MORE TROUBLE FOR THE POLICE

Monday Night, April 12th.
Tuesday Morning, April 13th.
Greeted at Headquarters that evening by the information that the staff of officers and their assistants were busily striving to locate one Arthur Turnbull, missing from the *Cedric* and one Mrs. Henrietta Sinclair, who had failed to come aboard the *Baledonia*, Inspector McNear clicked his tongue in a surprised manner and privately asked himself what nonsense his superior, Superintendent Welch, was up to now.

Nevertheless, whether Welch was up to nonsense or not, McNear was reluctant to leave for his country home, and the result was that after he had dinner at his favourite tavern he telephoned his wife that he would be late, and after an hour or so he returned through the brightly lighted streets to Headquarters.

"Find those two missing tourists?" he asked the brawny operator at the switchboard.

The operator wearily rubbed his forehead. "If they're at a hotel they're certainly under other names! At least, we can't locate them."

McNear chuckled, wondering what Welch would do if he found that his far-flung search interrupted an innocently blooming romance between the stout Mr. Turnbull and the tall Mrs. Sinclair. He went out into the hall.

Dr. Jenkins, his little black bag in his hand, nodded brusquely to McNear. As they went down the stairs together the Police Surgeon complained, "This job is taking up too much of my time.

131

Hardly have a moment any longer to myself. It's ruining my private practice, simply ruining it."

McNear nodded sympathetically. "We had a regular crime wave there for a while, but I think we've seen the last of it, Doctor."

"Humpf!" Jenkins snorted. "Just a minute ago I was called on the phone and ordered to take the ambulance to Court and Church Streets!"

"Accident?" McNear inquired.

"Fellow named Tom Henderson was found lying in the gutter with his head all but bashed in! With the man at the point of death, it doesn't sound like an accident to me!" Jenkins said caustically.

"Tom Henderson, eh," McNear muttered. "He's a bad egg, that one. I've had my hands on him two or three times."

As they reached the ambulance, McNear said to Jenkins, "I think I'll go along with you, Doctor, and take a look into this affair myself."

Near Church and Court Streets the helmet of a constable rising above a small crowd of curious onlookers showed them the object of their destination.

"Make way, make way!"

Dr. Jenkins pushed through the crowd, aided by the strong arms of McNear and the constable.

Kneeling beside the prostrate man's side, Jenkins' nimble fingers gently examined the wound which, even by flashlight, was seen to be bad.

"Emergency ward, straight away," Jenkins directed.

"That bad, Jenkins?" McNear looked grave.

"Not much hope," Jenkins answered in an undertone, and followed the stretcher on which Henderson was carried to the waiting ambulance.

McNear turned to the constable. "Webley, what do you know about this?"

Webley saluted. "Very little, sir. I was making my rounds and I came upon him just as you saw the man when you yourself arrived."

But one of the crowd shouldered forward and called, "Inspector—I'd like a little private talk with you, please."

McNear took hold of the man's arm and drew him to one side. "Speak up," he directed shortly.

"I don't know," the man began, "how that fellow was hurt, but I do know he was in the Bull Dog bar not half an hour ago, for I saw him there with my own eyes."

"And what was he up to in the Bull Dog bar?"

"Well, sir," his informant answered, "the fellow had a roll of notes that any man would be glad to have in his pocket, and he was buying drinks for everyone in the place."

McNear thanked him. He had never heard of Tom Henderson earning an honest shilling in his life. He walked directly to the Bull Dog bar to investigate.

The white-jacketed bartender was busily polishing glasses and setting them on the shelf opposite the cash drawer when McNear entered. Though catering for the poorer classes of the city, he had never run afoul of the law and he greeted the Inspector with easy cordiality.

"What can I do for you, sir?" he inquired.

"I hear Tom Henderson was in here a little while ago."

"About half an hour ago," the bartender admitted.

"Leave alone or didn't you notice?"

"Left by himself as far as I know. Joe!" the bartender raised his voice and a negro youth, who was sweeping the floor in what seemed to be an industrious and yet powerfully lazy manner, raised his head. "Joe! Did Tom Henderson go out of here alone?"

The boy nodded. "Yes, sare!" He kept his head raised but went on with his sweeping.

The bartender noticed McNear's heavy frown. "If I may be so bold as to ask, sir, what's wrong, Inspector?"

McNear answered shortly, "Henderson was found nearby with a broken skull."

"So that's all?" The bartender shrugged indifferently. "He had it comin' to him, if you ask me. Why, Inspector, he was flashing a roll of money when he was in here like that Rockefeller himself!"

McNear scowled in an angry, flabbergasted sort of way at the bar. "There's been a little too much of this criminal business around here lately. Who was in your bar while Henderson was here?"

The bartender slowly recited a list of names, each of which McNear carefully set down in his little grey notebook. From their reputations, McNear knew that most of the men who had been drinking with Henderson were shifty and brutal enough to have done him in for the amount of money he carried. "How much did Henderson spend here?"

"A little over two pounds—at least, I changed two one-pound notes for him," the bartender said calmly.

"Know which ones they were?" McNear inquired. "I'd like to have them for identification if you can single them out."

The Bull Dog bar saw pound notes rarely enough for their appearance to mark a special occasion. Turning to the cash register, the bartender pushed a lever. "Happened to notice," he said. "Not the Bermuda Government issue, but notes from the old country. And here they are."

McNear took them. "I'll borrow these temporarily. They, or the same amount, will be returned to you tomorrow."

He walked out into the night, which seemed especially dark and humid. He sighed a little and marched through the brightly lighted streets towards Headquarters, wondering if Henderson had yet regained consciousness and determined to see him and find out as soon as possible whether the man knew the name of his assailant.

"What's the news about Henderson?" he asked the Sergeant on duty.

The Sergeant shook his head. "Dr. Jenkins said he was in a bad way, sir. They operated, but it's touch and go whether he'll live or not."

McNear grunted sceptically. "His sort don't die off that easily. But it serves him right if he does—flashing his money about like that. No wonder one of those bar-flies at the Bull Dog popped him on the head. Some of them would do worse than that for a half-crown."

"You think he was attacked for his money, sir?" the Sergeant asked.

"What else?" McNear posed a question which to him had no other answer.

The Sergeant drew a long, dubious face. "Only this, sir. When they took off his clothes at the hospital they found a hundred and sixty pounds in his inside coat pocket!"

McNear threw up his hands in vexed bewilderment. "Damn it, man! If there's something mysterious about this Henderson business I—" But whatever his threat he sputtered off mildly and ended with a look of grim perplexity as the telephone, which he scarcely heard, began ringing on his desk. "Get the serial numbers on those notes for me."

"Right away, sir!"

"The telephone, Inspector," the Sergeant pointed out.

"Yes, yes, I know," McNear growled. He took up the receiver and his voice changed immediately.

"Mrs. Howe? Of course, Mrs. Howe. You say he hasn't come home yet? Well, ma'am, I wouldn't worry. We're pretty busy around here." He paused and looked up at the Sergeant.

"The Superintendent left about five o'clock or a little after," the Sergeant answered, "trying to get track of those people that missed their boats." McNear nodded and leaned toward the transmitter. "I think he's on a case, Mrs. Howe—no, that's all right. No trouble at all."

"That man'll wear himself to a shadow, working like this," McNear said, as he hung up the receiver.

The Sergeant smiled. "You haven't had much rest lately yourself, have you, sir?"

"I've got to get caught up with my duties—then I'll take a good rest," McNear said. "What about that fellow Davis that I brought in? Has he had anything to say?"

The Sergeant shook his head. "The Chief had another go at him before he left this afternoon, but the man was mum as a brick. Says he don't know how he got hold of those bonds."

McNear was sombrely thoughtful. If Davis were shielding an accomplice he must be under pressure to maintain silence in that regard. Because, in the circumstances, mere possession of the bonds would earn him a protracted prison sentence. Yet he kept reiterating his statement that he had had nothing to do with the robbery and was without any knowledge of how the bonds had come into his pocket. Meanwhile the case was open and Davis detained for ten days, having been sentenced to that term by the magistrate on McNear's charge of assault and resisting an officer.

"Well." McNear sighed and filled his huge churchwarden with fragrant tobacco. He leaned back in his chair only to sit up again. Through his window he could hear the sound of pattering in the courtyard. "Isn't that rain?"

"I hope so," the Sergeant answered concernedly, "my good lady said only this morning that if we didn't have rain soon our reservoirs would be bone dry."

"Umm," McNear said, lighting his pipe and puffing at it with deep appreciation. "No use going home in a downpour, is there?"

"Pretty late to go home now, anyway, sir," the Sergeant advised him, "living out in the country as you do."

McNear nodded as he looked at his watch. It was five minutes before midnight. However, the lateness of the hour and the fact that it was raining were not the reasons he rejected the idea of going home to his comfortable bed. It was his concern over Welch and the need he felt to get on with the Henderson investigation that kept him sitting in his office in the middle of the night.

"Think I'll stretch out here," he said, indicating his padded armchair. As the Sergeant turned to go McNear added, "Wake me up if you hear anything of Superintendent Welch."

"Yes, sir." The Sergeant saluted and closed the door.

McNear shaded the light to a soft, indirect glow and leaned back in his chair. He unbuttoned his tunic and comfortably arranged his legs. That the attack on Henderson pointed to still another extraordinary crime was exasperating to him, and he sought for reasons to explain the assault on grounds of simple robbery as he first had done. It was still possible, he argued with himself, that Henderson had been waylaid for his money and that the man's attacker had been frightened away by the footsteps of some approaching pedestrian, or by the sight of the constable, before he had a chance to make a search. That, he reasoned, would account for the banknotes being untouched in Henderson's pocket without giving rise to a complicated mystery. Still, how did the banknotes get in Henderson's pocket? And why were their serial numbers, which the Sergeant had procured for him, all consecutive?

That was his last thought when he dropped off to sleep and his first thought when he awoke at six next morning. Swinging quickly into action for the new day, he made a hasty toilet and, after a quick breakfast, returned in the direction of the Bull Dog bar to subject the proprietor to further questioning.

How long it had rained during the night he didn't know, but the air had that freshly washed appearance and the sidewalks shone clean and bright under the morning sun. At the Bull Dog he found the proprietor about to open his place for the day, and over a bottle of cold beer, which helped to make up for his scanty breakfast, McNear resumed his questioning of the night before.

"About this money Henderson had? Somebody mentioned a roll of it."

"A roll or a wad," the proprietor said; "I don't know which you'd call it, but it was all bunched together in pound and ten-shilling notes."

"Hmm," McNear said. "Sure of that?"

"Sure as I'm alive. Twice I seen him yank it out of his trouser pocket to pay for a round of drinks."

"Trouser pocket?" McNear repeated. "You're sure of that, too?"

"Absolutely," the proprietor answered quickly. "I remember thinking how big the roll must be, what with all the trouble he was having getting it in and out. Big enough to choke an ox."

"No sign of a wallet?"

"Not a sight of one, Mr. Inspector."

"Well," McNear arose. "I'll keep these two pound notes a while longer," he said.

"No hurry about that, sir," the proprietor assured him as he left McNear walked slowly up Front Street. He had his destination well in mind. It was the Bank of N. T. Butterfield and Son, but as it was too early for the doors to be open he loitered on farther down Front Street, sniffing with displeasure as he proceeded along that odoriferous avenue of decaying vegetables and overripe fruit. For

the appearance of Front Street was the *bête noir* of the Inspector's
life. How many times had he longed for the authority to demand
that certain merchants of that thoroughfare clean their respective
sidewalks at least once a month! A short stretch just opposite Wharf
Number One, where the stately *Queen of Bermuda* lay berthed,
was today, he noted, in a more disgraceful condition than ever.
Myriads of flies covered a display of vegetables so thickly that it
was impossible to distinguish onions from potatoes or carrots from
beets! In no other country, the patriotic Inspector reflected sadly,
would the front door through which every visitor must pass be allowed to remain in such a repugnant condition. If Paris were judged
by its Rue de la Paix, London by its Bond Street, New York by its
Fifth Avenue, he sincerely hoped that Bermuda would never be
similarly appraised by the untidiness of its principal street of trade.

Still seething at this state of affairs, McNear returned to
Butterfield's Bank. The place was not yet open to the public for
the day, but as McNear's cousin was a paying teller the Inspector
was well enough known to gain admission even without the aid of
the impressive uniform he wore.

His cousin, he saw, was at work behind the paying teller's window, and the janitor, at a nod from an official who had seen the
Inspector, swung open the bronze door for McNear and closed it
behind him as he stepped inside.

"Hello, Mac!" McNear's cousin, a grey-haired, twinkling-eyed
old man greeted him from his stool behind the barred cage. "What's
up? Come to borrow a million pounds this early in the morning?"

"Couldn't use a million, Joe," McNear answered cheerfully; "but
you might give me some information worth almost that much to
my peace of mind!"

Joe laughed. "Must be pretty expensive information. What is it?"

McNear passed the two banknotes and a slip of paper with the
serial numbers of the others on it through the wicket. "I noticed
there were consecutive numbers on these and they're both English
issue."

"So I see," his cousin said perplexedly.

"What does that mean to you?" McNear asked.

"Means the same to me that it means to you, I expect," his cousin answered, "and that is that these notes are fresh from a bank."

McNear was relieved. "I thought that's what it meant, but I wanted your opinion." He leaned over the counter and tapped the notes with his blunt finger. "Now the question is, Joe—what bank?"

Joe turned in silence and walked over to a nearby bookkeeper, with whom he began to peruse the pages of a massive ledger. After a few minutes he returned and announced:

"From our Bank, Mac. We gave them out on Saturday morning."

"Fine!" McNear congratulated him. "Who'd you give 'em to?"

Cousin or no, Joe was first of all a cautious officer in a bank. He pursed his lips. "A very good client, Mac. I'd want to be sure that this information wasn't against his interests before I told you."

"Interests or not," McNear stated firmly, "I want that man's name. We can make it regular and proper as you like, but I must get it. The Chief of Police will give you all the authority you need and I'll get it for you in black and white!"

Before his determination the paying teller relented. "It won't be necessary to do that, Mac. I'm the last one in the world to put obstacles in your way when you're doing your duty. But this particular client is a very good one and we shouldn't care to lose his account."

McNear nodded understandingly. "I see that, Joe. But if he's an honest man with nothing to fear I can't see what harm it'll do if I know his name." He waited expectantly.

After a thoughtful moment Joe said, "Very well, Mac. We gave them out to Henry Hastings, of Hastings and West."

"How much?" the Inspector asked.

Joe went back to the ledger and returned. "Two hundred pounds in one-pound notes."

"Whew!" McNear whistled. "That's a lot of money."

Joe smiled. "Hastings and West do a lot of business!"

"But," McNear protested, "does he usually draw out such sums?"

"Not usually," the paying teller admitted, "but all these wine merchants have dealings with people who don't take easily to cheques. Ever since prohibition in the States."

McNear nodded knowingly. "But I should think the bootleggers would pay him, not the other way round."

"It works both ways," the teller informed him. "Anything else I can do for you?"

"That's all," McNear thanked him, and made rapid tracks out the door and through the city to the offices of Hastings and West.

Soon he was sitting opposite Henry Hastings, puffing furiously at the cigar which had just been presented to him.

Hastings was very affable. "And now what can I do for you, Inspector?"

"Well, sir"—McNear looked apologetically at his excellent cigar—"it's a bit delicate, but do you by any chance know of a man named Tom Henderson?"

Hastings started, but quickly recovered his easy composure. "The name sounds a little familiar, Inspector. What about the fellow?"

"We found him last night—head bashed in. He was still alive this morning, but he'll have to be pretty tough to pull through."

"Very unfortunate," Hastings answered indifferently. "What has that to do with me?"

"Well, sir, you've had dealings with this man, haven't you?"

Hastings' face was blandly impassive. "None that I recall."

"Financial dealings, I mean," McNear continued.

"No," Hastings said with an easy flatness.

This blunt denial made the Inspector frown. "Mr. Hastings, last Saturday morning you drew two hundred pounds in cash from Butterfield's Bank."

"Very possibly I did," Hastings answered imperturbably. "I often use cash, and there are many calls to spend it."

"And what calls had you to spend this particular money?" McNear, who had become slightly nettled, asked.

Hastings flushed. "Really, Inspector, aren't you going a bit too far? I have submitted to your strange questioning without protest, but, after all, my business is certainly my personal affair, and I fail to see what the police have to do with it!"

"Ordinarily," McNear answered in an even voice, "you would be quite right. But ordinarily I shouldn't have come here. As I told you, the man Henderson is lying at the point of death. I must also tell you that in his pocket were found notes which had been drawn by you from Butterfield's Bank!"

Hastings sat and stared stonily at the window. "I have told you, Inspector, that I've had no financial dealings with this man. How or where he came into possession of the notes which you say I withdrew from Butterfield's I can't tell you. I must remind you, however, that notes are made for the express purpose of making money as easily negotiable as possible. Those notes may have gone through a dozen hands since they left mine!"

"A reasonable enough idea—ordinarily, but," the Inspector doggedly continued, "we found practically the full two hundred pounds in Henderson's pocket, Mr. Hastings. Now surely you can tell me who you paid that money to?"

Hastings tightened his lips. "I'm sorry, Inspector. I can tell you nothing of the sort!"

"Can't or won't?" McNear demanded grimly.

"Take it any way you like," Hastings answered. "You're inquiring into my private affairs, and I refuse to admit that you have any business to do it!"

McNear stood up. "I'm sorry you've taken this attitude, Mr. Hastings. I know you need to use ready money in your business. I admit it's no business of ours if you give large sums of cash to the bootleggers at St. George's. But your silence, when the police come to you for aid, does not set well with your reputation as a business leader of Hamilton. Good-day, Mr. Hastings!"

Hastings sat deep in thought. "Don't be huffy about it, Inspector. I just can't tell you, that's all."

"But if Tom Henderson dies, man!" McNear expostulated.

"If he dies," Hastings answered, "come back here. I don't promise, but I might tell you the name of the man I gave the money to.

Until then, however, I fail to see the connection between my disposal of the money and the attack on this man Henderson."

"And that's your last word?" McNear demanded.

"My last word!" Hastings said emphatically.

McNear left abruptly and with an irritable scowl.

For one of the business leaders of the Islands to refuse to co-operate with the police in a serious matter was an almost unheard of thing.

Passing back along Front Street the Inspector saw a fresh stream of American passengers disembarking from the newly docked *Monarch of Bermuda*. At the adjoining wharf lay the *Lady Somers*, lately arrived from Montreal and now loading for her return voyage. McNear groaned. "More tourists!" he muttered with dismay. For in their golden stream he could see only more trouble for the police.

However, there would be fresh news from the States. Stepping in at the Phoenix Drug Store, he bought a *New York Times* and a tabloid which he privately referred to as "that damned little ha'penny rag from New York." Leaving the busy news counter, he went toward Headquarters, scanning the news from America.

The Marsden child, he noted, was still missing. The innumerable clues and false leads which were continually cropping up had each led to a blank wall. The New York police seemed to have reached an impasse; even the murdered Pamela Hawkins was no longer mentioned in connection with the disappearance. From all of which McNear shrewdly suspected that the cablegram received by the Bermuda police from their New York colleagues ordering the detention of Miss Hawkins had been another wild shot in the dark.

15
A SUSPECT AT LAST

Tuesday Morning, April 13th.

Meanwhile Masters, having arrived at his office, had settled himself before a mass of executive paper work and was about to inquire for Superintendent Welch on a matter of routine when his door opened and a constable stood apologetically on the threshold.

"Pardon me, sir, but there's a call from the hospital. Henderson, the man who was attacked last night on Church Street, wants to make a statement to the police and particularly asked for you!"

Masters swore under his breath. "Wants me, does he?" Serious as the accident had been, he saw no reason why he should be taken away from pressing work to hear a tale from a shifty scoundrel such as Henderson was reputed to be. He looked up. "The man probably wants to give the name of his assailant. Better send Inspector McNear," he directed.

The constable remained motionless. "Inspector McNear left early, sir. Besides, I think"—the constable hesitated—"I think maybe it's about the murder, sir."

"Murder?" the Chief barked. "You mean the murder of that Hawkins girl?"

The constable nodded. "That's the message that came from the hospital, sir. Said it was very important, too. The Doctor said Henderson might sink back into his coma!"

"Coma?" Masters said interrogatively. "Anyway, whatever he sinks back into, have my carriage in front of the building in five minutes."

"Yes, sir!" The constable saluted and withdrew. Left to himself, Masters swore again. He was angrier now than ever. For if the Hawkins case were to be reopened after having been so nicely disposed of by the Coroner's jury it would mean a mountain of work and head-scratching on the part of himself and the rest of the force. But it was not the work he dreaded so much; it was the feeling that he was likely to pry up a corner of the lid, letting just enough light on the mystery to show how far wrong he had been in his beliefs.

A few minutes later his gleaming carriage drove through the flower-bordered entrance of the King Edward Hospital, and Masters saw Dr. Walters, the head of the institution, waiting for him on the steps.

"I presume you've come about Henderson?" Dr. Walters inquired. As the policeman nodded, the Doctor continued, "Peculiar case. Very. I should have said last night his chance of pulling through was one in a thousand. Yet he came out of the ether with a strong pulse and he's been conscious for a good half-hour."

"He must have had a miraculous escape, the rascal," the Chief of Police said. "Dr. Jenkins reported there was hardly any hope of his recovery. Evidently you've been to see him. What is it he has to say?"

"He won't say anything except to the police," Dr. Walters answered. "It sounds very mysterious, and I let him have a minute's talk with your man here that's on duty. He's still very weak and his mind may be temporarily unhinged, though I'll admit he talks clearly enough."

Masters walked beside Dr. Walters along the spotless white corridors till presently the Doctor stopped before a numbered door and quietly motioned for Masters to follow him inside.

His head swathed in bandages till only his eyes and nose were visible, Tom Henderson lay on a high, white bed near the window.

Masters came directly to the point. "Well, Henderson, I've heard you want to make a statement."

Henderson weakly inclined his head and said in a thin voice, "This is Mr. Masters, ain't it?"

"It is," the Chief said and seated himself beside the bed on a chair which the Doctor had brought before tiptoeing out of the room. "Now what's all this nonsense, Henderson?"

Henderson smiled feebly. "Ain't nonsense, sir. Not what I've got to tell!"

"Very well. Who struck you?"

"I don't know, sir," Henderson answered in his thin voice, "but I know why it was."

"That money you had in your pockets, eh?" the Chief said.

"Money?" Henderson said. "It wasn't the money; it was murder he was after."

"Murder?" Masters was incredulous.

"Ain't his fault I ain't pushin' up daisies," Henderson said.

"'He,' you say. You mean you know the hand that did it?"

"I don't know the hand that struck the blow, but I know the hand behind it," Henderson's voice though weak was none the less emphatic. He lay silent for a moment, looking up at the ceiling from beneath his bandages. "I know who stabbed that Hawkins girl and he knows I know it!"

"Who?" Masters demanded, sitting stiffer than ever and staring.

"The murderer," Henderson said.

An imprecation passed Masters' lips. "You know—the murderer—you say?"

"Last Friday night," Henderson began in his thin monotone, "I was takin' my evening glass at the Royal Palm bar, and while I was standin' there up comes a man and a girl. I'd seen the man before and I knew his name, but I'd never laid eyes on the girl. Well, they were pretty gay and flipperty and I says to myself, 'He's after that girl and he won't have no peace till he's got what he's after.' And sure enough I heard him askin' her to meet him the next morning for to go for a sail and a picnic at Port's Island. Well, after a while she says yes and I heard them agree to be at half-past six next morning at Darrell's Wharf. 'A picnic, me eye,' I said, but I didn't know then what that girl was up agin. I didn't know it was to be murder, Chief."

"The girl—you mean she was Pamela Hawkins?"

Henderson nodded a little.

"And the man—" Masters bent tensely forward.

"Mr. Henry Hastings."

"Hastings!" Masters was astounded. "No, man! You're not actually accusing Henry Hastings of murdering that girl!"

"I know," Henderson admitted in a plaintively understanding tone, "I know how the Coroner and the police all said it was a feller named Collins, but I wasn't havin' none of that. Happen I was born with sharp eyes and good ears and happen I got a right to use 'em. And I says to myself, 'You think you're a pretty smooth article, Henry Hastings, but you ain't quite smooth enough.'"

"So that's how he found out you had heard him," Masters said accusingly, "you tried to blackmail him!" His eyes narrowed suspiciously. "And if Mr. Hastings had paid you well enough you'd have held your tongue! Is that it?"

How Henderson, weak as he was, could contrive to make his voice sound so sullen was a mystery, but the tone was there as he answered, "You're wrong there, sir. Hastings give me two hundred pounds! But when he sends around to have me murdered I guess I've got a right to talk!"

Two hundred pounds! It was that fact that finally convinced Masters of the straightness of Henderson's story. Once decided, he acted at once. Going to the telephone before he left the hospital, he gave orders for Hastings to report to his office and to be held till he arrived. Then he hurried downstairs to his waiting carriage.

When Masters reached Headquarters he found Hastings waiting for him in his private office. Looking harassed but stubborn, the wine merchant started to rise up resentfully when Masters greeted him.

"Mr. Hastings," the Chief of Police began with little preliminaries, "I'm sorry to have to question you in this fashion, but there's no alternative. Two very serious charges have been made against you—accusations which you, yourself, if you're the sort of man I think you are, would want to see investigated at the earliest possible moment."

Hastings sat with his eyes aloof, gripping a cigar between his fingers. He said nothing.

"The first charge," Masters proceeded slowly, "is that, while on Good Friday last you spent some hours in the company of Miss Pamela Hawkins, you failed to inform the police of this fact!"

Hastings glanced fleetingly at the policeman. "Who told you that?" he challenged.

"A credible witness," Masters answered.

Hedging uncomfortably before this unnamed accuser and doubtless feeling that it could not be Henderson since he supposed the man still to be unconscious Hastings admitted, "It's true I was with a young woman last Friday evening. But I don't admit that it was Pamela Hawkins."

The Chief of Police smiled sceptically. "Doubtless you've some very good reason for putting your reply in just those words?"

"I have," Hastings said firmly. "I've the very good reason that I never found out her name!"

"Rather extraordinary, that," Masters commented. "Now just how couldn't you have known Miss Hawkins' name?"

Hastings flushed. "We met," he said, "as people often do. I smiled and spoke; she smiled and answered. I invited her to join me in a cocktail and that's all there was to it."

Masters looked gravely dubious. He was very much a family man and unused to such informal meetings. "Even so, isn't it a little surprising that in the course of an hour or more while you were together she did not tell you her name?"

"Surprising, perhaps, and unfortunate, perhaps, but it is still a fact."

"You asked her name, of course?"

"I did. And she refused to give it."

"Refused, eh? Humph!" Masters' doubt was growing. "Under such circumstances I should think a girl would at least give you her Christian name!"

"I have thought lately," Hastings replied, "that she was afraid if she told me her first name— Well, it's an unusual name and it's been in the Press in such an unfavourable light lately—"

Triumph gleamed in Masters' eyes. "Ah—" he began.

On the table beside him the telephone rang. He took it up irritably. "Yes?"

"Mrs. Howe calling, sir—Superintendent Welch's sister."

Annoyed by the interruption at that moment, Masters said hastily, "I'll talk to her later, operator." He hung up the receiver, then turned with suave satisfaction to Hastings. "You told me just a moment ago that you had no idea the girl was Pamela Hawkins!"

Hastings squirmed in the net of his own fabrication. "But I didn't know it at the time," he stammered. "Only lately, after I'd been thinking it over, did I come to the conclusion that the description of the girl I was with was the same as the dead girl's."

"Rather a weak explanation, Hastings," Masters observed. "However, we'll let it pass for the moment." Suddenly he demanded, "At what time Friday night did you leave Miss Hawkins?"

"About nine o'clock," Hastings said after a thoughtful pause.

"And you never saw her again?"

"Never."

"Humph!" his interrogator ejaculated. "But you expected to renew your acquaintance on some future occasion?"

"I had no such intention," Hastings said flatly. "The next morning—Saturday—I had business at St George's. The following day was Sunday—Easter Sunday—which I would naturally spend with my family. As for the day after that, I would be at my office; and since the girl told me her ship was to sail Monday afternoon I consequently would have had no chance of meeting her again."

"I see," Masters commented in the tone of one who doesn't see. He looked at Hastings severely, his tight lips drawn to a straight, reproving line:

"Mr. Hastings, you are a very poor liar. You have denied that you knew the girl was Pamela Hawkins—lie number one. You have just said you had no intention of meeting her again—lie number two. In fact, Mr. Hastings, it is difficult for me to believe a word of your story!"

The two men stared at each other till Hastings' brown eyes wavered.

"Hastings," Masters clipped his words, "I'll give you one more chance—and one only—to tell me the whole truth!"

Hastings bent his head toward the floor while he tried to regain composure. But the policeman's steel grey eyes continued to bore through his consciousness, and every moment of silence made him feel he was losing ground. Finally he burst out in an incoherent voice: "As God is my judge, I never knew on Good Friday that the girl was Pamela Hawkins. That's a fact. Anything else you have heard is a lie. But it's true we did make an engagement before I left her. It was for the next day."

"Well?" Masters, having the upper hand, sat waiting.

"But I didn't keep the appointment. I was going to meet her, yes. But as I told you I had important business in St. George's."

Masters looked as if he believed this. "I understand," he said. "Now, Mr. Hastings, if you'll continue to tell the truth it will be to your advantage. Where were you to meet Miss Hawkins?" Hastings' eyes fell again. He muttered the damning words faintly, "At half-past six on Darrell's Wharf."

"You know, of course," Masters said searchingly, "that Miss Hawkins was found dead within half a mile of your rendezvous and at that very hour!"

"I can only repeat," Hastings said desperately, "that I didn't see her again and that I was nowhere near that spot at the time!"

"Then, of course, you can tell me where you were at half-past six that Saturday morning. You've certainly witnesses for an alibi?"

The wine merchant fixed fascinated eyes on the Chief of Police's immobile face.

"I—I'm afraid not," he stuttered.

"No? Why not?" Masters demanded coolly.

"Well, sir," Hastings floundered, "you see, Mr. Masters, I got up very early that morning—at six, I should say. I had to be in St. George's. I left before the servants had arrived for the morning's work. For that reason there was nobody who saw me leave my house."

"Not even your wife?" Masters inquired.

Hastings shook his head. "She had gone to New York for a short visit."

"Then somebody on the train," Masters suggested impatiently. "Undoubtedly the train conductor would remember you made the trip and would testify he had seen you at that hour?"

Hastings glanced despairingly about the room. "No, sir, I'm afraid not. You see, I cycled. The train I meant to catch was the

6.25, but I missed it. I had very urgent business in St. George's, and rather than wait for the 7.30 train I decided to bicycle!"

"By how many minutes would you say you missed the 6.25?" Masters demanded.

"I can tell you that all right," Hastings answered. "I reached Hamilton Terminus at 6.29, just four minutes after the train had gone."

"So at 6.29 you started to bicycle to St. George's?"

Hastings moistened his lips nervously. "It was about that time."

"And you arrived at St. George's at what hour?"

"At half-past eight."

"You're a very slow cyclist?"

"No, sir."

"Then why," demanded the Chief of Police, who knew his Islands well, "did it take you two hours to make a trip which everybody else makes in a little more than an hour?"

Hastings looked unhappily at his cigar, which had long ago ceased to burn. "I stopped along the way to look at a house which my firm is thinking of turning into a bar."

"And there, no doubt, you at last saw someone who will testify to having seen you!"

But again Hastings shook his head. "I'm afraid not."

"What!" Masters demanded incredulously. "You mean to say you went all the way from Hamilton to St. George's without meeting up with a soul you knew?"

Hastings mumbled in excuse, "It was rather early—"

"So!" Masters said grimly. "So, Mr. Hastings! During that important hour—the hour you were to have met this girl, the hour, in fact, that she met her death—you were cycling to St. George's and saw nobody who would recognize you!"

Hastings fidgeted with his handkerchief and mopped his forehead. "But many people saw me at St. George's after 8.30. Isn't that enough?"

Masters laughed drily. Opening a drawer of his desk, he took out from a pile of papers a green timetable. "There is a train, as you have said, at 7.30 from the Hamilton Terminus. It is a train that the murderer would have had plenty of time to meet and arrive in St. George's before half-past eight—8.26, to be exact. Under these circumstances, Mr. Hastings, I hardly believe proving you were at St. George's at half-past eight is much of an alibi for the two preceding hours!"

Hastings rubbed his handkerchief between his moist palms. He was very pale, and when he tried to talk his facial muscles jerked out of his control. "Good God!" he said, "you're not accusing me of murdering the girl?"

"I've charged you with nothing—yet," Masters said stiffly. He leaned suddenly forward. "Now, what about this attack on Henderson?"

"Wh-y!" Hastings whistled feebly with overwhelming consternation. "I don't know anything about that."

"You won't deny," Masters asked gravely, "that you paid him two hundred pounds to hold his tongue!"

Hastings sank his head in his hands and murmured brokenly, "Yes, I paid him. I couldn't do anything else. I can't be denounced as a murderer. And there is my wife to think of—" His voice trailed off.

Like most Hamiltonians, Masters knew that all was not well in the Hastings household. His wife, an English-born woman, had brought him at the time of their marriage the money with which he had expanded his flourishing business. But the capital had remained in her name, and at this particular time an open rift in their frayed relationship, when Hastings had so many irons in the commercial fire, would have been more than calamitous.

"But why did you bribe him?" the policeman insisted.

Hastings flung out his hands desperately. "Because it was worth it!"

"Aye!" Masters sagely nodded his head. "Two hundred pounds to ease a guilty conscience! But it takes more drastic measures to make sure of silence. You found that out, eh?"

"Before God!" Hastings broke out in a frenzy, "you can't accuse me of that, Mr. Masters!"

The Chief of Police stared at him unsympathetically. "Hastings, you have put me in a very uncomfortable position. And it is entirely your own fault. You are a man of good standing in our community, but, whatever your reasons, you have not only failed to co-operate in upholding the law, you have, first by your silence and then by your downright lies, attempted to obstruct the carriage of justice. And"—he leaned over and touched a signal bell on his desk—"I am only doing my duty in holding you as a material witness."

"Good God!" Hastings exclaimed wildly.

"You should consider yourself lucky," Masters said gravely, "that the charge is not a more serious one!"

16

CRIMINALS AT LARGE

Tuesday Morning, April 13th.

Ordinarily, Superintendent Welch's failure to arrive at Headquarters that morning would have been passed by in silence. Being second-in-command of the Island's police force, he was, so far as his hours were concerned, less accountable than the Chief of Police himself. Like so many confirmed bachelors who live in a household run for their benefit, Welch was as considerately methodical as the most exemplary of husbands. And as he had specifically promised Mrs. Howe, his widowed sister who took care of him, that he would be home for dinner the previous evening, his absence had concerned her greatly.

But even aside from Mrs. Howe's worried telephone calls, the fact that Welch had not appeared next morning was a source of uneasy surprise to the members of the force. For a man who, the evening before, had turned the Island's constabulary upside down to search for two missing passengers from the cruise ships, not to return for information as to the results of the search, was peculiar and disconcerting.

Even so, his absence might have gone unchallenged. But with two people dead and a third brutally attacked within a period of less than seventy-two hours, the placid, slow-going representatives of order in quiet Bermuda had begun to feel that their Island was no safer than the bed of a Chicago gangster whom a rival gunman had determined to kill. And by the third time Mrs. Howe tried to reach Masters that morning by telephone, Inspector McNear was in a fine state of alarm.

"He's come to some harm, Mr. McNear," Mrs. Howe predicted lugubriously. "I've had a feeling of it in my bones ever since I finally had to put away the dinner I'd cooked for him last night."

"Don't worry, Mrs. Howe," McNear consoled her; "the Superintendent'll turn up safe and sound."

"But if he's not there, either," Mrs. Howe querulously protested, "where in the world can he be?"

"Now, now," McNear said, with much more assurance than he felt, "we'll find him safe enough, Mrs. Howe."

Slightly mollified by these words of assurance, Mrs. Howe rang off.

McNear shook his head worriedly and sought out his superior.

Infected by his subordinate's concern, Masters swung into action, and a few minutes later all the available constables were routed out of their routine duties and scattered over the Islands in diligent search.

"If Welch has been harmed—" McNear said, with a threat of vengeance in his voice.

His companion drummed nervously on the top of his splendidly polished table. "It is a mystery why he didn't report this morning," he admitted.

"First time since he's been on the force," McNear said.

He tramped restlessly from the office and continued inquiring where Welch had gone when he had left Headquarters the night before. So far nobody had been able to answer the question, but at about eleven o'clock McNear encountered the police stenographer who had copied the wireless messages for Welch.

"Let's see, now,"—the police stenographer wrinkled his forehead in a violent effort to recollect—"I remember he called up somebody just before he left. It was—bless me, if I can recollect who it was!" Seething with impatience, McNear stood grimly over him. "Take your time, man, but don't be all day about it!"

"Some real estate fellow," the stenographer said hesitantly after a long silence.

McNear grasped hastily for the telephone book. With his eyes fixed sharply on the stenographer, he read off one name after another:

"Mears and Wilson?"

The stenographer looked dumb.

"Frank T. Kent?"

"No, I think—"

"Bonnybright and Whelpley?"

"No, I know it wasn't that."

"Calloway, Gardiner and Co?"

The stenographer's brow cleared. "Gardiner! That's the man!" he said.

McNear took up the telephone and read the number to the operator. Half a minute later he was talking to Arthur Gardiner.

"Yes, yes," Gardiner said, "we had quite a chat together. He seemed very anxious to find a woman. Well, he left me saying he was going to visit the three houses our firm recently rented."

McNear fished hurriedly for his pencil. "If you'll give me the addresses, Mr. Gardiner, I'll trouble you no more."

In very brief order McNear wrote down the addresses of the three houses and hung up the telephone, only to take it up again and direct constables to investigate each of them.

"Now, it seems to me," he said to the Chief of Police, "that he'd go to the nearest one—which is Greenleaf."

Masters nodded confirmation. "Sounds reasonable."

"Yes, sir," McNear said emphatically. He jerked down the brim of his helmet. "I'll need a few policemen, sir."

"Take as many as you like," his Chief offered generously.

A few minutes later he was leading a squad of uniformed men past the Hamilton Hotel in the direction of Greenleaf. As he passed a new cottage which was still in process of construction, a man called in a startled voice, "I say!"

McNear stopped his procession. "What is it, my man?"

"I say," the man repeated, "there's not anything wrong up ahead, is there?"

McNear closed up to him. "You must have some reason asking me. What is it?"

The man laughed a little apologetically. "I'm John Hollis of the Customs Office," he identified himself. "I'm building a new house here. Last night I saw my friend Superintendent Welch going up the road, and this morning I see you and your men going the same way. I just wondered what kind of a neighbourhood I had come into, that's all."

McNear reared his head like a war-horse scenting powder. "Which way did he go, sir?" he demanded.

"Well," Hollis answered, "he was inquiring about the new tenant of Greenleaf—that's the little cottage down the road—you can see it from here."

"Come on," McNear said to his uniformed squad, and marched forward two hundred steps to the minute.

Deploying his men so as to encircle the house, McNear pushed through the gate and went up on the steps. He knocked peremptorily.

There was no answer.

He turned the knob, but the door held firm till, with a heave of his left shoulder, he splintered the panel. Reaching through the broken wood, he unfastened the lock and stepped inside.

The house was dark, gloomy and apparently deserted.

"Hmm!" McNear said, noting the closed shutters. He gave a sharp whistle, and two men, who had waited by the gate, came in quickly.

"Search the place," McNear directed.

The three men scattered into different rooms. One of them went upstairs.

McNear began flinging open the shutters. In the light of a full Bermuda day he could see that dust lay on part of the furniture, but had been wiped away from other pieces. The dining-room sideboard was covered with dust, but the table itself had been so recently used that there were particles of sugar to be seen on it. While he was puzzling over this a voice cried from upstairs.

"Damme! Well, look at this!" Heavy shoes sounded on the old wooden stairs, and one of the searching officers came down and stood holding out a policeman's helmet.

"Superintendent's name's in it, too! It was in a bolster on a bed!"

Spurred by this find, McNear called in the others he had brought, and the house fairly shook under their tramping feet as they ransacked the place from top to bottom.

McNear stood in the kitchen with one of his assistants, opening closets and vegetable bins. Bending near the floor, McNear suddenly exclaimed, "Good God!"

"What is it, sir?" his assistant asked in a startled voice.

"The trap to the reservoir!" McNear said, and pointed to the square of linoleum which, from its cut edges, was evidently removable. "If he's in there—"

The assistant said forebodingly, "And it rained last night, sir!"

McNear lifted the square with nerveless fingers. As he had expected, the concrete trap lay below it. He began to sweat and to make speechless calls on God.

The assisting constable came forward with his flashlight as McNear lifted the concrete slab.

The beam of light played over the deep water. From a far corner came a feeble cry.

"He's there—alive!" McNear said wiping the sweat from his forehead.

"Come here—all of you!" the Constable yelled to his comrades.

McNear stood up and yanked off his tunic, kicking meanwhile at his shoes. He stripped down with unsystematic and swift movements and, clad in his underclothes, lowered himself through the trap.

Guided by the ray of a flashlight held from above, he struck out in the water in the direction from which the cry had come. His hand touched a bare, half-lifeless shoulder, and, reaching out for support, he encountered the drain-pipe in the corner of the reservoir.

As other flashlights strengthened the lonely ray from the trap, McNear hooked one arm about the copper pipe and began to loosen the water-soaked knots in the belt with which Welch had bound himself to the drain when he had begun to feel his strength giving out. Meanwhile, Welch was stiff as a dead man, and in spite of the cry with which he had greeted the light, McNear had a ghastly feeling that he was rescuing a corpse.

"Welch," he muttered, finally getting the man loose.

There was no answer.

Manoeuvring on his side so that Welch's supine body could be supported by his left arm, McNear called, "I'm coming."

He struck out with his right arm, and eager hands reached down, waiting, from the trap while he made for the flashlights.

"Got him!" a constable said breathlessly, and McNear felt Welch's body grasped. He swam around in a narrow circle while the Superintendent was drawn up through the trap.

"All right, Inspector!"

He swam under the trap and raised his arm to a hand extended toward him. Shivering and scraped by the concrete edge, he was drawn to the kitchen floor.

Welch lay flat on his back, completely motionless, while two of the constables anxiously rubbed his naked body.

"G-get the am-m-bulance," McNear ordered through chattering teeth.

A constable rushed out to telephone, and while they waited the rest took turns massaging Welch's body.

McNear dressed slowly, with numb fingers. "He's alive, though?"

"Just unconscious," answered the constable who was rubbing his legs. "He'll come round."

McNear gave a sigh of relief and fumbled for his pipe. "If we hadn't come when we did," he muttered, then broke off and shook his head. "Pretty narrow squeak, all right!"

Out in front sounded a rumble as the ambulance drew up. Dr. Jenkins bustled in with his little black bag.

"What's this? What's this, Inspector?" he exclaimed in a querulous tone. "Great Scott, the Superintendent himself! What next? What next?"

He clicked his tongue in useless remonstrance at such happenings and bent down. The men watched him anxiously. His face was grave. Finally he stood up. "King Edward Hospital," he said to one of the stretcher-bearers who had followed him in; "that's the best place for this fellow for a while."

But to that Welch found voice to protest. "Home!" he said in a weak but determined voice.

McNear grinned, delighted and astonished. "There's spunk for you!" he observed, casting a glance about the constables as if to impress them with an object lesson.

"Home, is it?" Dr. Jenkins bent down and arranged the blankets which had been taken from an upstairs bed to cover Welch from his chin to his toes. "You'll do better in the hospital, my man!" At these words a more violent protest disturbed the heavily swathed figure. Dr. Jenkins leaned nearer, listened for a moment and smiled broadly.

"If you can swear like that, well, I think perhaps you aren't so bad but that you can be taken home, Superintendent."

McNear drew anxiously nearer. "Dr. Jenkins, might I ask a question of the Superintendent?"

Dr. Jenkins was thoughtful. "If you'll limit it to one, Inspector. I suppose you want to know who the responsible criminal is—as I do myself."

McNear nodded tensely. "Welch," he said, "how'd you get down there?"

Welch stirred restlessly, moving his head up from beneath the blanket. "That Sinclair woman—you've got to find her, Mac."

McNear braced himself. "And find her we will!" he vowed in an unexpectedly emotional outburst, then fidgeted angrily with his pipe.

The two stretcher-bearers went out with Welch to the ambulance. When the door had closed behind them, McNear turned to his constables. "And now, lads, for an eagle-eyed search of every inch of this foul place!"

"Well, sir," the youngest constable spoke up at once, "I found something a while ago. It may not be much and then again it may." He uncrumpled his fist and exhibited several ticket stubs of the Bermuda Railway for passage from St. George's.

McNear examined the stubs carefully. "Good!" he said, "we'll have our hands on that bloody-hearted woman before very long!"

17
THE PURPLE WRAPPING PAPER

Tuesday Afternoon, April 13th, until Wednesday Evening, April 14th.
Although the Bermuda police, led by Inspector McNear, instituted
an immediate search such as had never before taken place on the
Islands, the attempted murderess of Superintendent Welch remained elusive as smoke far off on the horizon.

Greenleaf Cottage, McNear discovered from Gardiner, had been
rented by a Mrs. Bigelow from the States; but evidently Welch had
seen the occupant and had from the description recognized her as
the missing Henrietta Sinclair.

However, a thorough examination of the cottage added little of
value to the investigation of the police. Apparently the woman had
brought only a little baggage for her sojourn in Bermuda. After
she had left there remained but two small suitcases filled with
clothing, all of which was of American manufacture. From this
McNear concluded that when she had disappeared she had taken
practically nothing with her but the clothes she wore.

But the baggage was a further indication that the woman was
Mrs. Sinclair. Because one of the constables pointed out, under
marks which had been made to obliterate them, gold "Esses"
stamped on the leather and bits of labels from the S.S. *Baledonia*
still on the luggage.

After more than three hours, in which he reassured himself that
he had left no clue behind, McNear left the house and walked back
past the new home of Mr. Hollis, thinking that the Customs official
might have seen the woman leave some time during the previous night.

160

But here, again, little developed to further McNear's search. For Mr. Hollis stated with conviction that from the time he had seen Superintendent Welch enter Greenleaf until he himself left at dark he had witnessed nobody come in or go out of the cottage. There was, however, he pointed out, a small lane leading through a vacant lot which the woman might have taken by way of her kitchen door. It would have led her to a road running parallel with the main road. Or, he suggested—as McNear had already concluded—that she had waited until nightfall before leaving the cottage. But neither of these surmises did anything to advance the cause of the police, with the result that McNear found himself no better equipped to set out for St. George's than he had been when the railway stubs were discovered.

As it was then late he decided he had better wait till morning before going to St. George's. And that involved a longer delay, for the absence of Welch had increased his duties and it was afternoon before he was free to leave Headquarters.

At Queen Street, McNear swung aboard a train, and finding a vacant corner seat he settled down to a thorough perusal of his *Royal Gazette* and *Colonist Daily*. He had no plan of action in mind except that he meant to find Mrs. Sinclair no matter what exertions the quest required of him; but till he got to the scene of action he saw no reason why he shouldn't employ his time and thoughts upon matters affecting the great empire in which he was one of His Majesty's subjects.

The Irish situation, he noted from the *Royal Gazette*, was still critical. But then, he thought, the Irish situation always had been and doubtless always would be critical. J. Ramsay MacDonald, he next observed, had rushed out with another Four-Power pact which was to stand between the civilized world and catastrophe. And McNear made the unspoken observation that J. Ramsay MacDonald and the Irish situation were at one in a certain respect, at any rate. Likewise Gandhi, who was entering his fortieth fast to the accompaniment of gravely spoken physicians' opinions that it would be the end of him.

From these commonplace topics McNear turned to the "They Say" column, which daily blossomed with subjects frivolous and stern.

THEY SAY:
That the police are doing some
prodigious thinking lately.

• • •

That the murder mystery is not as
settled as it might be.

• • •

That the matter is being hush-hushed
pending "developments."

• • •

That "developments" as every snap-shotter
knows frequently don't turn out.

• • •

That the old story of high prices is
worrying some of us again.

• • •

That the sight of the grocery advertisements in
New York papers makes one's mouth water.

• • •

That eggs are selling there for
twenty-one cents a dozen.

• • •

That the two-day sea voyage to Bermuda so
swells their heads that they won't be sold
here for less than sixty-five cents.

• • •

That a wise visitor has said our shop-keepers
have acquired a surfeit of "in-laws."

• • •

That too many wine-dealers, commission merchants, and grocery magnates have married the

daughters of wine-dealers, commission merchants,
and grocery magnates.

• • •

That their motto seems to be "United
we prosper, divided prices fall."

Familiar as he was with the local high cost of living, McNear
leaned back in his seat and laughed heartily.

He was still chuckling when the door to his compartment
opened and the conductor entered.

Watching McNear's mirth, the conductor wore a hopeful expression of sharing in it, an expression so human and naive that
McNear showed him the column and waited for the ticket-taker to
laugh with him.

On the contrary, the conductor was grave and thoughtful. "So
they believe that Collins man didn't murder that poor Miss
Hawkins, after all?" he asked.

"Well," McNear answered guardedly, "the department may have
some reason for further investigation."

"You see, sir," the conductor said, coughing a little apologetically, "I happen to have a special interest in this case—I took a
little part in it, as you might say. That red handbag that was tossed
off the train—"

"Oh, I see," McNear nodded with sudden comprehension.
"You're the conductor who told Superintendent Welch about seeing it fly through the window."

The conductor beamed. "That's it, sir! I'm Hedgelock on Number 14."

"Superintendent Welch sets great store by that clue you gave
him," McNear said in a friendly voice.

The conductor was delighted and a little surprised. "Does he,
sir? You know, I've been wondering. The Superintendent—and a
very civil spoken man he is, too—he said that if there was anything
at all I remembered, no matter how small it seemed to me, that I
should tell him about it."

"Yes?" McNear listened calmly.

"Well, sir. I know the Superintendent's a busy man and I'd rather not bother him with a trifle. But I've been racking my memory, sir, and it seems to me that there was a small child sittin' with that woman in the back seat of the first-class compartment."

McNear blinked. This information might be of the highest value, he could see. "You don't remember what the child or the woman looked like?"

The conductor laughed deprecatingly. "Well, sir, a passenger's not much more than a ticket to me, if they're strangers, that is. That's the reason I forgot about the child—because it was under age and rode free."

"Was the child a girl or a boy?" McNear asked.

The conductor scratched his ear. "It was too little for me to notice that, sir."

"And that's the only recollection you have?"

"The one and only," the conductor admitted. "But if you see the Superintendent and think it worth repeating—"

"I'll see him," McNear said gratefully, "and I'll certainly tell him. This may be very valuable, Mr. Hedgelock."

"I hope so," the conductor said and passed on. McNear sat thoughtfully considering this new bit of information. Was the woman who had been on the train the same woman who had tried to murder Welch? If that were true, then she must have been an accomplice to the murder. Or could she be the Marsden child's kidnapper? If not, then what crime had she been connected with? Was it the original bond theft in Boston, or the robbery from the *Baledonia*. Or had she, on the other hand, nothing to do with any of these crimes? If—was—or—but! McNear blinked. If she was not involved in any crimes, these or any others, then why had she tried to murder the first police officer who appeared at the cottage to question her?

McNear glanced out of the window of the slowly moving train. The blue and green panorama of sky and sea unrolled endlessly. From the high vantage of the railway bed he could see the full sweep of shoreline from Ireland Island to St. Catherine's Point.

A thousand ragged little coves, lusty mouthfuls bitten out by the avid jaws of time, indented the mainland. And, between the tracks and the water, hedges of varicoloured oleander spread great masses of pink and white and red over the countryside, brightening the prevailing hue of intensely green grass and shadow-soaked cedar.

Out to sea, which was calm and reflective as a mirror, the magnificent *Queen of Bermuda* slipped along the narrow channel, New York bound. Her three black and scarlet funnels poured out a light smoky haze against the sky as her smooth turbines increased their revolutions. Soon, only a little while after the train had dropped McNear at St. George's, the great liner would be only a faint grey dot on the enormous breadth of the Atlantic.

McNear watched the liner and thought grimly of the dark-faced woman. Somewhere on these small Islands she had gone into hiding. And on these Islands she would remain until she had been found. For, since she had left the cruise ship, she would be without a ticket entitling her to return to America. And all the shipping agents had been instructed, from the previous afternoon when the search had begun, to report immediately to Headquarters if an application was made to them for such passage.

This fact was further buttressed by a peculiarity of Bermuda law. And McNear, as he reflected on it, felt still more sure that the woman would have to remain on the Islands until discovered. For some years the local government and the shipping lines had been put to the expense of returning home indigent tourists from the States who had arrived in Bermuda with a one-way ticket and, promptly proceeding to spend what little money they had, had left the small matter of their return transportation in the lap of their guardian angels.

This had happened so frequently that at last the government decreed that nobody—British or foreigner, rich or poor—should be permitted to visit the Islands without a return ticket or a bona fide continuing passage to some other port.

A Bermudian, of course, was not bound by this restriction; it therefore followed that the buying by a non-resident of a one-way ticket to the outside world was a rare occurrence. And when that rare occurrence came, McNear knew, a constable would soon be at hand to investigate.

The train came to a jerky halt at Bailey's Bay and half the seats in McNear's compartment were emptied as the tourists crowded out on the platform and began to debate where they would go first—there was the Swizzle Inn for drink, the Castle Grotto and Leamington Cave for scenery and Tom Moore's house for literary history as well as food.

They were still pleasantly wrangling when the train started forward. McNear leaned out, watching them good-naturedly, and before he realized it he was closely approaching St. George's, the ancient capital of Bermuda.

Bidding good-bye to Hedgelock at the station, McNear walked briskly up Stile Hill, then made his way through York Street till he presently was within sight of the squat-faced police station of St. George's.

He was greeted by an involuntary murmur of surprise and mild consternation, for his sudden appearance usually indicated that he was on a visit of inspection.

The Sergeant in charge hurried forward to greet him with a very deferential salute.

"How are you, Inspector? Mighty glad to see you!"

They shook hands and McNear, glancing about, nodded warmly to the small group of constables who had been lounging about.

After a few minutes' attention to routine police affairs and a while longer of listening to those inter-family complaints which inevitably float upward through a police force, McNear briefly explained his business to the Sergeant in charge.

The Sergeant, a red-faced forthright man not unlike McNear himself, shook his head dubiously. "St. George's would be a harder place for the woman to hide in, sir, than Hamilton itself!" he pointed out. "We're smaller here. We don't get so many strangers as you do and people who don't belong here are noticed rather quickly."

"So much the better," McNear said. "'Twill make it that much easier to find her. The woman has been here, that we know from the railway stubs we found in her bedroom. She has been here three times in the past six days so there must be something more than mere sightseeing that brings her over here. Without insulting your fine old town, I might say that an ordinary tourist can see all there is to be seen in less time than that, eh?"

The Sergeant smiled broadly at this friendly dig. No love is lost between the inhabitants of the two principal places of trade in Bermuda. St. George's will never forget the ignominious day when the seat of government was removed over the fierce protests of her people, to the upstart town of Hamilton, which has since grown and flourished like the green bay tree. And Hamilton will long remember that from the time of prohibition in the States, St. George's captured almost the whole of the bootleg industry.

"Well, sir," the Sergeant said, "if she's here and if you can give us a hint of what she looks like I expect we'll find her."

"The description we have of her," McNear explained, "came from the Captain of the *Baledonia*." He took his little grey notebook and read a copy of the wireless aloud. "Not much to go on, I'll admit," he added.

"Not much," the Sergeant agreed. "Sort of a thin, sharp woman, eh? Well, I'll inquire around amongst the constables if they've seen anyone who looks like that."

McNear looked at his watch. It was twenty minutes past four. He put it away, saying, "I'll be back about six, Sergeant. Try to have all the information you can get hold of on hand for me." Stirred by the attack on Superintendent Welch, the Sergeant promised fervently and McNear knew he would do his best.

Leaving the police station, McNear walked through to Water Street and presently found himself on King Square. He was in search of information and eager to talk to anyone who might supply it. Seeing the beckoning sign of the Somers Inn, he crossed to it and went through the friendly tap-room to the still friendlier bar.

A bleak Scotsman with a Roman nose and shaggy beard was leaning against the bar and McNear recognized him as Colin Montross, an old acquaintance.

"Here," McNear said as he flipped a coin and nodded to the glass gripped in Montross's hand, "I'm paying for that one."

Montross winked toward the bartender and chuckled at McNear. "Ye pay for the next, Inspector, and I'll hae a guid drink!"

McNear laughed and they clinked glasses. "Here's how."

"Ne'er sae die!" Montross answered, squaring off so as the better to drain his liquor at a gulp.

"What's new around here?" McNear inquired when he had pushed his empty glass toward the bartender.

"'Tis the same auld thing—all St. George's worritin' their heids for the deepenin' of the channel sae that grand and bonnier bootleg ships can come up inta St. George's!"

McNear grinned. "That ought to interest you, too," he said. "Or aren't you still the agent for that Scotch distillery trust?"

"That I am," Montross answered. "And if the government itself should pay for the worrk 'twould be certainly bonny!"

"Why don't your people pay for it themselves?" McNear suggested. "Deepen the channel so you could bring ten thousand tonners up to the dock. Those little fifty-foot motor-boats you use now must cost you a good bit in money and lost time."

"'Tis a verra fine plan, Inspector," Montross said, "but I think ma people back home wouldna' find it a guid investment the noo. Fra' the looks o' things in the States I juist gi' ye a month a' most afore yon prohibeeshun is sent full packin'!"

"What a sad day for St. George's that will be!" McNear said. For, as was well known, if liquor were legally permitted in the States, then three-fourths of St. George's shipping would be lost and the thud of whiskey cases being brought from bonded warehouses would no longer make sweet music on St. George's quays.

"Verra bad for puir St. George's," Montross agreed, "but not sae bad for us, mon. When prohibeeshun's over in the States you'll find me in New York sellin' more in a day than we sell hereabouts in a week!"

"That I believe," McNear admitted, then asked casually, "Have you seen Henry Hastings lately?" "He's no' been here this past week!"

"You're sure?" McNear inquired.

"Hoots, mon, isna Hastings the local dealer wi' mae whiskies?"

"That's odd," McNear said thoughtfully, "he told me he was here last Tuesday."

"Ye must ha' mistaken him, Inspector. I spoke tae him o'er the telephone twice last Tuesday. He was in Hamilton all that day."

McNear meditated. He was not surprised by his companion's words.

"Well, it's of no consequence," he said finally. "Maybe I did misunderstand him."

The cocktail hour was near and the bar began to fill up. McNear was sipping his last glass of whiskey when the door leading from the upper quarters of the inn burst open and a square-shouldered, square-jawed old tar in a blue pea-jacket and a rolling seaman's gait, came clumping into the room.

Espying McNear and Montross, the seaman elbowed his way through the crowd and made a place for himself at the bar beside them.

Montross thwacked the sailor on his broad back. "Weel, weel, Captain! Glad tae see ye! How d'ye feel?"

"Never felt better in me life!" the Captain thundered. And as if to prove the truth of his words he shouted to the bartender, "Drinks for the whole house, blast it, and don't forget the drinkers in the tap-room!"

At these cheering words the bar suddenly teemed with liveliness and the tap-room grew loud with shouts and laughter.

"To Captain Hawks!" a wizened loiterer shouted, holding his glass high.

"Down the hatch to Captain Hawks!" the bar responded.

"God's teeth!" McNear muttered in an undertone to the scandalized Scotsman. "What's got into the man? There must be thirty people he's treating to free drinks!"

"Aye," Montross agreed. "He's damned hospeetable a' o' a sudden. Acts like he's come intae a fortune!"

Captain Hawks slapped the bar commandingly. "Fill 'em up again!"

McNear glanced curiously over Montross' shoulder at the seaman. By that time Hawks was paying the bill for sixty-odd drinks and he did it with an open-handed gesture, though there had been a little difficulty in getting the money out of his pocket, for the roll of American bills was sizeable enough to choke a horse.

McNear' drew Montross aside. "I know these rum-boat captains are well paid, but doesn't that seem like a lot of money for one of them to have?"

"That it is," Montross nodded. "I canna' understand it. The mon worrks for Hastings and West in conjunction wi' oor combine in Scotland and he gets no pay like that!"

"Oh, well," McNear said, not wishing to make too great a point of his suspicion, "perhaps he carries money enough on hand so that he can take care of the business dealings when he unloads his cargo."

Montross glanced at him with friendly scorn. "It's no' oor money. We wadna trust a rum-boat captain wi' al' that money as far as the corner pub—much less oot in the midst o' the Atlantic Ocean!"

"In that case," McNear commented thoughtfully, "it seems a little hard to account for."

"It is so. Oor ships have aboord a factor sent out fra Scotland tae mind the brass. The Captain gets a guid wage, a verra guid wage, but naething to encourage reckless spendin' like Master Hawks is indulgin' in!"

"Humph," McNear said. It had just occurred to him that several of the people connected with Henry Hastings were basking in the sunshine of considerable gold of late. "What boat is Hawks captain of?" he asked.

"The *Maria Alba*. Ane o' oor best vessels, a wee bit bigger than most, aboot a hundred tons, she is—and fast. She gaes the roond trip to St. Pierre and back in seven di'."

McNear permitted himself a cynical smile. There was one fiction that all rum-runners persisted in, which was that their ships went directly to their declared destination and then, without dallying off the American coast, directly returned. Thus it was a usual sight to see in the daily shipping news such items as "British M.V. *Rangoon*, Capt. Harry West, master, 60 tons displacement, with crew of six, sailed today for St. Pierre, Micquelon," and four days later the same paper would print an item that the M.V. *Rangoon*, etc., "with crew of six, arrived today from St. Pierre, Micquelon"—thus having achieved the miraculous feat of sailing to the Grand Banks, unloading, and returning the nine hundred odd miles to Bermuda all in the space of four days!

McNear looked up at the clock over the bar and saw it was three minutes of six. Much as he would have liked to learn more of Captain Hawks's sudden access to wealth, he saw no way of making an investigation, and, being anxious to find out if the St. George's constables had learned anything, he bade good-bye to the Scottish distillery agent and returned to the police station.

"I've some news for you, sir," the Sergeant greeted him as he entered.

"Good," McNear said, and looked expectantly at Constable Jackson, who was standing beside the Sergeant and fairly bursting to make his report.

"Inspector," Jackson began in a sort of flurry, "the Sergeant here gave me that description—said had I seen anything of such a woman around here. Well, sir, is that what you want to know?"

"It is," McNear said. "Have you seen her?"

"I—I remember a woman who looked something like that, sir."

McNear drew up a chair and said, not unkindly, "Out with it, man!"

"It was yesterday, sir. I was watching a man who seemed to be loitering suspicious-like near Todd's Wharf. I stepped up to him and he explained that he was waiting for his brother. He said his brother was with a gang of stevedores loading a boat nearby. His story was straight enough, and after I gave him a caution against trespass I turned to go away. That was when I saw the woman, sir."

"Where was she?" McNear demanded.

"Walkin' along the shore line and goin' pretty fast, as I remember it."

"Scared, would you say?" the Sergeant prompted.

WILLOUGHBY SHARP

"Not scared," the Constable answered, "but walkin' sort of businesslike, you know, as if she knew where she was going and had to get there. I watched her a little while, but she was soon out of sight behind a shed. Not thinking much of it, I went on about my patrol."

"Come, man," McNear said reprovingly, "it can't be a common occurrence around here for women to go disappearing behind sheds!"

The Constable held his ground. "No, sir, that's true. But this woman, there wasn't any hanky-panky about her, sir. She was goin' about her business."

McNear frowned. "There aren't any houses along the beach there, are there?"

Constable Jackson shook his head.

"Was she carrying any luggage?" McNear asked.

"No, sir, no luggage," the Constable replied. "I'm sure of that because she didn't have room for any."

McNear stared at him quizzically. "And what do you mean by that?"

"You see," Constable Jackson explained, "she was carrying a parcel in both hands."

"What kind of a parcel?" McNear demanded. The matter of this strange woman walking rapidly along the waterfront was growing more and more absorbing.

"I don't know what kind," Jackson answered stolidly, "but it was wrapped up in purple paper."

"Purple paper?" McNear repeated incredulously. "Surely not purple paper!"

"Yes, sir," the Constable affirmed. "And it was the first paper of that shade I'd ever seen around here, sir."

"Hmmm," McNear said. "Shouldn't be hard to discover whether any of the St George's shops use purple wrapping paper for their parcels." He turned to the Sergeant and muttered, "Mrs. Sinclair left Greenleaf without any baggage. If she's the woman the Constable saw, that parcel may very well have contained some clothing. And in that case we ought to be able to find out where she bought it."

"That's true enough," the Sergeant agreed. "But it's after six o'clock and I'm afraid we won't be able to do anything about it till tomorrow, much as I'd like to get it over with tonight, for the shops are all closed."

"Excuse me," the Constable interrupted, "but I don't think, sir, that there was clothing in the package the woman was carrying."

"How do you come to that conclusion?" the Sergeant demanded with a superior air.

"Because," Constable Jackson explained, "it was a heavy, bulky package, sir. The woman held it upright in her two hands."

"Then it certainly wasn't clothing," McNear acknowledged, though his admission made him cast aside the little theory he had built. "Sounds more like something she was afraid might drop and break."

"That's right, sir," Constable Jackson nodded respectfully.

"Well, whatever the contents," said the Sergeant, who was growing hungry for his evening meal, "I'm afraid we'll have to wait till morning. And that being the case, Inspector, I can assure you of a welcome in my home for the night!"

"That's very kind of you," McNear accepted with a smile. "I'll ring up my wife and tell her not to wait up for me, because I want to get on with this business as soon as the stores open up in the morning, and it will be very handy if I stay here tonight."

Instructing the Constable to begin his search for the store from which the purple wrapping paper came early in the morning, the Sergeant and McNear left the police station for the Sergeant's house. There, after a hearty dinner, they spent the evening sitting about and smoking.

"Sergeant, do you know Captain Hawks?" McNear inquired after the Sergeant's wife had gone upstairs to bed.

The Sergeant knocked the ashes from his pipe. "You mean that rum-boat fellow?"

McNear nodded. "In command of the *Maria Alba*."

"Know him? Known him man and boy these twenty-five years. Matter of fact, when he was married a year ago, the wife and I attended his wedding."

"That so? Married a Bermuda girl, did he?"

"Married Susie Hartwell."

"Well, well," McNear was mildly surprised. "You don't mean old John Hartwell's daughter up near Printer's Alley?"

"The same."

"Well, well," McNear repeated. "I used to know Susie. So she's married, eh? Now there was a fiery little red-head for you, say fifteen years back!"

"That she was," the Sergeant agreed.

"Still live hereabouts?" McNear inquired.

"No," the Sergeant answered. "About a month ago she went off to Montreal to be with her sister Josie who owns a house up there."

"Hawks seems to be pretty well in funds," McNear commented. "I saw him at the Somers Inn bar this evening treating that whole crowd to drinks."

"So?" The Sergeant's voice was gravely thoughtful. "Only a few days ago I heard him complaining of hard times!"

"I don't believe it. He must have been humbugging you. But I will admit from the way he was handling his money," McNear said, "I imagined he hadn't had it very long—and that he wouldn't have it very long."

Beneath a yawn the Sergeant observed, "Easy come—easy go."

"Easy come," McNear answered, "but from where? That's what I want to know!"

Meanwhile it had grown late and the Sergeant was the kind of man who had gone to bed early and slept soundly so many nights of his quiet life that he would have been exhausted the next day if he had stayed up later than ten o'clock the night before. He yawned again. "Sorry, Inspector," he said, his facial muscles still contorted.

McNear took pity on him. "Show me to my bed, man!"

The Sergeant escorted him upstairs to his room, and while McNear was still contemplating the old-fashioned nightshirt which lay on the foot of the bed, the Sergeant yawningly departed for the night.

"Oh, well," McNear thought disappointedly as he was forced to close his investigations for the day, "maybe I'll make more headway in the morning." He tried to think, but suddenly found himself dozing without the strength to keep his eyes awake, and the next thing he realized it was morning with bright sunlight and the smell of kidney pie ascending from the kitchen.

The Sergeant and McNear were still at breakfast when there was a knock at the door and Constable Jackson arrived with his colleague, Constable Jones.

"It's about that purple wrapping paper, sir," Jones explained apologetically when the Sergeant's wife had led him into the dining-room. "I thought I remembered there was one place in St. George's where I'd seen that colour, so the first thing this morning I went there and routed out the proprietor from his bed up over the shop. And here it is, sir."

He handed McNear a large purple paper bag of fairly heavy construction. McNear looked up at Jackson. "This seem to be the same sort of thing that was wrapped around whatever the woman was carrying?"

"That it does, sir," Jackson answered.

"And does the proprietor remember the woman?"

"Yes, sir."

"And whatever it was she bought?"

"Yes, sir."

"What sort of shop is it, Constable?"

"It's the little dairy on Old Maid's Lane, sir, and what the woman bought was five bottles of milk."

18
SUPERCARGO ON THE *MARIA ALBA*

Thursday Morning, April 15th.

McNear jumped up and hurried for his helmet. Five bottles of milk! That signified a child! And the woman was escaping with it because she was the Marsden kidnapper? The solution struck him like a thunderclap. "Take me to where you last saw this woman," he directed Constable Jackson.

"Yes, sir." The Constable led the way down the street briskly.

In a few minutes they had reached Todd's Wharf and had turned aside along the beach.

"Is this the place where you lost sight of the woman?" McNear inquired as they halted near a ramshackly-looking shed.

"Yes, sir," Constable Jackson affirmed. "I was standing right over there"—he pointed to a spot a few yards distant—"when she passed out of sight behind that shed."

Inspector McNear walked over toward the dilapidated building. Its door swung with a sagging motion on corroded hinges; the window panes had been shattered by mischievous prowlers, and from inside came a mouldy breath of long disuse.

McNear gave a shove to the rickety door. At one time, evidently many years before, the shed had been used as a storehouse for a ship-chandler. There were piles of rotting canvas lying in untidy heaps, while strands of rotten rope festooned the walls. And now, added to the mouldy smell, was the odour of dried-up paint standing in rusty tins.

The policemen poked through the pieces of worthless junk.

"Nothing here, Constable," McNear muttered vexedly. "Let's look outside."

They emerged into the welcome sunlight. Glancing around, McNear took stock of their position.

There was a road overgrown with weeds and underbrush which ran in front of the shed toward the edge of the shore.

"Come on," McNear said, and led the way along it till the narrowing path disappeared in a thicket. McNear paused and scratched his ear. "Now where the devil are we?" he muttered.

"Must be near the water, sir," the Constable encouraged him.

McNear pushed his way through the scratchy tangle. After some minutes of slow movements he found himself standing on the edge of a quay.

The quay projected some distance out into the placid waters of the harbour and there was nothing in sight on either side.

"Here's where she must have come," the Constable said, "but what in the world she come here for is a mystery to me."

"Didn't you say," McNear thoughtfully demanded, "that a boat was loading near here when you saw her?"

"That's a fact," the Constable admitted, chagrined. "There was one—a bit to the east of here."

"Any other rum-boats about at that time?"

"As I said yesterday," the Constable answered, "I seem to remember a couple more masts sticking up out of the weeds around here—but I'm not sure."

"It doesn't matter—we can find out about that," McNear said shortly, and led the way back through the thicket. That the woman was now definitely traced to the rum-boats seemed pretty certain in his mind.

Striking the path, he walked rapidly to Water Street and along to the police station. He went inside and took up the telephone, at which he impatiently waited for a call to be put through to the King's Harbour Master.

The connection was made, and he said, "McNear speaking. Did any rummies sail last night, John?"

Evidently the answer pleased him.

"Fine," McNear said after a pause. "Not till this afternoon, eh?"

"Any other smaller craft dear during the night?" he asked next. That answer was also gratifying. "Much obliged, John."

Replacing the receiver, McNear turned to the Sergeant "That woman must have boarded one of the two or three ships that were loading yesterday up near Baxter's Bay."

"I'm glad you're getting somewhere, sir," the Sergeant complimented him.

McNear rubbed his hands together with unrestrained anticipation. "And now to find her!"

"You'll want a few constables to go with you, I presume?" the Sergeant suggested.

"Yes," McNear replied, "but not just yet—the rum-boats don't sail till late this afternoon."

"You don't want to let her get away from you, sir," the Sergeant said anxiously.

McNear smiled and rubbed his hands together again. "She won't get away."

The Harbour Master had informed him that three of the rum fleet were due to sail that afternoon at four o'clock. A glance at his watch showed McNear that it was now ten. Obviously, the woman intended to make her escape from the Islands in one of these ships and McNear had six hours in which to lay plans to prevent her.

Still holding the little grey notebook, which he had taken out to write down the names of the ships and their masters, McNear read to himself: "The *Henry VIII*, Captain Winscomb; the *Good Hope*, Captain Follansbee; the *Maria Alba*, Captain Hawks. Hmmm," he muttered to himself, "Captain Hawks again, eh?"

Leaving the police station, he set off at a leisurely pace towards King's Square. From there he could see the masts of three loading ships standing beside the long row of bonded warehouses. That they were the three boats named by the Harbour Master he had no doubt. But instead of continuing on in the direction of the waterfront, McNear turned abruptly and went toward the Somers Inn. As he crossed the square he chuckled in spite of himself, for he suddenly realized that nearly every clue he had come upon had been presented to him by a bartender or in a bar; and this, for a temperate drinking churchgoer, was a little disconcerting—but that was Bermuda!

It was early, and neither in bar nor tap-room was there any of that blustering good-fellowship of the previous evening. Save for a straggling few who leaned against the bar, the place was deserted.

McNear went to the middle of the bar and waited. When the bartender, having detached himself from the man he was talking to at the farther end of the bar, came up for his order, McNear said, "One small beer."

He leaned pensively on an elbow, and while the bartender turned to the beer spigot McNear thoughtfully surveyed the oil painting which, behind an array of enticing bottles, portrayed the piratical days of yore.

"Quiet today?" he engaged the barman in conversation when his drink was set before him.

"It is that," the barman agreed. "Always quiet of a morning. But if it was afternoon, now, it would be different. Three of 'em"— he jerked his thumb over his shoulder in the direction of which the three rum-boats were loading—"are goin' out on the slack tide and every man in the crews'll be in here for a last drink before they raise anchor."

"Well," McNear said, "they've a long trip ahead of them."

The bartender held up to the light a glass which he had been industriously polishing. Satisfied by its brilliance, he replaced it in one of the gleaming rows behind the bar. "They're a thirsty lot," he said in a philosophical voice. "You'd think they'd have enough of liquor, loadin' it, carryin' it, unloadin' it and comin' back for more. Every trip they go out with thousands of cases in the hold. But to watch 'em come in here for their last drink you'd think liquor was something new to 'em, not their bread and butter at all."

McNear chuckled. "They say familiarity breeds contempt—but not familiarity with liquor."

The bartender shook his head slowly, as if he found the contradictions of human nature too involved to cope with. "It's a funny world!"

McNear set his glass on the bar. "I suppose you know most of the men in the crews loading up for this afternoon?"

"Every man jack of 'em," the bartender declared. "Been here ten years now and it's few new faces I've seen in that time. You take the average sailor on a rum-boat and you'll find him stickin' pretty close to his job. Once he knows his way around, he gets good pay and he knows it's steady year-round work. Sure, I expect I could name off most of the crews to you, right out of my head."

That was a little farther than McNear needed the bartender to go. "Any of the *Maria Alba's* crew around now?" he inquired.

The bartender glanced about the room. "Don't see any of 'em this minute. But I'll stake my bottom shilling there'll be some of 'em in soon."

"Good," McNear said and leaned closer. "I've a little job of work on," he said confidentially, "and I need your help."

The bartender nodded. "Just tell me what to do, Inspector."

"When one of the crew from the *Maria Alba* comes in," McNear explained in a low voice, "I want you to point him out to me."

Again the bartender nodded. "Like to talk to him, would you?"

"I would," McNear admitted.

"I'll put him right alongside you," the bartender promised.

McNear ordered another small beer and waited. After about twenty minutes the door banged open and a man with a fresh thirst burst in.

The bartender gave McNear a surreptitious wink. The newcomer strode up to the brass rail, and the bartender, who was old at his trade, moved toward McNear, which swung the new man directly beside him.

"Morton, you're loaded early," the bartender said.

"Ah, I've just run in to wet my whistle," Morton answered, wiping the perspiration off his forehead. "Gimme a long, cool one."

The bartender turned away and concocted a frosted drink which he brought back and set before the sailor. "Morton," he said, "meet Inspector McNear."

Morton wiped his thick-palmed hand and thrust it forward. "Glad to have the pleasure—Inspector, lemme buy you a drink!"

McNear beamed genially. "If you'll let me buy the next one."

"I'll do that," Morton promised. "Never throwed a drink over my shoulder since I been big enough to hold a glass in one hand."

Thus established in that atmosphere of cameraderie which drinking establishments seem inevitably to produce in their patrons' bosoms, McNear and Morton began an amiable give and take of talk and fresh drinks.

"So you're going out on the slack tide?" McNear asked.

Morton nodded. "Yes, and it looks like we're in for dirty weather. The glass has been fallin' all day."

"I hope not," McNear commented sympathetically. "It must be pretty uncomfortable aboard those little cockleshells in a bad blow. Not much room to move about in, eh?"

"That's the word for it," Morton agreed. "Hell, you couldn't swing a cat below decks. And now, by Jeez, there won't be as much room as we had before." McNear's hand shook slightly as he lifted his glass, but he managed to keep his tone no more than ordinarily curious as he asked, "Extra cargo, I expect?"

Morton wiped his mouth. "The old man's wife—she's aboard this trip."

"Mrs. Hawks?" McNear inquired. "I should think you boys would be pleased to have a fine-looking woman like her aboard."

"Well," Morton said, "I guess I ain't got much of an eye for females, but—no disrespect, you understand—I wouldn't say there was anything very fine lookin' about Mrs. Hawks. Downright plain, I'd call her."

"Now that's a shame!" McNear looked disturbed. "I'll admit it's been some years since I've seen Mrs. Hawks—Susie Hartwell, as she was then—but she was pretty as a picture. She certainly must have changed."

"Can't say as to that," Morton answered indifferently. "I never laid eyes on her till last Tuesday night when she came aboard with the kid and had to have a special cabin rigged up for the both of 'em."

The kid! McNear's heart thumped fiercely. From all he had learned it seemed impossible that the woman aboard the *Maria*

Alba could be Mrs. Hawks. On the contrary, he was virtually certain she must be the missing Henrietta Sinclair. And the child, he felt certain he would discover, was the kidnapped Marsden baby. He said, "It must be a pretty baby if it's got red hair like its mother."

"Red hair?" The sailor looked astonished. "Did you say red hair like its mother?"

"I did," McNear asseverated. "What's so surprising about that?"

Morton bent his head and mulled over his drink a while. "Well, I can't say as to the kid—kids ain't much in my line and I wouldn't know even if it had green hair—but I can tell you right now that Mrs. Hawks ain't got red hair!"

McNear tried to look abashed. "Maybe you're right," he conceded. "I expect I was thinking of her red-headed sister. I know one of those Hartwell girls had red hair."

"Well, it wasn't the one the skipper married," Morton said morosely. "That Mrs. Hawks has got hair as black as our cat's. And I'll say she looks like a cat to me."

Black hair! McNear hesitated only long enough not to cause Morton to feel that he had been questioned. After ordering another drink and switching the conversation to the engrossing topic of the repeal of prohibition in the States, he excused himself and started for the police station, as morally certain that he was on the right track as if he had come face to face with the woman who was masquerading as the wife of Captain Hawks.

When the Sergeant heard the corroborating evidence McNear had gathered, he said, "Now, sir, hadn't we better get to business?"

McNear put a restraining hand on the Sergeant's arm. "Plenty of time, man. We'll give Hawks rope enough to hang himself. Then we'll cut him down."

The Sergeant stared, shuddering a little at McNear's cold-blooded phraseology. "But if he don't hang himself, sir?"

McNear chuckled. "He will, in a manner of speaking. We'll let him cast off just as he plans to do. Then, when he gets up past Ordnance Island where he can no longer deny that the means to take the woman off the Islands, we'll stop him and make him stand to while we climb aboard."

"I see, sir," the Sergeant admitted respectfully. "Only I hope if that woman's the one who tried to murder Superintendent Welch that she don't slip through our fingers!"

McNear was confident. "She won't!"

"And now"—McNear stood up—"to find a motor launch."

The Sergeant knew of several belonging to residents of St. George's, and they set out to commandeer one that would be suitable for size and speed.

But this was no easy matter and they were both reduced to grumbling over the fact that the Bermuda police had no harbour patrol. However, they found a trim, neat craft at last and with it the owner's permission to use the boat for as long as necessary.

By that time it was the middle of the afternoon and McNear began to choose his crew from among the available constables.

At ten minutes to four the Inspector, the Sergeant and six men went down to Commercial Wharf and began to climb aboard the borrowed motor-boat. They settled themselves in the cramped cockpit and waited expectantly.

"They're a tough lot, those rum-boat crews," the Sergeant said uneasily.

"We're all right," McNear quieted him. "If the whole crew were mixed up in this it might be different, but I think Hawks and the woman are the only two who know they're breaking the law."

They sat waiting for the shrill blending of whistles which would sound at four o'clock. Every week this parting salute rose from the harbour and filled the air above the stately, hill-terraced town of St. George. It was a message from all the craft in the harbour bidding Godspeed and good luck to their northbound rum-boat comrades, a message similar in sound and portent to what was heard in St. George's years ago, during the war between the American States, when the old port was the rendezvous of blockade runners to Confederate waters.

A whistle shrilled, another joined, the sound welled into such a blast that it was like a great organ with all stops jerked open at once.

Sitting in the cockpit, McNear could see the *Maria Alba* slowly warping away from her dock and falling in at the end of the little rum-boat armada heading toward the open sea.

"Push off," McNear commanded.

"Put-put-put," sounded the motor-launch's exhaust as the bow swung in a half-circle and headed outward.

The motor-boat drew nearer the *Maria Alba* as the rum-boat approached the Town Cut Channel.

"Overhaul her," McNear said, and the motor-boat spurted ahead till it was alongside the larger vessel.

"Stand by!" McNear bellowed from the bow to the *Maria Alba*.

The engines of the rum-boat slowed down and two constables began in a businesslike manner to lash the motor-boat fast to the *Maria Alba's* side.

McNear gave a jump and clambered up over the low deck.

Captain Hawks rolled toward him like an angry cloud, cursing. "What in hell's the meaning of this?"

"You'll soon find out!" McNear promised grimly, while the Sergeant and his constables started over the ship.

"Where's your clearance manifest?" McNear demanded.

Hawks turned sullenly and went below. He came back with the desired papers.

McNear scrutinized them. "I see you have one passenger."

"Aye!" Hawks muttered in a surly voice. "My wife!"

"Your wife, eh?" McNear challenged.

"Your wife," the Sergeant echoed. "Man, don't you mind not a month back when you told me your wife had gone to Montreal?"

Hawks glanced away in a furtive rage.

"Bring her up," McNear commanded.

"Come and see for yourselves!" Hawks sneered.

Closely followed by the Sergeant, McNear went below, close on the heels of Hawks.

"She's in yonder!" Hawks pointed to a cabin on the port side.

McNear approached the door and tapped. There was no answer. He rapped more loudly. Still there was no answer. Grasping the knob, he opened the door.

The room was empty.

McNear turned an accusing eye on Captain Hawks. "What's the meaning of this?" he thundered. "Where is this woman you call your wife?"

Hawks glared at him. "Find her yourself! She was in there a while back."

"Of course," McNear accused him, "you don't know where she is! Come, my man, you can't get away with such a cock and bull story!"

Jerking his whistle out of his tunic pocket McNear blew loudly.

Two constables came running up.

"Search this vessel from stem to stern," McNear roared, "and if there's any hindrance we'll turn the ship back to the docks!"

Reinforced by the others, the constables scattered about the small craft, digging among the bunks and cargo.

Meanwhile McNear and the Sergeant sat guarding Hawks in the latter's strangely deserted cabin.

Time passed. Hawks seemed to take up courage. "What d'ye think them constables'll find?" he jeered.

"The woman you call your wife," McNear answered imperturbably.

The Sergeant eyed Hawks sternly. He knew that the constables were then searching the hold and, being acquainted with rum-boats, he knew that the hold was filled with thousands of cases and burlap bags of liquor and wine. "They're doing a thorough job of it!" he warned Hawks.

Of a sudden there was a shout from below. Along the companion-way came sounds of a furious scuffle and the muttering of excited voices.

"Looks like they found her!" the Sergeant said.

Meanwhile McNear had sprung to the door.

Two husky constables were on either side, of the long-sought, black-haired Mrs. Henrietta Sinclair. Her sallow face was twisted with fury. Between kicks and attempted scratches she was making herself as troublesome as possible to her unhappy captors, who, pushing her through the doorway, stepped back with expressions of profound relief.

Still farther along the companionway came another constable, carrying a small bundle in his arms, from which could be heard infuriated wails.

"So you're found at last, Mrs. Sinclair!" McNear accused her. "And a pretty chase we've had to get you!"

The woman clamped her thin lips tight, but darted an apprehensive glance in the direction of the bundled child, which continued to scream in the constable's arms.

"Yes," McNear eyed her grimly, "you're soon going to learn that you can't go about hitting police superintendents over the head, madam!"

Mrs. Sinclair glared her silence.

"Sulky, eh?" McNear said in a goading tone. "Well, our questions can wait!"

Mrs. Sinclair's compressed lips moved slightly. "I want a lawyer!"

"You'll need one, especially when you try to explain how you came by that child!" McNear said grimly. Mrs. Sinclair turned on him, her hands like claws. "You—" The constables tightened their hold on her arms. McNear turned toward the Sergeant asking, "Where are the rest of the men?"

One of the constables answered. "They're going through the hold, Inspector. We found her in a little closet off the crew's quarters, and I guess the others are still looking for her."

"Call the men up," McNear directed. "And you, Constable Jackson," he charged the flustered young man who held the baby, "take good care of that child."

One of the constables departed on this errand. He had scarcely left the cabin when there were heavy footsteps and panting heard outside.

The constable returned, backing into the cabin and staring at an object which was being dragged along the companionway.

McNear ran to the door. "What's up?" he demanded.

Two of the brawny constables were carrying a hatless, plump little man with curly brown hair and a vacuous, almost child-like expression, on his unconscious face. His eyes were closed, and there was a smell of chloroform about his clothing.

"Damme, what's this?" McNear shouted and turned to the woman.

She stared sullenly at him. "I've never seen him before."

"No?" McNear shot at her. "Just enough to drug him with chloroform, eh?" A thought struck him. The man, in spite of his disheveled appearance, was not unlike the description of the Arthur Turnbull who was missing from the *Cedric*. "Oh, your accomplice, eh?"

The woman refused to let McNear meet her eyes.

"Bring him along," McNear directed. "And Hawks, my man, you too are going to see the inside of the Hamilton gaol!"

19

THE ARMCHAIR INVESTIGATOR

Thursday Night, April 15th.

Restraining his exuberance, Inspector McNear, out of consideration for his ailing friend, tapped on the panel of Welch's cottage door very gently. He held his helmet under his arm, and, while there was a look of ready commiseration on his face, his smile was broadly confident. For, in the flash of cablegrams and wireless conversations between New York and Bermuda, the Marsden child had been almost positively identified. Also, Captain Hawks and Mrs. Sinclair had been securely lodged behind steel bars in the Hamilton gaol; the man suspected of being the missing Turnbull from the *Cedric* was under heavy guard in the hospital. And Henry Hastings, though he had been released from his cell, was under a bond of a thousand pounds. After so many baffling results of the last few days it was a great relief and not a little source of pride for Inspector McNear to have so many suspects within reach. Moreover, he was anticipating the privilege of telling the Superintendent that his vicious assailant had been captured.

Mrs. Howe came to the door. Her preoccupied frown cleared a little as she recognized the visitor.

"Come in, Inspector," she invited McNear. "The Superintendent is sitting up, and I hope it will do him good to see you—very restless he is!"

"He'll be the better for this visit, ma'am," McNear said, bubbling with confidence. "I have much to tell him that he'll be glad to hear!"

"No doubt!" Mrs. Howe said a little dubiously. "But he must not be excited, Inspector. Those were Dr. Jenkins's particular orders!"

"That he won't be," McNear promised meekly. Finally he was let into the house and shepherded up the stairs to Welch's bedroom, where he found his friend looking more like an invalid than he had feared.

Welch sat wanly in an armchair. He was wearing a dressing gown and was swaddled with quilts and hot water bottles. His head was profusely bandaged, but there was a pleased, excited gleam in his eyes as he saw Inspector McNear.

"Sit down, Mac! Thought you'd come to bury me, eh? Is that what you look so delighted about? Out with it!"

"It's all over but the finish!" McNear beamed. "We found the Sinclair woman trying to escape from the Islands on a rummy, and she had the Marsden baby with her! Got her locked up now! Matter of fact, we've bagged them all!"

Welch grasped the Inspector's hand in a warm, congratulatory clasp.

"How'd you do it?" Welch leaned forward, listening closely and anxiously to the Inspector's account of the capture.

At last, when McNear had finished, Welch said, "So now you suspect that Sinclair woman of a third crime—since Pamela Hawkins was the Marsden child's nurse?"

"Right." McNear was triumphant. "And when we can make that Turnbull talk I think we'll be able to pin the murder on the two of them."

"They had a motive all right," Welch admitted cautiously.

"Sure," McNear agreed with conviction, "the Sinclair woman comes here with the Marsden kid, expecting to hide until the ransom is paid. She'd have gotten away with it, too, if the nurse hadn't recognized her—and that was the end of Pamela Hawkins!"

"Umm," Welch considered. "If this fellow Turnbull was in on it, he'd have recognized Pamela Hawkins on the *Cedric*." He paused. "Turnbull's description fits the missing man's, does it?"

"To a T," McNear assured him. "And I'll tell you something else—My guess is that they'll squeal on each other when we get 'em up before the Chief of Police."

"You mean," Welch asked, "because you found Turnbull chloroformed?"

McNear nodded. "They'd evidently fallen out and she was trying to get rid of him."

"It would seem that way," Welch answered noncommittally.

His silence irritated McNear. "There's no doubt that's the way it was," McNear said a little impatiently.

"You hadn't any doubt about Collins either," Welch reminded him.

McNear grinned, shamefaced. "We've got something to go on this time," he defended himself. "Plain sailing, too," he went on. "You're just not well; otherwise you'd see it right off!" But in spite of himself, McNear looked at Welch a little uncertainly.

Welch smiled. "I hope you're right, Mac. But if you had some proof that Turnbull had access to those lilies in Collins' cabin and knew about the bonds I'd feel more sure of it."

"We'll get all that tomorrow!" McNear said confidently.

"Then you don't suspect Henry Hastings any more?" Welch asked slyly.

McNear looked moody. "I must say," he muttered, "Henry Hastings acted pretty queer—but I guess you can explain that by his habit of trifling with the ladies."

"According to the Chief of Police," Welch mused aloud, with a private little smile, "Hastings lied like a trooper, and not a very good one. And every time he'd try to work himself out of one tight corner he'd get himself stuck in another one. Now, I'm not saying you're wrong to suspect Turnbull. But I do say that Hastings made some admissions there that any jury could look at only in one way— guilty without the shadow of a doubt."

McNear squirmed uncomfortably on the straight-backed Windsor chair. "But you don't think Henry Hastings is guilty?" he challenged.

"Of Pamela Hawkins's murder?" Welch asked quietly. "He admitted he had a date with her at half-past six at Darrell's Wharf on the morning she was killed."

McNear looked at him sharply. "But you don't think that means anything?"

"On the contrary," Welch said seriously, "I think it means a devil of a lot."

"But he didn't keep the date," McNear protested.

"He hasn't proved he didn't keep it," Welch countered.

McNear nodded reluctantly.

"By his own admission," Welch went on, "he knew that the girl was to be at Darrell's Wharf at that time. And as Masters pointed out, he could have committed the murder, he could have taken the train he said he missed at the Hamilton Terminus, he could have got off at the Aquarium Station to dispose of the bag, he could have gone back to the station and picked up the next train, which would have got him into St. George's before half-past eight that morning. As a matter of fact, it looks pretty black for him."

"And there's another thing," McNear added, falling in with Welch's train of reasoning, "the *Maria Alba*—that's Captain Hawks' ship—carried consignments of Hastings and West's liquor!"

Welch acknowledged this contribution with an amused smile. "That's true. Also, Hastings has the familiarity with the Islands which the murderer must have had."

"That's a fact," McNear added. "I expect he's bicycled over every acre of ground that has a road running through it."

"Also," Welch proceeded, "it could probably be proved that he had easy access to the *Baledonia*. A man like that who makes it a business of meeting the tourists would have been entertained as much aboard the cruise ships as he entertained passengers ashore."

"I don't doubt that," McNear agreed.

Welch suddenly laughed outright. "Which is it, then, Hastings or Turnbull?"

McNear looked embarrassed and scratched his head. "You got me all turned around, didn't you? What're you trying to prove, anyway?"

Welch grew sober. "I'm trying to show you that whoever committed the murder—whether it was Turnbull, Hastings or someone unknown—was able to get into Collins' cabin without much trouble, and unless we can prove that against one of the suspects we haven't any case."

"But that cabin was broken into, man!" McNear reminded him. "It could have been done by a visitor from ashore as easily as by a passenger."

Welch demurred. "The cabin," he pointed out, "was broken into the *second* time it was entered, but not the first time." He leaned forward, letting the pillows slip from behind his head. "Whoever removed those lilies from Collins' cabin must have had a key!"

"Hell!" McNear scratched his cheek. "I'd forgotten about that!" He puffed away perplexedly. "Then who—?" he burst out.

"I'm not saying Hastings isn't guilty," Welch said; "I'm only pointing out one or two pieces of evidence that don't seem to fit."

McNear jerked exasperatedly at his ear. "But, Welch," he protested, "you've got to admit that somebody killed that poor Hawkins girl!"

"The man I'm looking for," Welch replied imperturbably, "is the man who knew about those bonds—"

"Collins?" McNear interrupted, with a startled gasp.

Welch shook his head. "Collins is dead and buried. The man we want is, I hope, still very much alive. And he knew a good deal more about those bonds than Collins knew—he knew the ones that were registered and the ones that weren't."

"But, Welch," McNear interrupted again, "you're not suspecting anyone at Headquarters, are you?"

"If the trail leads to Headquarters, I am," Welch answered. "But so far I don't see any indication of it."

McNear laughed ruefully. "Nor I."

"The man I'm looking for—" Welch began again.

This time it was the turning of the door-knob to his bedroom that interrupted him.

Mrs. Howe came inside and surveyed the Inspector sternly. "Do you know what time it is?"

Welch tried to forestall her. "Official business! Official business!" he defended himself.

"Your official grandmother!" Mrs. Howe surveyed him with quiet steadfastness. "It's ten o'clock and you two have been talking for hours! Inspector, it's time this man was in bed."

"Nonsense," Welch protested.

"Call it nonsense to Dr. Jenkins," Mrs. Howe challenged. "Inspector, off you go!"

McNear stood up embarrassedly and tucked his helmet under his arm. "Well," he said, with an attempt to regain his cocksure manner, "we've got two of 'em in gaol, another one under guard in the hospital and a fourth one under heavy bond."

"But that," Welch observed stubbornly, "doesn't solve the murder of Pamela Hawkins—"

McNear shook his head in bewildered agreement and turned toward the door.

"Oh, by the way—" Welch called after him.

"Not another word!" Mrs. Howe said firmly.

"—if you happen to see Hastings before he's called into the Chief's office, ask him why he chose such an out-of-the-way place as Darrell's Wharf for his date with Miss Hawkins."

"I'll let you know," McNear answered, and disappeared swiftly from Mrs. Howe's imminent reproaches.

20

TWO HANDFULS OF PRISONERS

Friday Morning, April 16th.

That morning Headquarters was exceptionally still, with a quietness foreboding an impending storm of guilty revelations. From the Sergeant in charge, behind the iron wicket of his desk, to the bedraggled janitor who moved about with mop and pail, everybody was covertly watchful and talk was at a whispered minimum.

In the main hall, on a straight-backed chair outside the office of the Sergeant in charge, Henry Hastings sat stiffly, trying to assume an air of composure, but unable to keep from turning his head to left and right and fiddling with his neatly fitting necktie and collar.

Walking quietly, Inspector McNear approached him.

Hastings sprang up.

"Sit down," McNear said in a low voice. "I'll let you know when the Chief is ready for you."

Hastings dropped to the chair again.

McNear stood watching him. Finally, he said, "Mr. Hastings, I've a question to ask!"

Hastings' lips crumpled nervelessly, and he put up his hand to steady them. "Ask it, Inspector."

"I want to know," McNear said, "how it was that you and Miss Hawkins happened to fix on Darrell's Wharf as a meeting place that morning?"

Hastings gave a sickly grin. "Why, she—she said she had an important engagement near there. It was the excuse she gave for

194

not meeting me when I first asked her to—and I said, 'Well, that's all right, I can meet you there as well as any other place, and we can have a picnic somewhere around there.'"

"I see," McNear muttered, though he didn't see at all.

"That clear things up?" Hastings asked with piteous hope.

McNear nodded non-committally. "You'll find that out soon."

Leaving Hastings, he walked to the telephone and called Welch.

Mrs. Howe demurred at first at calling the convalescing man to the telephone, but yielded finally when McNear stressed the urgency of the matter. Welch, apparently, had been close at hand, for he answered almost immediately.

McNear repeated what Hastings had told him and was further mystified to hear Welch say in a tone of satisfaction, "Just what I thought!"

"Now you know who the murderer is, I suppose?" McNear said sarcastically over the wire.

"No, damn it!" he heard Welch mutter. "I don't!"

McNear backed away from the telephone and wandered about the hall, looking at his watch. A few minutes later he went quietly upstairs and opened the Chief of Police's door.

Masters, lean and stiff in his tight blue uniform, sat before his flat-topped desk, preparing his examination with the grimness of a Grand Inquisitor. He nodded sharply to McNear, saying, "Bring in the Sinclair woman!"

McNear turned back to the door.

"And, McNear," the Chief of Police added, "fetch the stenographer as well."

McNear saluted and went downstairs again to one of the cells under the charge of the Police Matron.

Mrs. Sinclair prowled restlessly from one barred wall to another, her fingers gripped tensely as curved steel talons.

The turnkey, who had come with McNear, opened the door and stood aside while the prisoner passed by. With a stealthy pace, she followed McNear down the corridor.

They passed the open door of the detention-room where Arthur Turnbull reclined on a couch under the guard of a constable.

Turnbull, McNear noted, looked dazed, his plump, baby face a sickly grey.

McNear turned the knob to Masters' office, and Mrs. Sinclair swished past him.

The night's detention had apparently made no impression on either the spirits or the appearance of Mrs. Sinclair. She was still the cold, steel traplike person of the previous day. Even the sombre black garments which she affected were in as good order as if they had just come from the tailor's iron. Her raven hair, combed into a severe, old-fashioned coiffure, the sinister appearance of her thin face and her green eyes, had a malignant glitter as she faced the trim, blue-jacketed figure behind the desk.

"Take a chair, madam," Masters directed sternly.

The woman seated herself with the angular stiffness of a rusty jack-knife.

"Mrs. Henrietta Sinclair," Masters began, "you are accused of feloniously attacking our Superintendent of Police; you are accused of entering this colony without adhering to our immigration laws; and, finally, you are accused of inducing Captain Hawks to swear to an untrue manifest to enable you to escape from our jurisdiction!"

The woman listened with a scornful smile, but said nothing.

"Have you anything to say to these charges?" Masters demanded.

Mrs. Sinclair glared at him. "I didn't attack your Superintendent of Police," she answered in a rasping voice. "If I broke your fool immigration laws it was because I didn't know about them. I missed my ship through no fault of my own, and when I wished to leave this Island I arranged with Captain Hawks to take me to St. Pierre. There's no Bermuda law, I presume," she asked acidly, "that says what ship I had to leave on?"

"No, madam, there is none. But I must ask why you persuaded Captain Hawks to claim you as his wife if you were not leaving these Islands as a fugitive?"

The woman's only reply was an evil glare.

"Moreover," Masters continued, "we have Hawks' statement that you paid him a thousand dollars as passage money. Any of the regular ship-lines would have returned you to New York for about forty dollars. Now, don't you think that's an extraordinary procedure to pay so much—"

"I didn't want to go to New York," Mrs. Sinclair broke in angrily.

"Ah!" Masters dexterously caught her unintentional admission. "You didn't want to go back to New York! Why?"

Mrs. Sinclair tightened her lips in fierce vexation and said nothing.

"Never mind," Masters said, with satanic leniency, "you feared discovery, was that it?"

Mrs. Sinclair continued silent.

"You feared discovery in New York and yet you were so anxious to leave Bermuda that you paid a thousand dollars for passage to St. Pierre. Madam," he said coldly, "you are in a rather bad position!"

Mrs. Sinclair merely glared.

"Bring in the man Turnbull," Masters said abruptly, and leaned back in his chair, waiting.

A few minutes later the arrival of Turnbull broke the tense atmosphere. He walked in groggily, on the arm of a constable, and sat down in the first chair he came to.

Masters stiffened behind his desk and fixed Turnbull with stern, cold eyes. "Your name is Arthur Turnbull?"

The man nodded.

"Turnbull, you are charged with having entered this colony without having adhered to our immigration laws. What have you to say for yourself?"

"It's true," Turnbull murmured unhappily.

"And you were later found trying to escape as a stowaway—in the company, of your fellow-criminal, Mrs. Sinclair!"

Before Turnbull could answer, Mrs. Sinclair stood up angrily. "If you mix me up with that fool, you're crazy!"

"Sit down!" the Chief of Police roared. He turned to Turnbull, who was sitting in meek silence, holding his head with both hands. "My man!" he sternly began, taking the line that there had been a falling out between the woman and Turnbull, "you doubtless realize what you're up against. There has been murder done. It lies between you and your accomplice there. Now, the sooner you tell the truth, the better! Who—killed—Pamela—Hawkins?"

To this menacing attack Arthur Turnbull reacted surprisingly. "Go gently," he pleaded in a low, harassed voice. "I'll explain, but oh! my head, my head!"

"Ah!" Masters' little breath of satisfaction as he sat dominating the scene was quite audible.

But to the astonishment of everyone, Turnbull leaned forward and began to unfasten his shoe. Unlaced, he gave a short but weary tug and pulled it off. Setting the shoe on his knee and without so much as a by-your-leave, he reached for the paper-cutter from the desk and began to pry up the inner lining of the sole.

"What the devil!" Masters exploded irritably.

The constable, acting on the supposition that Turnbull was about to produce a poison with which he would do away with himself, sprang forward and grasped the man's arms.

"Please!" Turnbull objected weakly. "My head!"

At a sign from his superior the constable released him, and Turnbull took out a wad of tightly pressed paper from which dangled a red seal and began to unfold it with fussy carefulness.

"I'll take that, please!" Masters held his hand forth authoritatively.

Mrs. Sinclair started involuntarily at Turnbull's actions. She watched the paper with sullen, suspicious eyes.

Taking the paper, which Turnbull gave up with a sigh of relief, Masters' perusing eyes flashed out a swift series of expressions so that it was impossible even to guess the import of what he read. But his final and most lasting emotion was chagrin.

"Well, sir," he said in a dry, exasperated voice, "perhaps you'll now tell me the meaning of this!"

"If it wasn't for my head—" Turnbull answered, and cast a look of weary loathing at Mrs. Sinclair. "Damn it, madam," he complained, "do you know you almost killed me with the strength of that chloroform!"

The woman glared at him in silence.

"Here," Masters said, and took out of his drawer a whiskey flask which he handed to Turnbull.

Turnbull drank it eagerly. He announced as he carefully wiped his lips, "Feel a little better now." He meekly looked from one person to another, all of whom were staring at him as if he were a composite of an ancient Egyptian mummy and a purple cow.

"It all started," Turnbull began with a sad, shamefaced air, "when someone—an American passenger from the *Cedric*—pointed out Pamela Hawkins to me aboard the tender that was taking me to shore—"

To McNear the name of the murdered girl was like an electric shock. He sat bolt upright, staring.

"Up to that time," Turnbull continued, "I had expected to spent a quiet week-end vacation in Bermuda. But the fact that the girl had been the Marsden nurse set me to watching her pretty closely—so that when our tender came up to the wharf a minute or so behind the tender from the *Baledonia* and Miss Hawkins suddenly grasped the rail and went white as a sheet, I began to look about and see what had startled her so."

Turnbull paused and glanced at Mrs. Sinclair. "Obviously it was someone who had got off the *Baledonia's* tender, and it didn't take long to guess who it was—because in the middle of the crowd was a woman carrying a small child in her arms." Indicating Mrs. Sinclair, the Chief of Police demanded sharply, "It was this woman that you saw?"

"It was," Turnbull answered. "And if she hadn't gone off in a carriage just as our tender was landing I fancy most of the crimes of the past week would have been prevented—because I'd have had the lady cooped up in gaol awaiting the arrival of the New York police!"

McNear stared wonderingly at Turnbull, trying to guess who the man might be.

It was Masters who enlightened McNear by saying to Turnbull, "You should have come to us, Chief-Inspector! To play a lone hand at a time like that was a very risky business."

McNear gaped. "Inspector!"

Masters answered coldly, "Chief-Inspector Arthur Turnbull of the Montreal police." McNear sat back in astonished silence.

"I know," Turnbull humbly admitted, "I should have told you, even though it was only a suspicion of mine. There was no proof that the child was the Marsden baby. And I'm too old a hand to leap to conclusions without more proof than a strange agitation on the part of an ex-nursemaid. Also, I must confess that it was my greed held me back as much as anything—you see, once started on the clue, I wanted the reward for myself."

"Ah, yes," Masters said, "the reward!"

"Anyway," Turnbull defended himself, "I'd lost her—and though I saw her again the next day—the day, by the way, that poor Pamela Hawkins was murdered—she managed to elude me. And that, without ever knowing that I was following her." He paused and turned suddenly on Mrs.. Sinclair, demanding, "Or did you?"

The woman arched like a spring, malignant fury burning in her eyes. But she held her tongue.

"You saw this woman," Masters demanded sternly, "the day Miss Hawkins was murdered?"

"Yes," Turnbull said, then quickly added, "but it was not till the following Monday that I knew she had been murdered—in fact, it wasn't till I read it in the Hamilton paper. And by that time, unfortunately, I had lost track of Mrs. Sinclair."

"And where did you see her?"

"On the railway train that goes to St. George's," Turnbull answered. "It was about half-past seven in the morning and I was walking along Front Street, looking out in the bay for the *Queen of Bermuda* which was due to dock that morning. I happened to turn as the train went past and I saw Mrs. Sinclair's face in one of the compartment windows."

McNear crossed over and bent down toward Masters, whispering in his ear, "Shall I get Hedgelock, Chief? That's the train the handbag was thrown from and he was the conductor who told us about it."

Masters shook his head and murmured, "As I recall it, the statement he made to Welch didn't assert that he had seen the woman actually throw the bag, so he couldn't prove any more than Inspector Turnbull has already proved—that she was aboard the train."

The Chief of Police looked up after his *sotto voce* conversation and addressed Turnbull, "You are positive of the time?"

"Perfectly," Turnbull replied. "Because the *Queen of Bermuda* was to dock at eight o'clock and she was nearly in."

Masters looked at him accusingly. "That's the time you should have come to us!"

"Granted," Turnbull agreed; "but you must remember I could then see no connection between the woman and the murder—in fact, it was only a couple of days ago when I read of the bag being found that I saw any connection at all. You must remember that this woman sat behind me in the railway carriage, therefore I did not see her throw anything from the window. Meanwhile, even the identity of the child was uncertain. I would have made a great fool of myself if, after coming to you and telling you the child was Marcia Marsden, it was later found to be Mrs. Sinclair's own offspring."

Mrs. Sinclair sat back with a complacent sneer.

"It was only after we had got on the boat, when I heard her talking to Hawks, that I was positive she had the kidnapped child."

Mrs. Sinclair's sneer became a feeble grimace.

"Well," Masters said, "we expect Mr. Marsden to arrive on Monday morning."

To that Mrs. Sinclair merely sneered again, though none too convincingly.

There was a discreet tapping at the door and a constable looked inside.

"Yes!" Masters said sharply.

"The people from the cruise ship, sir," the constable replied, "to identify the woman."

"Ask them to wait," the Chief instructed, and turned again to Turnbull. "I don't mean to belittle your accomplishment, Inspector, but as a Montreal police official—in fact, even as a private citizen—it is a pity that you let hope of the reward influence you to such an extent. And the result of all your secrecy is the death of Miss Hawkins, which might have been prevented, likewise Mrs. Sinclair's assault on Superintendent Welch! However, before you finally tracked this woman to the *Maria Alba*, did you discover anything that might connect her with the murder? Apart, I mean, from seeing her that time in the railway train."

"No," Turnbull answered reluctantly, "I'm sorry to say that I didn't."

McNear and Masters exchanged long looks of complete exasperation. For they both realized that the paramount question was the same now as it had been on the morning Pamela Hawkins' body had been found. It was, simply, where is the murderer?

There sounded a rapping at the door again and the constable apologetically peeped in. "If you please, sir, the cruise ship people—"

Masters bit vexatiously at his cigar. "Send them in," he said irritably. "Send them in—and as soon as they leave we'll have Hastings up here."

21
MURDER WILL OUT

Friday Morning, April 16th.
After his brief but satisfactory conversation with McNear, Welch hung up the telephone.

"The idea!" stormed Mrs. Howe as he guiltily shuffled past her toward his bedroom. "I told you not to get out of bed, and now look at you!"

"Official business," her brother protested by way of explanation. "Official business!"

"Official your grandmother!" Mrs. Howe grumbled, following him up the stairs. "Besides, it's time for your nine o'clock medicine!"

To Welch the voice of female persuasion was a power before which he could only submit. Getting quietly under the bedclothes, he meekly accepted his sister's ministrations.

"There," Mrs. Howe said, collecting glass, spoon and bottle, "and now stay in bed."

Welch lay still so long as his nurse remained within sight, but as soon as she left the room he sat up and began fiddling with the radio set which she had brought up by his bedside.

He had every reason to be proud of this set. Some weeks earlier, while reading his *New York Times*, he had seen an advertisement offering a well-known and expensive radio set at a ridiculously low price. It had been guaranteed to bring in all foreign stations and it was, according to Mrs. Howe, for whom the purchase had been made as a present, entirely satisfactory in that respect.

London, Paris, Rome and Berlin were received with the same case
and clarity at New York, Havana and Montreal.

Welch drew his dressing-gown more closely round him and sat
looking at the radio while he thought of the implications of what
McNear had told him. The fact that Pamela Hawkins had had a
previous engagement near the scene of the murder was an important clue. And the more he considered it the more important it
seemed. It was, he thought, as essential to an understanding of
the case as the discovery of the lilies. It was much more important
than the hat label. For that bit of cloth, he realized, was no sure
indication toward the murderer. It could have been sewn on the
hat by anyone whose interest it was to give the impression that the
girl had been in Bermuda for some time—that is, that she had not
come from one of the cruise ships. Moreover, it was not impossible that the girl had, as Masters had maintained, sewn on the
false label herself.

But that out-of-the-way meeting place! Welch frowned, exasperated with himself that he could make no definite connection
between this fact and the other clues at hand. Finally, in a kind of
desperation, he turned on the radio.

Music swelled forth. First, a piano duet, then a talk on home
economics followed by advertising, followed by a Spanish lesson,
followed by more advertising and finally topped off with hints on
cookery—all the usual, uninteresting programmes offered the
morning listener.

It was more than boring. Heretofore the press of business and
then his injury had kept Welch from anything but a cursory investigation of the radio's possibilities. He had often regretted it, but
with such a programme he regretted it no longer.

Still, with the insane perseverance that overtakes radio owners, he began turning the dial back and forth, going slowly up to
the highest kilowatt station and then, pausing a moment at each
broadcast, turning it slowly down again.

Lower and lower the numbers appeared on the dial. Still there
was nothing of interest, not even a croon from Rudy Vallee. He
realized, of course, that the time of day was unpropitious for a

broadcast of any pretension, but he did hope for some mildly acceptable entertainment. With the nervous impatience of the bedridden, he fumbled with the dial in a last frantic endeavour to find something to which he could listen without wanting to throw a shoe.

At the lowest wave length a tense stream of talk burst forth, one lone voice reaching across the Atlantic.

Welch listened idly. . . . And then some strange note in the broadcast struck response in his active mind. With the easily aroused interest of a radio fan he leaned forward, his boredom converted into rapt attention.

The voice droned on and on. But Welch sat stupefied with amazement, leaning nearer and nearer to the loud-speaker.

Drawn by the sound of the radio, Mrs. Howe came bustling in. As she saw Welch so actively employed she began to scold, "Back to your bed! Get under the covers!"

For once Welch failed to heed her. And there was something in his expression which made her join him and stand listening:

> "General Motors at 38
> Delaware and Hudson at 110
> Canadian Pacific at 26
> Lambert at 80
> Standard Oil at California at 49
> R. H. Macy at 90
> United Aircraft at 46
> North American at 50
> Chrysler at 48
> Pennsylva—"

Mrs. Howe stared at her brother in amazement. "Of all the non-sense!" she burst out, and abruptly snapped off the electric current.

"A fine thing for you to get yourself worked up over!" she scolded him. "A poor policeman listening to the stock market! Back to bed with you!"

As if entranced, Welch merely reached forward and turned the radio on again.

"Well!" Mrs. Howe said in an affronted voice. "The very idea!" She turned and stamped out of the sick-room, muttering retaliations when Dr. Jenkins arrived for his afternoon call.

Welch continued to listen to the rest of the stock quotations, and then to the four minutes of hurried speech that followed.

The Superintendent owned no stocks. The share markets of the world were as unfamiliar to him as to the veriest child. Yet this strange voice which came unbidden out of the ether, this voice of a man who was not even remotely concerned with any of the investigations of the Bermuda police, or with Pamela Hawkins, or with George Collins, the dead cashier—this voice which spoke of nothing but stock exchange affairs, made as dear as hot sunlight all there was to know of the bond theft aboard the *Baledonia*—and, by Welch's reasoning, the murder of Pamela Hawkins as well.

He jumped up and began dressing with a song in his heart and the name of the robber and murderer on his lips.

"Rowena!" he called to his scandalized sister, "I want a carriage!"

She came hurrying down the hall. "You'll get no such thing! You go back to bed!"

"I want a carriage!" he repeated firmly. "Hurry and order it or I'll have to walk!"

Their eyes met and clashed. Finally, comprehending the urgency of his actions, she gave in.

"Hurry!" he called after her and continued dressing.

Ten minutes later, in a brand new uniform, he went down the steps and through the garden gate to the carriage as it drove up. And the driver, giving his whip an extra flourish, started along the straight limestone highway, lined by grey, moss-encrusted walls and covered with flowering bougainvillæa and morning glory.

Welch reached Headquarters as a constable was escorting Henry Hastings up the steps to the Chief of Police's office. He followed quietly in the rear.

The door opened, then closed behind Hastings. During that brief moment Welch had a glimpse of Purser John McKnight and

one of the *Baledonia's* stewardesses. McKnight was standing in a
jaunty manner and the stewardess was making a half-curtsey before Masters who was questioning her.

"This is the woman," Masters was asking the stewardess, "who
occupied one of your cabins on the previous trip down—the woman
who so unfortunately missed the ship?"

"Yes, sir," the stewardess answered. "The lady was in 64-C, her
and her baby."

"You're positive of this?" Masters inquired.

Before the woman could repeat her assertion, Welch stepped
inside and looked around the room, smiling.

Masters' frown at the interruption broke into pleased surprise
as he recognized Welch. "Glad to see you back, Superintendent.
We've missed you. You're just in time to hear some interesting
revelations."

Welch asked in quick surprise, "You've got the murderer?"

"No," Masters said grimly, "but we've got his accomplice!"

Welch stepped farther into the room. He stood looking slowly
from one person to the other. Finally he said, "I think you've got
the murderer here, too, Chief!"

At these words the gasps of surprise and consternation were
like a sudden gust of air. Then the room became painfully tense
and silent.

"By ingenious efforts," Welch's sharp voice cut the stillness,
"Pamela Hawkins' murderer almost convinced the police that her
death was due to suicide. Later, through these same efforts, the
blame was shifted to the innocent shoulders of a dead man. Both
of these plans nearly succeeded. It was only the discovery of the
murdered girl's handbag far from the scene of the murder that
proved George Collins, even if guilty, must have had an accomplice who threw the bag along the railway track."

"We now know who tried to dispose of that bag," interrupted
the Chief of Police. Masters nodded tersely and then indicated
Inspector Turnbull. "This is the man who saw her on the train from
which it was thrown, Chief-Inspector Turnbull of the Montreal
police."

Too intent on his own story to be surprised at the identity of Turnbull, Welch briefly acknowledged the introduction and proceeded, glancing at Mrs. Sinclair as he began to speak:

"Last Friday afternoon the *Baledonia* docked for the week-end. That Friday night three people we should have been especially interested in stayed ashore till the next morning. George Collins went to the Blazing Star. Miss Hawkins, I think it can be proved, registered at one of our hotels. And Mrs. Sinclair, as a Mrs. Bigelow, rented Greenleaf Cottage."

Mrs. Sinclair, plucking nervously at her dress, refused to meet Welch's eyes. He continued, turning his gaze toward Henry Hastings:

"During that Friday night Miss Hawkins was seen by another person in whose movements we have become particularly interested. You saw Miss Hawkins," Welch demanded, turning on Hastings, "and talked to her, I believe, Mr. Hastings, and made an engagement to meet her next morning?"

Hastings bowed his head in a mournful nod. "Yes," he whispered.

"Before that, however," Welch continued, "Miss Hawkins had met ashore still another person whose movements are of the greatest interest to us—because, as I long suspected from the fact that the meeting place was so out of the way, Miss Hawkins had made a previous engagement to be at or near Darrell's Wharf at about six-thirty Saturday morning. How that person had made the acquaintance of Pamela Hawkins, and what excuse he gave for their early morning meeting, can be at present only conjecture. But possibly, being told by Mrs. Sinclair that Pamela had obviously recognized the child on the ship's tender, he may have sent word to the unfortunate girl that he also had discovered the kidnapper's presence and that he needed Pamela's aid in clinching the baby's identification."

Welch paused again and there were grim lines about his mouth. "We now come to that Saturday morning—the morning of the murder. People were stirring early that day, as early as dawn itself. Miss Hawkins had arrayed herself and had set out for her first appointment—which I rather think she approached with a troubled, but not suspicious, mind. Mr. Hastings, as he has told us, was bicycling to St. George's, having missed the six-thirty train. Mrs. Sinclair was also up and about; in fact, she was at the waterfront waiting for someone around seven o'clock.

"Only," Welch went on, looking about the tense assemblage, "only George Collins was still in bed—some miles away in his room at the Blazing Star. But while he slept, or tragically meditated on his crime, someone was stirring in his cabin on the *Baledonia* very early. At six, or even before, someone unlocked Collins's cabin, stole a bouquet of lilies—which suited his purpose—and left in a motor-boat, bound through Granaway Deep to Darrell's Wharf, where he docked a little before half-past six.

"And now"—Welch's blue eyes glittered ominously—"we are tracing the movements of the man whose acts are the most interesting to us, for this man is the murderer. With a long stiletto fitted in among the lilies, this man left his motor-boat and walked from Darrell's Wharf to Snake Road, where, as had been agreed upon, Miss Hawkins met him.

"The last scene we can readily picture. The unfortunate girl coming down the road, seeing the person she had agreed to meet, but no doubt deeply troubled by the gravity of the subject she had come to discuss. Then, the bouquet offered as an unexpected present. The girl reaching out her arm to receive it, perhaps with a little cry of pleasure. Then the cry turning to a death rattle as the murderer savagely pushed the hidden steel against her breast!"

Mrs. Sinclair shivered in spite of herself. Hastings held his head in his hands. McKnight, the purser, stared into the lining of his upturned cap. Chief Masters and McNear, along with Turnbull, watched Welch as if they were witnessing a grisly conjuring act.

"That, gentlemen," Welch continued, "is how Miss Hawkins was murdered. Whether her murderer stayed there long enough to sew that hat label in her dress or whether the girl had done it herself, I can't say. We know, however, that the murderer snatched up the girl's handbag and that he was so undecided what to do with it that he still had it in his possession when he met his accomplice,

Mrs. Sinclair, by previous agreement, that morning between seven and half-past.

"Nor," Welch went on, "can I account for all the various movements that took place from the time the murderer went on about his business until he made his first false step—but as that fatal mis-step was made the day following the murder, perhaps I won't need to.

"George Collins committed suicide on Saturday afternoon and his body was found late that night. Previously, however, Inspector McNear had traced the lilies at my suggestion, and had discovered they came from Collins's cabin—"

At this statement regarding the lilies Inspector Turnbull scratched his head and had such an expression of perplexity that McNear, in a brusquely muttered aside, said he would later explain to him how Welch had discovered the lilies were imported and therefore traceable to the cruise ships.

"And Collins's cabin," Welch continued, "had been locked. That key had been put in Purser McKnight's safe. However, between Saturday afternoon and Sunday morning, Collins' cabin was re-entered, ransacked and the bonds he had stolen from the Boston bank had disappeared. Very neatly, in place of the bonds, in the trunk from which they had been taken, was found the scabbard to the stiletto which had killed Miss Hawkins.

"Now that, I contend," Welch said with leisurely satisfaction of a hunter who had dropped his quarry and has only to stoop to bag it, "was a fatal mistake on the murderer's part. Knowing that Collins was suspected, he opened the trunk to put the scabbard in it, therefore increasing suspicion against Collins. And to his great surprise, and to what must soon be his great regret, he found hundreds of thousands in negotiable bonds and his cupidity was too great to leave them there. He stole those bonds—otherwise he might still be free of suspicion.

"Sooner or later," Welch continued, "those bonds would have been traced to the man who stole them. Due to the fact that ten of the bonds were registered and that those ten certificates were found on the person of Davis, the steward, discovery was sooner, that's all.

"For a while the finding of the bonds on Davis confused me, but not for long. I was favourably impressed with the man's story. For it seemed on the face of it wildly absurd that the man should have set off on a spree with precisely those bonds which were non-negotiable and which the Bermuda police had a record of! And from that the conclusion that someone had put them in his pocket while Davis was drunk was obvious."

"Ah, ha!" McNear boomed in a voice of triumphant awakening. "Ah, ha!"

"Exactly!" Welch said, following McNear's eyes to the Purser. "John McKnight, I hereby arrest you in the name of His Majesty the King and charge you with the murder of Pamela Hawkins, the theft of the bonds from George Collins's cabin and the kidnapping of Marcia—"

The Purser swung viciously around, his fist narrowly missing the Superintendent's chin. Before he could draw back again McNear and the burly police stenographer had started toward him.

McKnight's right hand, as he backed toward the door, crept menacingly toward his hip-pocket.

"Look out!" shouted Turnbull, and ignoring his own words leaped forward, striking McKnight's arm as he was about to level the pistol.

Meanwhile a constable had stepped forward with a lifted club, under the weight of which McKnight sagged to the floor.

22

THE WHYS AND WHEREFORES

Friday Morning, April 16th {continued).
Masters stood in the middle of his room and surveyed the little
company with a quizzical smile.

McKnight, heavily handcuffed, had been led away; Mrs. Sinclair
had been returned to her cell to await the arrival of the Marsdens;
Hawks had been remanded for a hearing before a magistrate; and
Hastings, with unconcealed joy, had been permitted to leave, the
clouds of suspicion cleared from about him.

"And now," Masters demanded of Welch, "how did you do it?"

Welch grinned. "I'd never have known except for this cracked
skull of mine."

"You mean," Turnbull suggested, "you had a lot of time for
thinking?"

"Thinking," Welch nodded, "but, more important, also for hearing."

His listeners sat at attention.

"As you probably know," Welch said, "anyone in Bermuda or
on a nearby ship can hear all wireless conversations from New York
simply by means of a short-wave wireless receiver. In other words,
our radio-telephone company hasn't yet gone to the expense of a
scrambler—a machine that makes the sound of the human voice
into an unrecognizable jumble while it's being carried through the
air and reconstructs it into normal tones when it's transferred to
the land wires.

"Well, one of the greatest mysteries in this case was how, when the telephone conversation from the New York police giving the numbers of those registered bonds was known only to us at Headquarters, how could these numbers have been known to an outsider—which was undoubtedly the case since those bonds and those only were found in Davis' pocket?

"It was the answer to that that solved the mystery. This morning I was lying in bed, listening to the radio and trying to get a decent programme. Finally I got disgusted and was about to switch it off when I heard a most peculiar broadcast. A voice would ask a question, then there would be a pause, and, without the first question having been answered, the voice would ask another. Then the voice recited a long list of stock quotations, followed by more questions interspersed with pauses. At last came the word that gave the solution. It was 'goodbye.'"

"Of course!" Masters ejaculated. "The wireless telephone!"

Welch nodded. "Someone here in Bermuda was instructing his New York broker to buy or sell at certain figures and I suddenly realized that was how the numbers of those certificates had been discovered. Somebody had been listening in on your wireless conversation with the Boston police!

"And then I remembered McKnight's interest in wireless, his continual presence in the wireless room of the *Baledonia*! And I knew that he was our man. Who else, I asked myself, would have been in so ideal a position to enter Collins' cabin. He already had the key which Inspector McNear had given him to put away for safe keeping till Collins returned, and even if he had been noticed entering or leaving the stateroom nobody aboard would have thought there was anything suspicious about it! And, as I have already pointed out, the man who stole the bonds must have been the man who put the scabbard, with its fingermarks wiped off, in Collins' trunk, and the man who put the scabbard in the trunk could be nobody but the murderer!"

"You're right," McNear said, gazing admiringly at Welch. "And I can tell you when he put the marked bonds in Davis' pocket—it was Easter Sunday, when I went with him to arrest Davis who was on a drunken spree, and in the scuffle McKnight slipped the package into Davis' pocket!"

"But why do you suppose," McNear continued, "that they picked on Bermuda as a hiding place for the child? There must be thousands of safer places for kidnappers to hide in the States. And how did the Sinclair woman manage to get on board with the child at New York with the police watching all embarkations?"

"The latter *is* rather puzzling," conceded the Chief of Police, "but you must remember that the inquiry is already over two months old, and you can't keep up a red hot search for ever. Crime doesn't stand still while you put all your men on one job, especially in the States. And in any case McKnight probably knew the detective scrutinizing the passenger list, and the woman could quite easily get through on his say-so. As for your first point, it has been brought to my notice pretty forcibly during the last few days that, in many respects, Bermuda is the criminal's ideal hide-out. Hundreds of houses are let out here every season to people who are unknown to the agents, and nobody bothers much about references and inquiries as long as the prospective tenant puts down the cash. McKnight having made so many trips here, knew the surroundings and the conditions, and also would be able to get his accomplice and the child off the boat and into Hamilton much easier than he could have done it anywhere else. And once here a woman living quietly with a small child would cause no comment."

McNear nodded that he was convinced. "But why did McKnight come here so readily this morning when he knew we'd found Mrs. Sinclair?"

"What else could he do?" said Welch readily. "It would have been casting suspicion on himself to have shown any sign of panic. He wasn't to know that we knew anything about Mrs. Sinclair except that she was missing from the *Baledonia*, and he himself had told us that early in the inquiry. He probably knows her well enough to know that she wouldn't talk, and, as a matter of fact, she hasn't. I expect he came down with the idea of staging a nice little comedy, identifying the missing passenger and all that, and she, of course, would have played up to it with some cock and bull story. You must also remember that, to everybody but ourselves, the case of the murder of Pamela Hawkins was closed with the verdict of the Coroner's jury last Monday. McKnight probably thought himself as safe as houses, and so, if I hadn't overheard those scraps of talk over the radio, he would have been."

"I'm still rather puzzled," said the obstinate McNear, "about that hat label in the girl's dress."

"I don't believe that has any significance at all. She probably really did sew it in herself in order to impress somebody when she got back. Only she didn't get back, poor thing. As to where she originally got the hat label, goodness knows, but probably there are thousands of that particular brand of Sports Shop hat drifting about the States. It might have been one Mrs. Marsden had given her, or somebody she'd got friendly with on the boat. All that label did or could do for us was to waste a lot of our time."

"That chap Hastings," Turnbull quietly observed, "got quite a scare out of it."

"His troubles," the Chief of Police answered in a highly moral tone, "were of his own making and we needn't waste sympathy on him. Of course, it's evident now that Henderson was robbed by one of those hangers-on at the Bull Dog bar. And as for that, Henderson also got no more than he deserved!" He paused. "In fact, the only question that remains open is—what about those rewards and who is to get them?"

Welch said promptly, "It was McNear that rescued the child."

McNear embarrassedly scratched his cheek. "So far as that goes, Turnbull here found her first. I wouldn't have found her at all if you hadn't tracked her to Greenleaf, Superintendent."

"That's true," Masters agreed as arbiter, "and of course it was Welch who arrested McKnight!"

"Yes," McNear said, "and it was Welch who traced the crime to the ship in the first place. If it hadn't been for him seeing that those lilies weren't Bermuda flowers we'd never have tracked the crime to the cruise ships at all!"

Welch laughed. "I guess there'll be enough for us all—"

"My sentiments exactly," Turnbull said.

"Shake on it," McNear said.

Masters smiled. Reaching beneath his desk he drew forth an enticing bottle of Highland Nectar whiskey. "Well, gentlemen—"

APPENDIX

Dead Men Tell No Tales:
A Story of Circumstantial Evidence

Munsey's Magazine, June 1921

DEAD MEN TELL NO TALES: A STORY OF CIRCUMSTANTIAL EVIDENCE

I

HE HAD two hours to live. In a huddled heap he lay on the hard bench, his old face deep-lined, his legs drawn tight against his body, his arms folded across his chest.

And this was to be the end ignoble death in the electric chair. In the corridor outside the cell relentless footsteps beat steadily, unceasingly. To the man, their dull, mechanical thuds symbolized the dreadful power that was hurrying him to the grave—that awful thing, fate, which cares not for the cries of the unfortunate or the pleas of the desolate.

A wild frenzy struck the prisoner. It wasn't right; it wasn't fair!

"I didn't kill him! I didn't kill him!" he wailed, as his old body swayed backward and forward in the agony of emotion. "Cyrus Townsend could tell you—Cyrus—Cyrus!"

His voice trailed away into nothingness. He lay limply on the bench, like a bundle of wet rags.

Cyrus Townsend was dead, and would never speak. Dead men tell no tales. It was useless to strive against fate.

The gray walls faded away, and in their place came scenes of the previous month, like a hideous motion-picture from hell.

There was the district attorney summing up his case.

"Gentlemen, the affair is now in your hands; I await your answer with complete confidence."

It was all so clear to the man in the cell—the crowded court-room, the inquisitive faces, the terrible overhanging dread. There was the district attorney sitting down pompously. Now he was mechanically shuffling a pack of legal documents on the table before him.

As a child, the prisoner had had a passion for the game of solitaire. He played against the devil, his mother used to tell him. He had often wondered about this devil who was so marvelously adept at cards. He had wondered how the Evil One looked. It had been a foolish, childish fancy; but now he knew what his youthful mind could not fashion. The district attorney, playing a winning hand for a human life with his pack of legal documents, was the incarnation of the devil in all his fiendishness.

A new scene took its place on the wall. In the center of it was the judge. His figure stood out like a black cameo. Vaguely the prisoner heard him droning out his charge to the jury.

"You are concerned with but two degrees of murder, gentlemen. It is for you to decide which. If, in your estimation, the prisoner deliberately preconceived and enacted this crime with malice aforethought, it is plainly your duty to render the verdict of murder in the first degree. Should you determine, however, that the act was unpremeditated but intentional, your duty is equally evident— to pronounce the prisoner guilty of murder in the second degree."

The judge cleared his throat and continued his charge.

"On the morning of Friday, the 18th of May, Cyrus Townsend, president of the Ajax Copper Corporation, was murdered in his office on the twelfth floor of the Municipal Building. Before him was spread his luncheon, which he had ordered, as usual, from the restaurant in the basement. On his desk a pile of papers awaited his signature. He had dismissed the stenographer to whom he had been dictating. He had urged her to rush through her meal, since he had important business to complete. He was alone in the office except for the defendant, his clerk; the remainder of the office force being absent for the noon interim. On their return, Cyrus Townsend was found dead. The coroner has declared that death was due to the introduction of cyanide of hydrogen, or prussic acid, as it is more commonly known, into the digestive system. He has further testified that death was instantaneous.

"The defendant was arrested. On his person the police found ten thousand dollars in cash and forty thousand in bonds, which were known to have been in the desk of the murdered man. This is the evidence complete. I deliver the case into your hands."

The judge resumed his motionless attitude as the jury filed slowly out of the room. A ripple of conversation in the back seats was sharply quelled by the black-robed figure.

The prisoner sank down in his chair, his face resting on cupped palms. His lawyer's words of cheerful exhortation made not the least impression on him. If anything, they only served to increase his gloom.

The chatter resumed in the court-room. The judge had retired to his chambers to await the verdict; but he was not absent long. Presently there was a hush, a craning of necks. The judge appeared once more on the bench; he rapped again for order. In filed the jury. They took their places in the box, standing like lamp-posts, unemotionally, lifelessly.

"Gentlemen," said the judge, "have you reached a decision?"

"We have," replied the foreman.

The judge adjusted his spectacles, fumbled among the papers before him, and took up the jury's sealed communication. With nerve-racking deliberation he cut open the envelope, glanced through the contents, and looked up. It was one of those moments when the true majesty of the law is felt towering above the petty trivialities of life.

The judge spoke.

"The jury has found the prisoner guilty of murder in the first degree."

For a moment a fateful quiet settled on the court-room. Then the counsel for the defense was on his feet.

"May it please you honor to allow the prisoner to address the court before the pronouncement of sentence?"

The judge nodded.

"It pleases the court."

The counsel for the defense turned to his client and helped him to his feet. As he stood there, the prisoner's age showed more strikingly than before. The thin hands, feeble body, tired eyes, all told of dead years.

II

"YOUR HONOR," he began, "I should like to state here in court just what I saw and did in that half-hour when I was alone with my employer, Cyrus Townsend. I had considered what I am about to relate to you in the light of a confidence never to be divulged. I have kept silent, hoping that an acquittal might save me from violating my solemn word; but now I have been convicted. I cannot believe that Cyrus Townsend would wish me to die rather than tell what I know about his death. Have I the court's permission to speak?"

"It is your privilege," replied the judge, "to address the court."

The prisoner continued.

"The prosecution has maintained that I poisoned the food which I brought to Mr. Townsend from the restaurant. That is a lie. There was no poison in the food. I brought the luncheon into the private office, and set the tray down before him. I turned to leave the room, but he called me back.

"'Johnson,' said Mr. Townsend, 'how many years have you been in my employ?'

"'Fifteen, sir,' I answered.

"'And in that time have you not come to look upon me as a friend, and do you not consider my word law?'

"'Of course, sir.'

"'You would not dispute a decision I had made?'

"'No, sir.'

"'You would respect anything I may tell you as confidential?'

"'Of course, sir.'

"'Johnson,' said Mr. Townsend abruptly, 'I am about to kill myself.'

"I could hardly speak, I was so bewildered. I reached out toward him and entreated:

"'But, sir, with your wealth, happiness, and—'

"'Stop!' he commanded. 'Remember your promise. My word is law.'

"I stood gaping at him, knocked speechless by his words.

"'For several good and sufficient reasons, Johnson, I am about to kill myself. The causes which have led me to this point would be of no interest to you. It is not for you to argue. Please bring me a ball of wrapping-twine.'

"I obeyed automatically, like a walking doll under the fingers of a child. I watched him, fascinated, as he walked to an open window and leaned out. I half started forward. It came to my mind that he was about to throw himself out before my very eyes.

"He turned quickly and reassured me.

"'Do not be alarmed. I will use a bit more finesse than that. I was merely looking at the clock. My watch has stopped, and one ought to know the approximate time of one's passing on, Johnson. You see, St. Peter might ask me when I left the earth. It would be annoying not to know.'

"Then I understood his action. On the side of the Municipal Building, just one flight below where we stood, there was a great clock, the official timepiece of the city. By the bidding of its hands the cogs of government regulated their daily operations. By leaning out of any of the front windows of our suite and looking down, one could read the hour.

"Mr. Townsend was very calm. He unwound about fifteen feet from the ball of twine I had handed him. It was a strong variety— of the kind used to tie large parcel-post packages. He cut the cord and walked over to his desk, where he picked up a bronze statue— an Oriental idol—and held it up to me.

"'This little god has brought me success in life; may he bring me success in death!'

"I couldn't understand. I just stood gazing at him, not knowing what to do. I dared not leave him, for I was afraid he would kill himself in my absence; and we were alone in the office. He took up the Oriental piece and tied one end of the twine around the idol's fat neck; then he went to the window and hung it over the sill. He walked to his desk, still holding on to the other end of the cord. He sat down; then he turned to me.

"'Johnson, you are to forget everything you have seen me do in this office. Do you understand? I am about to die of heart failure. There is to be no suspicion of suicide. It might have a disastrous effect on the affairs of my business associates. It is to be the every-day occurrence of an overworked man dying in a natural way. There will be no investigation. I have let it be known that my heart is weak. It will be a shock to my friends, but not a surprise. You have served me well, Johnson. I have not forgotten you in my will; but in addition to this legacy I want you to accept a further token of my gratitude.'

"He opened a drawer, from which he drew out a bundle of bonds and a package of currency.

"'But, sir—' I ventured.

"'Silence!' he thundered. 'Do as I say! Take them!'

"He held them out, and I stuffed them into a pocket. Mr. Townsend was dominating me by his personality, as he had ruled every one with whom he had ever come in contact. In the face of death I was helpless.

"'To the world, Johnson,' he said evenly, 'I shall have died from heart trouble. See to it that no adverse rumors spread about.'

"With that he reached into his waistcoat and took out a bottle about three inches high. It was filled with a pale-colored substance.

"'Prussic acid, Johnson,' he informed me. 'I shall be dead before I can swallow the contents of this little vial.'

"He looked up and smiled. 'Good-by,' he said.

"I didn't move, so he spoke again, this time more sharply.

"'Leave the room!'

"But I couldn't leave him. I held out my hands imploringly. His eyes grew cold. I was the full length of the room from him, but I measured my chances, and rushed toward him with all the strength of my horror-stricken body. He stood up quickly and grasped my arm. I was an infant in his grip; I could not stir. How I longed then for the muscle of Hercules! Mr. Townsend loosed me, as if he knew my puny strength and did not fear it. Then, sitting down once more, he pointed to the door.

"There was nothing to do but obey. As I passed out, I glanced over my shoulder. He was sitting at his desk. In one hand he held the little bottle. He was staring at it quizzically, as a child inspects some new plaything. There was a smile on his face. In the other hand he held the long cord which led to the Oriental idol hanging over the window-sill. Then I closed the door."

The prisoner faced the judge, and held out one of his thin arms. "And that's the truth, your honor, so help me God."

III

THE DISTRICT ATTORNEY sprang to his feet. "I request to be allowed to cross-examine the prisoner," he demanded.

"The request is granted," replied the judge.

With a dramatic gesture, the prosecuting attorney pointed an accusing finger at the man on the witness-stand.

"You say Cyrus Townsend killed himself. Then where is the bottle or vial which contained the poison? It has never been found. Where is that bottle which you claim Cyrus Townsend clasped in his hand as he ordered you from the room?"

"I do not know," replied the prisoner.

"Your honor," continued the district attorney, "the power of cyanide of hydrogen, or prussic acid, is well known to you. Its effect is practically instantaneous. If Cyrus Townsend killed himself, what happened to the vial that held the prussic acid? He could not have disposed of it himself; no traces of poison were found on any of the dishes or glasses on the murdered man's luncheon-tray. What happened to it? The prisoner states that he does not know.

"He lies! He knows he placed the poison in his employer's food; he knows he washed the plate in which the poisoned food was placed; he knows he opened the windows, so that the sickly odor of the acid would be carried away; he knows he rid himself of the missing bottle before the rest of the office force returned from their lunch-hour."

The district attorney waved his finger dramatically at the prisoner.

"And this cock-and-bull story of his about the piece of twine with an Oriental idol on one end of it—does he expect any jury to believe that? Where did the bronze idol go? If the prisoner says that Cyrus Townsend hung it out of the window by a string, he intimates that the murdered man was insane. He can mean nothing else. Cyrus Townsend was beyond the baby stage. He didn't play childish tricks such as the prisoner has described.

"And if the idol had dropped from the twelfth floor of the Municipal Building, don't you suppose it would have fallen in the street? Where else could it fall to? And if it hit the pavement, how long do you think an object like that would lie there? Not ten seconds, your honor. This story of the Oriental statue is also a lie. It is a wild tale to explain the open window, which he had forgotten, in the enormity of his crime, to shut. It is a base falsehood made up out of the terror-stricken mind of a murderer!"

The district attorney took his seat, and the attorney for the defense addressed the court.

"I move," he petitioned, "that, in view of the newly offered evidence, the court order a retrial of this case."

The judge did not deliberate long.

"Motion overruled. The new evidence has not been substantiated by proof. Cyrus Townsend has been dead a month; none of the offered evidence—the idol and the poison vial—has been found. In the estimation of this court there is not sufficient ground to permit of a retrial."

He silenced a flurry in the court-room with a vigorous smash of the mallet. There was a hush. The judge turned to the jury.

"Gentlemen, you have found the prisoner guilty of murder in the first degree. I have been shown no legal reason why this verdict should be set aside. Therefore I sentence the prisoner to death by means of electricity—the order of this court to be carried out at twelve o'clock noon on Thursday, the first day of July."

IV

THE JUDGE'S VOICE melted away. His figure became indistinct; in its place was the gray wall of the cell. The prisoner, huddled in his corner, shivered with fear. The two hours must be almost gone!

He heard rough footsteps in the corridor, and then a key rattled in a lock. A priest stood by his side.

"Courage, friend, courage!"

Then they led him toward the little door of the black room into which men enter but never return.

The prisoner collapsed as he entered the somber chamber. Even the rough prison attendants, inured to death from innumerable contacts, felt an almost uncontrollable pity for the aged man. He was out of the usual run of murderers—not a degenerate gunman, not a bestial wife-killer, only a pitiful old wreck.

But law is law. Sentiment can find no secure spot to lay her head in the death-chamber. The ghastly preparations for the last rite commenced. The priest consoled the prisoner as the leather straps were being adjusted; the hushed singsong of the confessional eddied into the darkened corners.

A hard-mouthed official stood, handkerchief and watch in hand, before a barred window; an electrician waited expectantly by a giant switch. All was ready. The official was still staring out of the window to where the face of the Municipal Building clock surveyed the housetops.

He frowned.

"My watch must be wrong," he whispered to a companion. "It says twelve o'clock, but the clock on the Municipal Building reads eleven fifty-five. We'll have to wait!"

No stillness exceeds that which reigns in the presence of the death-chair. Through the minds of the officials, as well as that of the doomed man, there came surging, like the visions of a drowning soul, tender memories, vain regrets, useless fears.

"My God!" ejaculated the man with the handkerchief and watch. "The clock has stopped! It is still at eleven fifty-five. It is the official timepiece of the city; we cannot proceed!"

He turned a nervous countenance to the prison attendants who had crowded around him, and were staring amazedly out of the window.

The dread of the supernatural is installed in the heart of every living person. The men in the death-room, shaken already by the prospect of the sight they must soon witness, stood aghast. Even time itself was arraying himself on the side of the doomed man.

"Telephone," some one weakly suggested. "Ask what's the matter."

The superintendent of the Municipal Building, sitting in the cool serenity of his inner office, was startled by an agitated voice over the wire.

"What? Stopped!" he shouted.

He dropped the receiver in his haste. The superintendent was greatly excited. The clock was sacred; all the watches of the city were set by its dictum. He might lose his position if it was any fault of his. He had a soft job, and he knew it.

He acted with unusual celerity. He sent electricians and machinists hurrying aloft. The intricate machinery was in perfect order, the main-spring was well oiled, and yet the hands would not move. A courageous machinist was sent to explore the face. The trouble was soon found.

A long piece of cord, whipped by the wind, had been wrapped around and around the hour and minute hands, binding them fast together in a position that indicated five minutes to twelve. It seemed as if the coiled twine had striven against fate to hold the hands from the hour of noon. On one end of the queerly placed cord was an Oriental idol; on the other, a little bottle, smelling faintly of almonds.

COACHWHIP PUBLICATIONS

COACHWHIPBOOKS.COM

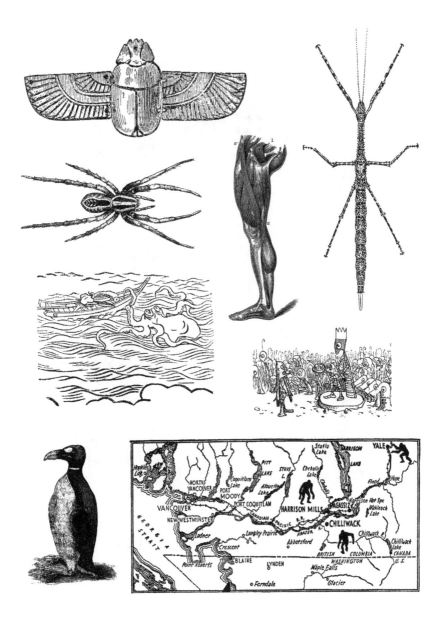

COACHWHIP PUBLICATIONS

COACHWHIPBOOKS.COM

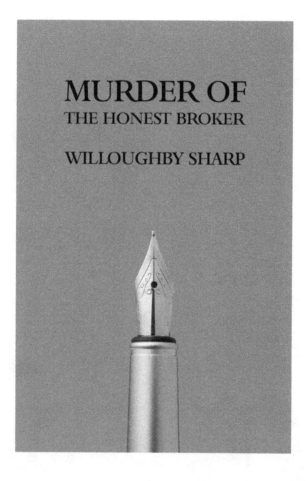

MURDER OF
THE HONEST BROKER

WILLOUGHBY SHARP

ISBN 978-1-61646-211-6

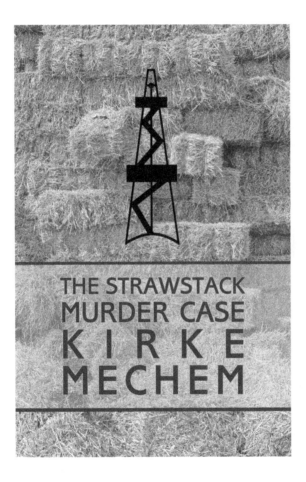

THE STRAWSTACK
MURDER CASE
KIRKE
MECHEM

ISBN 978-1-61646-179-9

Coachwhip Publications

CoachwhipBooks.com

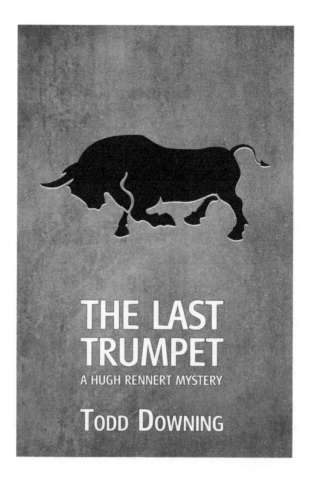

THE LAST
TRUMPET
A HUGH RENNERT MYSTERY

TODD DOWNING

ISBN 978-1-61646-152-2

CLUES AND CORPSES
The Detective Fiction and
Mystery Criticism of Todd Downing
CURTIS EVANS

ISBN 978-1-61646-145-4

CPSIA information can be obtained
at www.ICGtesting.com
Printed in the USA
BVHW070811011219
565288BV00002B/193/P